Infinity and Always

Blackrock series 3

E.A. Weston

Table of Contents

First Edition
Frist Printing 2015
ISBN-13: 978-1514112366
ISBN-10: 1514112361

Cover Design by RLD Print

Elizabeth Kelly

Infinity and Always

Blackrock series 3

Chapter 1

Reaching over, I silence the alarm on my phone. Knox's arm tightens around my waist and he groans at me in protest.

"No, darlin'."

Sliding from his grasp, I swing my legs over the side of the bed and yawn. The sun hasn't come up yet, but I don't care; I like to run in the dark.

"Bailey, please you promised," Knox whispers.

Turning, I find him watching me with a sad look on his face.

"I'll be back soon."

Climbing off the bed, I get dressed; grab my phone and running armband from the nightstand, and head for the door.

"You promised," he says, more forcefully.

"No, I said I'd try Knox and I did, but it's not working."

Reaching for the handle, I pull open the door and walk outside. I quickly drink some water and walk to the door to put on my shoes. Knox exits the bedroom rubbing his face while watching me tie my laces.

"You didn't try hard enough darlin'."

"Jesus Christ, Knox! Would you leave me alone!" I yell at him, as I force my hair into a ponytail.

"Fine, if you want to be like that then fine!" he shouts at me. I can see the hurt and anger mixed on his face, but I don't care. I need to get out of here.

"I have to go, Knox, I'll see you later."

"If you walk out that door Bailey…"

"What?" I ask, turning back to him.

"Don't come back," he whispers, begging me with his eyes to stay. My heart is already numb, the only person who could actually hurt me just did.

"Okay."

Opening the door, I slam it behind me as I leave the apartment. Stepping out in the cool morning air, I take a deep breath and start to run. I was only planning on doing a few laps around the football field, but after another morning of Knox, I decide to run up to the lake.

I have my music loud as I run. The hills are starting to take a toll on my body now. Reaching the lake I notice my Dad's house is still in darkness, so I do a lap around the lake. When I arrive back at his property line, I find him standing on the back porch waiting for me.

"Morning, sweetheart."

"Dad," I answer, taking the bottle of water from him. "Thanks."

"So you're up here again?"

Rolling my eyes I look at him, "Where else would I be?"

"I don't know, in school, with your fiancé."

I snort at my Dad and shake my head, "No on all counts Dad, and speaking of my wonderful fiancé," I say with sarcasm. "I suppose he called you to rat me out again."

"He's just worried about you sweetheart."

"No Dad, he thinks he is."

"No Bailey, he is, trust me I see him every day."

I can't help but get angrier with Knox; he has totally pissed me off by calling my Dad at this hour.

"Aren't you getting ready for work?" I ask, taking a seat on the chair.

"No, I'm taking a leaf out of my daughter's book."

Looking over at him I frown. "And what would that be?"

"I'm playing hooky," he says, smiling at me. "I was thinking I could give up on my life and let the business go down the drain and just for fun, I might go to Vegas and blow all my money on the slot machines." He nods to himself.

"Seriously Dad, you're going to try to pull that shit on me?"

He looks down at me and crosses his arms. His face is a mask of emotion. He must have gotten schooled by Knox in that art form. I watch him watching me.

"What do you want me to say, Dad?"

"I want you to tell me what's going on with you. Why are you skipping classes?"

"Dad please, just leave it. I get enough of this crap from Knox and I don't need you on my case too."

He walks back into the house without another word. Closing my eyes, I lean back in the chair and let out a deep sigh. Why the hell does life have to fuck me over all the time? Why is everything I want so damn hard? Standing up, I walk inside and up to my room. After a quick shower, I join my Dad in the kitchen watching as he reads over some papers.

"Are you really staying home from work today?" I ask because he has never stayed home before.

"Yes I am, why, does that bother you?"

"Nope. If you want we can do something," I offer, taking a seat beside him.

"No thanks sweetheart, I have plans."

"With who?" I stare at him in disbelief.

"Well, I can't tell you because you will only get mad and then you will probably break something and I will have to kick you out of the house." He smiles at me.

"Yeah, you wouldn't be the first one today," I mutter.

"Ah, so he finally told you to get out, huh?" he asks, looking at me with a slight smirk on his lips.

"Yeah, so can I have my old room back?" I ask, hoping he won't kick me out too.

"On two conditions," he answers.

Looking at him I frown, but shrug my shoulders, pretending that I don't care either way.

"You go back to school and you talk to Knox."

Unbelievable! I bet those two planned out this whole scenario. "Fine, but I get a condition of my own." My Dad purses his lips before nodding at me. "I get my car back starting today."

"Deal," he says, shaking my hand, "now hurry up we have classes to attend and I have a day with my future son-in-law."

3

We arrive at campus just after eight am and Dad makes sure that I sign up for all my classes and copies my schedule so he knows when I should be in class. I feel like I am in high school again, well, I had more freedom then.

"Where to now?" I ask as we walk back to the car.

"You can drop me off with Knox and you can enjoy your last free day." He smiles at me.

Pulling into the parking lot of the apartment, I see both Knox and Max waiting by the truck. Knox stands up when he sees my car and frowns when I pull in beside them.

We climb out, Dad says hello to them, but I just walk away towards the apartment. I grab a box and begin to pack up my school stuff, notes, books, and my computer.

"What are you doing?"

"Packing."

"I can see that, but why are you packing?"

Sighing, I sit on the bed. "Knox, you told me not to come back. I'm getting some stuff then I'll be out of your way."

He crosses his arms and stands there, looking at me. I can see how tired he is from the dark circles under his eyes and I know I caused them. Guilt burns through me like a wildfire and I have to look away.

"I was angry darlin'," he says in a low voice. "I don't want you to leave. I just want you back."

"I haven't gone anywhere, Knox."

Standing, I begin to grab some clothes from the closet. Knox catches my elbow and turns me to face him.

"Don't do this, please darlin', I want the girl I fell in love with to come back."

Pulling my arm out of his grasp I stomp into the bathroom, muttering curses at him. He follows me around the apartment begging me to stay, but I can't, he pushed me too far this time and I need space. I need to get out of my own head and find that peace again.

"I'll see you around."

Grabbing my stuff, I walk out to the car finding my Dad and Max standing by the truck. My Dad gives me a sad smile and a shake of his head, but Max looks gutted; his face is distraught and he runs his hand through his hair.

"Sis, what are you doing?"

"I'm going home Max, you're welcome to visit."

"Aw Bailey, come on, this isn't fair. You know he only worries about you."

My heart hurts, but I need to get away from everyone. Pulling Max into a hug I squeeze him tight. "I still love you, bro."

"But not me?"

Knox's hurt voice sounds from behind. Letting Max go I turn to face him. Both Dad and Max climb into the truck to leave us alone.

"I do you love you, Knox, but you're driving me crazy and I need to be alone right now."

Stepping over to me he wraps me in his arms and I can't help but melt into him. I really do love him.

"It's not over darlin', you promised me forever."

Swallowing the lump in my throat, I step away from him, unable to reply. I keep my head down and climb into my car. Pulling out of the lot I finally let the tears fall. What the fuck am I doing? How can I love someone so much and want to run away from him too? I take the day to rest, to unwind, and let life pass me by. I turn off my phone and go for a walk around the lake; everything is changing. My life is slipping again and I know I am to blame, but not all of the blame lands on me, there are other parties involved.

Once I'm back in the house, I turn my phone on, receiving a voicemail from my new attorney, Rachel. I fired my uncle last year, much to the family's annoyance, but I had to. He was too close to me to see what I saw and I honestly think he didn't give a shit because I have money and his kids don't.

Listening to the voicemail, I call her back. "This is Rachel Osborne, how can I help?"

"Hi Rachel, It's Bailey."

She tells me that sentencing for Ben will be in a few weeks and asks if I will be coming to court. Shit! Why now? Just as I signed up for classes again.

"Yeah I'll be there."

"Okay I will see you then, call me if you need anything else."

We say goodbye and I dial my Dad.

"Yes sweetheart?" he answers.

"Dad, I hate to break up the bromance, but what time will you be home?"

"Not sure, why?"

"I just spoke to Rachel and I have to go, Dad, I need to be there."

He lets out a long sigh and I can picture him pinching the bridge of his nose; it's a new thing he does when I upset him or he is having a hard time with me.

"Okay, we can talk over dinner. Did she say when?"

I fill him in on the time frame and he argues with me about school. I can't do it again, the waiting is torture, and the sleepless nights are even worse. He agrees to hear me out later and we hang up. I spend a few hours cleaning my room and flipping through my textbooks. The last year of college should be a fun experience, but I'm dreading it. Knox and Max graduated last year so I have been on my own around campus for a while now. I still have Abbey and Becky and we hang out after practice, but that's about it. All I have in my life lately is football.

When Dad arrives home, he brings Knox and Max with him. I can hear them laughing in the kitchen. Walking down the back stairs I say hello to them, Knox nods at me and Max grins.

"What's up sis?"

"Nothing much Max, what about you?"

He shrugs, "The usual."

I start getting dinner ready while the three of them hang out on the back deck. I assume they are all staying for dinner. Once I have it ready, I walk outside carrying the plates.

"Need help?" Knox asks.

"Sure," I reply.

Walking back inside, that's what we have been reduced to, one-word answers. He grabs the salad bowl and the garlic bread. I know he wants to talk to me, but he is holding out. After dinner Dad asks me about my call with Rachel, I really want to slap him for asking with Knox here.

"She said the sentencing is coming up."

6

"Oh okay, well hopefully he gets what he deserves," Dad replies.

Max looks over to his brother who is clenching his fists. I know this is pissing him off, but right now it's not about him.

"I'm going Dad, I'm not arguing about it."

Once the words leave my mouth, Knox shoots up out of his chair and stalks over to the lake. Max and Dad both look at me.

"What? I'm not going over there."

"Bailey please, I love you just as much as I love my brother, but you're hurting him right now and you promised me years ago that you wouldn't."

Shaking my head, I stand up and brace myself for the argument I know is coming. I walk across the garden towards him, reaching his side I stay a few feet away.

"You okay?" I ask, crossing my arms.

He lets out a sigh and runs his hand through his hair, messing it up even more. I have to restrain myself from reaching over and fixing it.

"I don't get it, Bailey."

I guess he is more pissed than I first thought. He's using my name.

"I mean, I know you want to know what is going on in court, but I don't get why you have to go there."

"You know why," I whisper. I have explained it to him so many times before.

"Jesus Christ, can't you trust your attorney to tell you what is happening? I haven't seen you for months. I go to bed alone, most mornings I wake up alone, where the fuck are you?"

"What! You know I sleep with you every night." I snap at him.

"Do I? Because from where I'm standing I pretty much don't have a damn clue where you are or who you're with."

"Don't be such an asshole, Knox, I'm in bed with you and only you. I get up a six for my run, you stay in bed until eight."

"Yeah, running, that's all you do!" he shouts at me, "Have you looked in the mirror lately? All you are is bones." He flips up my t-shirt, and I smack his hand away from me.

7

"And that," he whispers, shaking his head. "You barely let me touch you anymore."

"Knox..."

"No Bailey, I don't want to hear it."

He looks ready to cry as he walks away from me. Taking a seat on the lounge chair, I stare out at the lake. I don't get why he doesn't understand that I have to be at the court. I want to see that asshole get sentenced for what he did to me, it's been two years already, and finally the case is going ahead.

I hear the truck doors slam and the crunch of gravel as they leave. If my heart weren't so hardened, I would probably be crying about now.

"So what was that about?" Dad asks, sitting next to me.

"He doesn't get it, Dad."

"So what are you going to do about it?"

"I don't know, I just want to see his face when they send him to prison, I need that."

"I understand sweetheart, but I meant about Knox?"

Groaning, I scrub my face with my hands. "I don't know, I guess he thinks I don't love him anymore or I am playing around on him."

"Are you Bailey?"

"What! Dad no, what the fuck? I would never do that him." I can't believe he would even ask me that.

"Well, when was the last time you told him you loved him?" he asks, looking out over the lake.

"Why are you asking me all these questions? Are you reporting back him too? Are both of you ratting to each other about me?"

"Stop getting upset sweetheart, I am only looking out for you. I know how much you love each other and how much this trial has taken out of you, but in a relationship you're supposed to lean on the one closest to you."

"I know, but what if that person doesn't agree with you? How can I lean on him when he thinks I'm crazy for going to all the court dates? He doesn't understand."

Standing, I walk away from him and take the trail around the lake. My body is numb and I hate who I have become. We were doing so good for a while - Knox and me, we had so

8

much fun together. He took me on a road trip on his bike last summer; we drove to Vegas and gambled a little. We even played around with the idea of eloping but decided we wanted a proper wedding. Now though, I think we will be lucky if we even stay friends.

I find myself standing on the far side of the lake, looking over at my Dad still sitting on the lounge chair. I feel guilty for just walking away. I want them to understand me. I want them to support me, but I can't see it. My Dad hasn't objected yet, but I know Knox, and he is so against me going back to Grove.

"Are you here to view the property?" A voice from behind me asks.

Turning, I frown at the guy standing there. "No, what?"

"The house," he points behind him, "my Mom is selling it and I thought you were checking out the garden," he smiles.

"Oh sorry," I answer, realizing I am actually standing in his garden.

"It's okay, I just thought we were getting a break." He smiles as he backs away.

"What do you mean?" I ask, following him.

"Oh, it's just been on the market for a while and well…" he looks over at me and his cheeks are tinted pink. "We kind of need the money."

"Oh, I didn't know any of the homes were for sale," I reply, "but I can take a look." I smile, falling in step beside him.

He shows me around the house, and it needs some serious work but I like it, it has character. He takes me upstairs to the master bedroom and brings me out onto the deck. It looks over the lake but is hidden from neighbors by fully-grown, big leaf maple trees.

"Wow, this is an amazing view. In all the years, I've run around this lake I have never noticed this balcony." I smile at him.

"Yeah, my dad built it so they would have some privacy." He looks sad as he turns to face the water.

"I can see my dad from here," I smile and point to him.

"He can't see you though."

We walk through the upstairs and back down to the back garden. "Well, I hope you liked the tour, I'm Will, by the way." He shakes his head as he holds out his hand to me.

"Bailey," I smile, taking his hand. "Do you have a realtor?" I ask, looking back up at the house again.

"Nah, we just want a quick sale."

I get his phone number and agree to call him in a few days. When I reach Dad, he is looking a little pissed off at me, "Who was that guy?"

Wrapping my arms around his neck, I press my head against his. "That Dad, was Will and I think I just found my dream house."

My dad leans away from me and looks at me, smiling for the first time in months. I smile back at him. He agrees to take a look at the house tomorrow if I can get Will to agree. Dad and I sit out by the lake for a while longer until he yawns and calls it a night.

"Night Dad, love you."

"Love you too, sweetheart."

Chapter 2

Walking into class after such a long absence is weird. I find a seat at the front of the class feeling a bit lonely without Paige by my side.

"Holy shit balls!"

Looking up, I see Ryan barreling through the students, headed straight for me. Standing up I smile as he reaches down, pulling me off my feet in a bear hug.

"Damn I missed you, girl," he says, putting me back on my feet.

"Missed you too, buddy."

Ryan takes the seat beside me, smiling. We get through our first two classes together and he joins me for lunch.

"So are you going to try out for your spot on the team again?" he asks.

"Don't know," I shrug, looking around the quad. I have so many great memories here, which make me sad too. Ryan talks about football and why I need to be back on the girl's team, and how they suck balls without me.

"Ryan, you do know we only had our last game two months ago?" I laugh at him.

"Yeah, but some of the chicks are crap, you should see them," he shivers.

I laugh at him and his description of some of the girls he watched try out last week. He drags me over to the football field and we watch a few girls run drills. I see Abbey and Becky and smile. Once they spot me on the bleachers, they both scream and run at me.

"Oh my God, you made it!" Abbey grabs me in a hug, "Come on, today is the last day of tryouts."

"Oh, I was just watching," I answer, cutting her smile right off her face.

"I don't think so, Bailey," Becky says, shaking her head at me, "We are not losing our star, wide receiver in senior year.

Get your boney ass onto that field now and fucking make us proud."

"Yeah! You tell her."

Ryan agrees and pushes me onto the grass, just in time for our coach to see me. After the first year of the league, the college took over our sponsorship and allowed us to practice here instead of the high school.

"Hi, Bailey."

"Hey coach," I answer, walking over to her. She knows my situation and has helped me in the past.

"So am I getting lucky and getting my best wide receiver back?" she asks, with a hopeful expression. I explain what is going on with the case now and how the girls wanted me to try out.

"Do you want to be on the team?" she asks, looking at me.

"Yeah, I miss it if I'm honest," I answer, looking around me.

"Well, practice is the same, Wednesday nights. I expect you there every week except when you'll be in Grove." She smiles.

"Shouldn't I try out?" I ask, frowning at her.

She gives me a pointed look before wrapping her arm around my shoulders. "No, you don't. You are one of the best girls I ever had on my team, but I need you to do something for me."

"Sure."

"I need you to put on some weight," she says as she looks at me sadly. "I know you're stressed out, but you've lost too much weight and I'm afraid you'll get hurt in the game."

"Okay," I agree and give her a hug. Walking back over to the girls I can see they look pissed off.

"Bailing on us senior year, huh?" Becky says, kicking the dirt at her feet.

"Please," I answer, "I'm so good I don't have to try out."

Both girls and Ryan scream and jump on me. We roll around on the grass for a few minutes before heading back to class. The afternoon goes by fast and I agree to meet Abbey and Becky for a pre-practice workout on Wednesday. Arriving home, I find my Dad in the kitchen.

"Hi Dad, what are you doing home this early?"

"Well," he smiles at me, "today your fiancé made his first pitch and nailed it. He was good Bailey. You should be proud of him."

The smile on my dad's face tells me how proud he is of Knox and I didn't even know he was doing this today. I feel like shit.

"Is he at home?"

"No, he and Max went out to celebrate." He gives me a sad smile as he stands.

We walk over to meet Will and look at the house again. On our way back, dad puts his arm around my shoulders.

"So how was class? You look sad."

"It feels good to be back. I got back on the team." I smile.

"Well look at that," he smiles at me. "Looks like you too have a reason for celebration."

"Yeah I guess," I sigh, leaning my head on his shoulder.

"They just went to the bar for a drink," he says, pushing me towards the garage.

"Thanks, Dad." Reaching up I kiss his cheek.

Running up to my room I change into jeans and a tank, then drive down to George's. Walking into the bar always amazes me that it is always full. Looking around I find them sitting in a booth by the back wall. I wave to Amber, and she smiles at me as I walk over to them.

"Hi, mind if I join you?" I ask, biting my lip. Knox looks a little shocked and Max just smirks at me.

"Sure," Knox answers, sliding out so I can get in beside him. I wait for Amber to bring me my drink before I speak again. My eyes rake over Knox, he looks so good in his suit.

"Here babe, it's good seeing you again." Amber smiles when she leaves my drink.

"So," I say, lifting my glass, "Congratulations on your first big win."

Reaching over I clink my glass against Knox's beer and he tries to hide his smile, but fails.

"Thanks."

Max winks at me then decides he has to check the delivery order for tomorrow. Knox argues that he has it done, but Max walks away. "Fucking asshole," Knox complains. I can't help but laugh out loud and Knox turns to look at me.

"What are you laughing at?"

"Nothing," I clear my throat and take a sip of my soda.

"I'm joking," he says, leaning down to me. "How did classes go today?"

"Fine, I got my spot back on the team." I smile at him.

"Yeah," he smiles, looking happy, "that's good darlin'."

"I'm proud of you, Knox."

He just shrugs taking a sip of his beer, "I thought I'd feel different."

"How so?" I ask.

"I thought I would feel high and have a crazy celebration." He chuckles, peeling the label off the beer bottle.

"What's stopping you?"

He looks at me for a few minutes, before brushing a loose piece of hair behind my shoulder. His eyes look sad even though he smiles at me, and we just stare at each other for a few minutes.

"I better get going, I have homework to do. You're lucky you graduated already," I sigh. Knox slides out of the booth to let me out and walks me to my car in silence.

"Okay, have a goodnight."

"Yeah," he sighs, stepping closer to me and taking my left hand in his. "You don't wear it anymore." He whispers, rubbing his thumb across my ring finger.

"It doesn't fit," I explain, again.

"I know. I'm proud of you too, darlin', for going back to school and getting on the team. You are pretty good at that."

"Thanks."

He pulls me into him, hugging me tight. Wrapping my arms around him I hug him back. He kisses my temple "night darlin'."

"Night babe," I reply automatically.

He lets me go, watching as I drive away.

When I get home, I fill the rest of the night with assignments and reading. I make it my mission to graduate. I want to do something with my life.

14

By Saturday morning my body is sore; we worked out hard on Wednesday night and I have to agree with Knox and my coach, I have lost too much weight. When the elevator opens, I step out and walk into my office, finding stacks of paperwork on the desk.

"Jesus," I moan, as I plop down in my chair. Pulling the first stack towards me, I start to read through it and sign where I need to. After a few hours I make my way down to the employee café, grabbing a sandwich and coffee. Looking around I spot Knox sitting with some of the engineers and their new assistant, Meagan.

"Hi." I wave and I take a seat at the next table. Knox excuses himself and joins me. "What are you doing here on a Saturday?" I ask him.

"Just going over some stuff for Monday."

"Oh okay, you can sit with them you know."

"I know," he sighs, "but I don't want too. I didn't think you'd be in today."

"Yeah well, just because my dad owns the place doesn't mean I can slack off."

He smiles at me and shakes his head. "I know, Frank can be a bit hard at times."

"Hey Knox, we are going back down now," Meagan smiles as she lays her hand on his shoulder.

Rolling my eyes, I bite my sandwich and take out my protein shake.

"Okay thanks," he answers.

She looks between us, and then leaves, pouting. I can't hold my laughter anymore and crack up just as she reaches the door.

"Darlin' please," Knox hangs his head in embarrassment.

"Aw, what's wrong babe? Don't you want her to know you're engaged to the boss' daughter?"

Knox looks up at me and frowns. "I'll leave you to finish your lunch."

Standing, he picks up my protein shake and reads the label before putting it down and walking away. Grabbing the bottle,

I throw away my lunch and head back to my office, picking up the phone as I dial.

"Hello."

"Hey, Paige."

"Hey Bailey, is it Saturday already? I feel like we just talked yesterday," she laughs.

"Wow, the party was that good?" I question, remembering she was out last night.

We talk for about an hour, which we do every Saturday. I tell her about my life and she tells me about hers.

"Damn Bailey, I'd go down to the dungeon and bust his ass," she sighs.

"Yeah, maybe I'll take a walk in a bit."

After another few minutes, we hang up and I decide to drop into the engineering department in the basement. I call it the dungeon, but it's not really. The space is an open plan with desks all around and huge bright lights overhead. When I walk into the room, Meagan smiles at me.

"Good afternoon Miss Mortenson."

"Meagan, how are you?" I ask, but I really don't give a shit. She has only been here three weeks and she already asked both Knox and Max out on dates.

"I'm good, can I help you with anything?" she asks, giving me a tight smile.

I know from Max that she thinks this room is hers and that all the guys are hers too.

"No," I answer and walk away.

"So, checking up on me?" Knox asks from behind me.

I keep walking, checking out the designs as I go. "No, just looking, checking on the family business."

"Yeah, is that what you call it?" he asks again, stopping at his desk.

I just smile and keep going until I reach Byron, one of my Dad's oldest and friendliest employees.

"Hi Byron," I smile at him.

"Hey boss lady," he winks at me.

He has called me that since I started working here three years ago. I stop beside him and give him a hug. He shows me what he is working on and I smile at him.

16

"I think I should be calling you Boss," I tease him and he howls out a laugh. I talk with Byron for a while, asking about his family. We say goodbye and I hug him again, walking back over to Knox. He keeps his head down while he works and I peek over his shoulder.

"Can I help you?" he asks.

"No, just saying goodbye," I answer, leaving him alone.

Passing Meagan she plasters on her smile and says goodbye. She actually reminds me of my Mom. Back in my office, I get through all the papers and finish up just after three o'clock. Stretching out on my sofa I open my protein shake and chug it. Looking around my walls, I can't help but feel like shit. Every picture I have is of Knox and I. The one of us on the beach celebrating my birthday two years ago is my favorite. I had it blown up and hung it in here because I loved it so much.

I walk over to it and stare at it, running my fingers across Knox's face. Our life seemed so simple then, he was mine and I was his. But now, I have no idea where I stand. Well maybe I do, but I just don't want to see it.

"You were happy then."

His voice sounds from behind me. I quickly wipe my eyes and turn around to face him.

"I'm happy now," I smile, walking over to my desk to get my bag.

Knox steps into the office and closes the door, "Can we talk?"

Nodding, I sit on the sofa and he sits across from me on the chair. He looks at me for a while before speaking.

"How are you doing?" he asks.

"Fine," I reply, a little confused at his formality.

"Good, I'm happy you are doing better, Bailey. Do you know when this court case is happening?"

"No, not yet. I haven't heard from Rachel since the other day."

I sigh, kicking my feet up onto the coffee table. Knox stands and walks around to me. Taking a seat beside me he lifts my legs onto his lap.

"How was practice?"

17

"Painful, I forgot how hard Becky hits," I chuckle.

We stay silent for a minute, both of us lost in our own minds. My door flies open revealing Meagan.

"Oh I'm sorry, I thought you were gone already," she says, looking between us.

"If I were gone, Meagan, my door would be locked and you would have had known that if you bothered to knock," I snap at her.

"Yes, sorry about that," she says, playing the young innocent secretary with the big scary boss.

"What did you want?" I ask.

"Oh, I forgot to give this to you when you visited earlier," she leans over Knox to hand me a file.

"Thanks, Meagan." Taking the file from her, I flick through it quickly. It's nothing important and I don't even have to sign it. Lifting my head I tune into her and Knox, she is talking about going to the bar tonight and asking if he will be there.

"I'm always there," he answers.

I take my feet off of his lap and put my shoes back on, "Okay, well you can both bugger off since I'm going home." I announce, grabbing my purse off the floor again.

"Oh me too, see you later." She smiles at Knox.

I just close my office door and lock it throwing the file she gave me into my dad's mail slot on my way past his door. The elevator ride down to the garage is silent and awkward. Once we arrive, I walk past both of them to my car.

"Wait up, darlin'," Knox calls, jogging after me. "Can I get a ride home?" he asks.

I am about to answer when Meagan offers to take him home. "Problem solved," I answer climbing into my car. He jumps into the passenger seat.

"Now it is," he smiles over at me.

We arrive at the apartment and he asks me to come up to talk. Following him I feel sad when I walk in. This has been my home for three years and I have to admit, it feels horrible being away from it.

"You want some dinner?" he asks.

"No, thanks. I just had a shake."

I automatically sit on my side of the sofa and kick off my shoes while pulling the throw over myself. I snuggle down. Knox brings me in a cup of hot chocolate and stops when he sees me. He looks confused and puts the drink down on the table.

"You okay?" I ask, watching him.

"Yeah, it just brings back memories seeing you like that."

"Oh sorry," I quickly pull off the throw and sit up putting my shoes back on. "Thanks for the drink."

"I didn't mean for you to get up, Bailey."

I wave him off and take a sip of the hot liquid. I don't know why I even came here.

"I want to come with you," he blurts out.

"Excuse me?" I ask, looking over at him, wondering why he has decided to be by my side now.

"I mean go to Grove with you."

"I know what you meant," I smirk at him. "I just don't know why now."

"I've been thinking about things lately, and I know I have been acting like an overprotective ass. I just want to keep you safe darlin', that's all I ever wanted since seeing you after that last time in court. I couldn't take it anymore. He fucked you up again, and I lost you."

I remember that last day I was in court and I had to Provide testimony against Ben. He sat in the courtroom with a smug look on his face as I relived what he did to me. His attorney tried to make out that I provoked him and I hit him first, but it was his word against mine. I was a wreck afterward. I stayed in bed for weeks and wouldn't talk to anyone or let Knox near me. My nightmares even came back, adding to the list of problems.

"Bailey?"

Turning, I find Knox staring at me with a worried expression. "I'm fine Knox. I should go."

"No, I don't want you to go," he says taking hold of my arm. "I'm sorry darlin', I miss you like crazy, and I know I shouldn't have told you leave. I was just angry and hurt and…" he closes his eyes and sighs. "I want you back, all of you,

Bailey, not just the shell. I love you so much darlin', this is killing me."

"Me too, but I don't trust myself, Knox. I don't know if I can give you everything again."

"I still have everything, darlin'. I never gave it back, so you can't justify that answer."

I can't help but smile. I know he owns every piece of my heart and soul, but I also know that over the next few weeks I won't be what he wants me to be.

"You know how this will play out Knox. I don't think you understand just how much Ben has affected my life. Every part of me hurts from him and therapy helped, but it didn't heal me. I don't think anything can."

"I can darlin'. I promise I can. Just let me in," he begs. "Baby," he whispers.

Closing my eyes, I fight hard to keep him out. I feel like I'm drowning without him, but drifting out to sea when we are together.

"Don't darlin', don't shut me out."

Opening my eyes, I look at him for a long time. I want so much to crawl back into his arms, but my resolve builds again, one brick at a time and Knox deflates. I can see it in his face the minute I harden my heart against his words. He lets my hands drop and falls back against the sofa, rubbing his face. I walk out of the apartment without another word, only stopping on the stairs, ready to run back to him. But I force me feet forward and drive home, mentally healing the wound I just caused myself.

Chapter 3

Over the last few weeks, I have pushed myself in my classes and practice. The date for the court has been set for November 5th. Pulling into the office, I go straight up to my dad's and sink down into the chair.

"Hi, sweetheart."

"Hi, Dad."

"Good news," he smiles at me, pulling out a large envelope from the drawer and handing it over. Opening it, I pull out the papers and read through them.

"No, way!" I scream. Jumping up, I dance around my dad's office laughing and waving the papers above my head. My dad is smiling at me and I pull him up to swing him around with me.

"Oh, Dad, I can't believe it."

"Believe it, you are now the proud owner of 5811 Lakeview Crest."

I dance around some more and hug the papers close to my chest. "Oh wow," I breathe.

"You deserve it, sweetheart," Dad says, hugging me.

"Do you think I should share my news?"

I told my Dad about my talk with Knox. He said he understood where I was coming from, but he also knows what it's like to be on the receiving end. I was absolutely wrecked when he told me my Mom treated him the way I am treating Knox, but he did say Knox had a part to play in it too.

"Sure, I think he'd like to see you."

I haven't actually set eyes on Knox since that day and I really want to share this with him. I leave my dad's office

21

before I change my mind and tap my foot the whole way down the elevator. Stepping out, I rush into the dungeon and Meagan stands up when I approach, but I blow past her, not giving her a minute to kill my buzz. I spot Knox and Max down the back of the room bending over Max's desk and take off running. The sound of my heels tapping on the floor has heads turning.

Reaching them, Knox looks up, and frowns but I don't care, he is not killing my buzz either. I launch myself into his arms and he stumbles back a little.

"Are you okay, Bailey?" he asks.

"Yes," I breathe, taking a step back. Max taps my shoulder and pouts at me. Laughing, I grab him too, hugging him tight.

"Well, it's nice to see you, sis, it's been a while," he says to me.

"I know, I'm sorry. I just have had so many things to get through lately."

"What's with the whole jumping into his arms?" he flips his thumb towards Knox. Looking around, I notice a few people watching us and straighten myself away from them. I wave my envelope and smile.

"Can you come up to my office in a bit?" I ask Knox.

"I'm kind of busy," he answers, wiping the smile from my face.

"Oh okay, sorry I never thought of that."

Turning, I walk out of the room with my head lowered feeling like a tool for even thinking he would want to share this with me.

"Hold up darlin'."

Turning, I find both of them standing waiting for me to speak. "Well?" he asks, nodding to the envelope in my hand. My mood is slightly less jovial now.

"Come on sis, spill the goods."

Smiling, I pull out the paperwork and hand them over to Knox, biting my lip as he reads over them. Once he is finished, he looks up at me, and my heart pounds waiting for any sign of life from his handsome face. Max grabs the papers from him and begins to read them.

"Congratulations," Knox says, his voice is neutral as he turns to leave. I watch him walk away and feel the sting of tears. Max hands the papers back to me with a hug.

"Congrats sis."

I just nod and clutch them to my chest, pressing the button on the elevator. A lone tear slips from my eye and Max brushes it away. When the door opens I step inside, keeping my back to him. I press the button and wait until I'm moving before I allow the rest of my tears to fall.

Once in my office I lock the door and get to work, drying my face and giving myself a pep talk. Reasoning that this is why I closed myself off again because the people you love the most are the ones that hurt you the most.

Max

"Wow, bro."

He looks up at me and sighs then continues to draw out his plans. "Aren't you going to say anything to her?" I ask.

"No, why would I? Clearly she is fine being alone."

"Clearly you still haven't got a fucking clue. I thought you knew how to read your girl."

"Max, shut the fuck up and get back to work," he says, turning away from me.

I love my brother, but I want to slap his dumbass right now. I take a stroll over to my desk and sit down. I can't concentrate anymore, so I grab my stuff and head up to Frank. I knock on the door and let myself in.

"Hey, Frank."

"Max," he frowns, taking off his glasses.

"I saw Bailey's deeds," I smile, taking a seat opposite him.

A big grin splits his face and he nods, "Yeah, I'm proud of her. It was a quick sale and last minute so she was lucky to have gotten it."

I can tell by the way he talks about Bailey how proud he is of her. I just wish my brother would grow up and get with the program.

"You should have seen her," he continues chuckling, "I haven't seen that smile for a long time and the dancing," he shakes his head laughing this time.

"Yeah she looked happy," I answer.

"She is, so tell me, how did Knox take it?"

Rolling my eyes, I snort. "He's an ass. He thinks she is moving on without him."

"Oh, those two need to be locked in a room together for a few days," he sighs.

"I'm game if you are," I grin at him.

"Don't tempt me, Max, don't tempt me," he says, shaking his head at the situation. I say goodbye and head to the bar to open up.

Bailey

Getting through work is hard, all I can think about is the fact that I own my own house now. Ben and his attempt at getting my money failed miserably. So I'm happy to say at twenty-three years old, I'm a home-owner, and he can go fuck himself.

Then there's my moody, handsome fiancé if he is even that anymore. I honestly don't know. Going through my work emails bore's me, so I turn to the security program I'm developing and get some hours done on that. By the time I look up from the screen, the world has gone dark. Checking my watch, I sigh when I see it is nine thirty on a Friday night. Gathering my bag and jacket, I make my way home.

Driving through the strip, I frown at all the college students out having fun, while I'm headed home to sit alone. Passing the bar, I see a line outside the door and decide to pull in and check it out. Walking around to the front I smile at Junior, the weekend doorman, and he smiles back and opens the door for me. Inside is full and I now realize why; Knox and Max are on stage.

They only play one gig a month now and the crowd apparently likes it. "Hi Amber," I call out, as I round the bar to take a seat. When she sees me, she walks over to give me a hug.

"Hey, I miss you around here Bailey. What's going on with you and the boss?"

"I have no idea, Amber," I answer honestly.

She looks a little pissed, but smiles anyway then brings me a drink. I watch Knox sing. The memories I have of being in here with him make me smile. I miss hanging out with both of them and Paige. Pulling out my phone I video chat her, and when she answers she frowns pointing to her ear to indicate she can't hear me. I mouth 'I know' then flip the camera so she can see the stage.

Neither of us bothers trying to talk. We just sit and listen, when they stop for a break, I flip her back to me.

"Shit, now you just ruined my weekend," she says, wiping her eyes.

"Sorry, I just haven't seen them play for a few months," I answer her.

"Yeah I know that feeling."

We both stare at each other before she waves and hangs up. I know how she is feeling so I understand, and I'll call her tomorrow anyway.

"What is this?" Max shouts when he sees me sitting at the end of the bar.

"I felt like a drink. I didn't know you were playing tonight."

"Yeah we decided to do a surprise gig," he smiles at me. "Coming in for some food?" he nods to the kitchen and I follow him.

Knox didn't notice me when he walked by me a few minutes ago, he was too busy texting. I take a seat at the table while they get their dinner ready.

"Did you see Meagan out there?" Max asks.

"Yeah, how could you not? Did you see the shirt she is wearing?" Knox answers, shaking his head. Max's eyes bug out, and slaps Knox across the back of the head and points to me. Knox turns, seeing me for the first time, and crosses his arms.

"So Meagan, huh?" I ask.

25

He turns away without answering me and grabs his food from the microwave. He chooses to stand by the sink to eat while Max takes the seat beside me.

"Are you going to ignore me?" I ask, looking at him.

Again he looks at me then bends his head down to eat. "Are you fucking serious?" I shout at him, getting his full attention.

"Sis," Max sighs.

"No Max, he does not get to kick me out of my home and then beg me to come back, but then decides to date the damn secretary!"

My anger escalates quickly and I stand up sending the chair crashing to the floor. "You know I'm trying. I came to you today to share something important, but I guess we have different definitions of forever, Knox!"

Grabbing my purse, I walk out of the kitchen and through the side door of the bar. I am quickly yanked back inside by Knox, who looks just as pissed as me.

"I am not fucking dating Meagan!" he shouts at me. "How many times do we have to do this?"

I take a step back away from him and shake my head. "You tell me, Knox, you're the one who started this, not me."

"Fuck! When the fuck are you going to realize that all I want is us?"

"When you start acting like it," I whisper.

"You make me so damn mad, darlin'," he sighs.

We stand facing each other for a few minutes before we both smile, and start to laugh. He pulls me into a hug and holds me. "Baby, I love you."

"You've been pulling out the baby card a lot lately," I whisper to him.

"Because, I need too, I need too..." he sighs.

I move back from him and reach for the door. "Are you leaving?" he asks, and I nod. He reaches for me again and pulls me close. "I'm sorry about today darlin', I'm happy for you."

"Thanks." It doesn't even matter anymore; the joy faded when I left his office earlier today. "I better go, I have a meeting with an architect I know in the morning," I smile.

"Dad? He never said he was in town."

"He gets back later. I emailed him and caught him at the airport."

"Oh okay. How about you stay for a while and have a drink?"

I don't know what to do. I want to stay, but I also don't want to get my heart stomped on again. Knox smiles his beautiful smile at me and pulls me back into the bar. Before returning to the stage, he makes me a drink and kisses my head. I watch him sing and play the guitar effortlessly. His biceps are much bigger than they used to be and I'm sure that the t-shirt he is wearing is about to burst at the seams.

I can't help but smile at him, which he catches and smiles back. He strums the guitar and starts to sing 'If you ever come back' by the Script. He hasn't sung this song for a long time and it hits me square in the chest. Knox keeps his eyes on me while he sings. Max looks over at me and sticks out his tongue. I sing along to the chorus and watch Knox smile. If only things were as simple as they used to be.

"Aw, see that's what I like to see, my boss and his girl making goo-goo eyes at each other," Amber announces, stopping beside me.

"What? We were not making anything with each other."

"That's the problem!" she laughs and I push her away.

When they finish singing, Knox takes a seat beside me and has a beer.

"Thanks for staying."

"I had fun. I miss seeing you guys play," I answer.

"Yeah it's been too long, maybe I could get my father-in-law to let me have a few days off," he says, rubbing his face.

"You can always ask, there is no harm in that."

He chuckles at me while nodding his head, finishing his drink I watch him. He looks tired and he has a permanent frown causing lines on his forehead. Reaching over I smooth my thumb across his forehead to his temple, he sighs and leans into my hand.

"You getting a headache?" I ask, noticing the bloodshot eyes.

"I've had a headache."

27

Max starts to clear the bar with Chase while Knox stands to close up the cash register. He gives my shoulder a squeeze as he passes and kisses the top of my head. Once the bar is empty Max takes the seat beside me.

"So, when I do get to see this new house of ours?"

"Ours?"

He laughs at me. "Hell yeah sis, you really think you're going to get rid of me?"

"I don't want to get rid of you, Max," I smile and lean on his shoulder. Both Knox and Max pull out their phones and announce at the same time.

"Dad's home."

I laugh at them and Knox winks at me. "Text him back that I expect him bright and early," I tease.

"Oh I get it," Max says. "You invite my dad to our new house but not us," he points between himself and Knox.

"I never said you weren't invited; you can come by with your dad tomorrow if you like."

Max agrees and gets off the stool to clean up. Grabbing my purse, I yawn.

"Well, I'm out folks since I have an early morning."

Knox walks over to me taking my hand in his. "Are you okay to drive? You look tired."

"I'm fine, you look tired."

He nods and yawns. "I'm beat," he sighs, rubbing his face again.

"Hurry up and I'll drive you over."

I watch him finish up with the cash drawer and call out to Max that he is leaving. I drive around to the apartment and pull into my spot beside his Harley. Knox takes my hand in his and looks over at me.

"Are you coming up?"

"No, it's not really a good idea," I answer.

He nods and climbs out of the car, walking around the back he opens my door and holds out his hand. "Come on darlin'."

"Knox, I don't want to fight with you, so it's better if I go now."

28

Bending down he reaches over to release my seatbelt and tugs my hand until I get out of the car. We walk into the apartment and the familiar smell makes me smile.

"You made lasagna?"

"Yeah for tomorrow," he takes my hand and leads me into our room, opening my shirt as he goes.

"Knox."

"No darlin', you're staying tonight."

After he successfully gets my shirt off, he falls back onto the bed yawning. Kicking his leg gently, I smile at him then go to wash my face. When I come back, he is asleep where he fell. Bending down, I take his boots off.

"Hey Knox wake up, take off your clothes," I call, shaking him.

He mumbles and then sits up to get undressed. I watch him and help when he gets stuck in his own t-shirt. His hands grip mine until I am in the bed beside him.

"Don't leave me in the morning," he says, pulling me closer to him.

Chapter 4

I wake up before the sun again but decide to stay in bed with Knox. I can't sleep so after a while I get up to make breakfast. In the kitchen, I go through the mail while the coffee is brewing and Knox's pancakes and bacon are warming. I miss being with him every day. It's hard to be away from him, but I know we both need this until the court case is over. Hopefully, once it is, I can relax and start to feel better.

"I thought you left."

Knox frightens me from the door and I scream, dropping the cup of coffee into the sink.

"Jesus Knox!" I shout at him, running my hand under the cold water. He rushes over to me checking my hand.

"I'm sorry darlin'," he says, taking my hand and kissing it.

Pointing to the table, I make him sit down and eat. He watches me drink coffee, but doesn't say anything. I steal a strip of bacon from him and chew it while I text his dad.

"Richard will be at the house by ten," I announce.

"What is he doing there?"

"It needs a lot of work, but it's perfect. I can't wait to move in," I smile at him.

"Sounds good darlin'," he looks sad as he speaks.

"Are you coming to see it?" I can't keep the hopeful tone from my voice.

"Do you want me too?"

"What? Of course I want you too, don't be stupid. I mean unless you want to wait until it's done."

I really want him to want to come with me to share this experience. I don't want him to feel left out of anything.

"Sure, I guess I could come up." He answers, finishing his coffee. "Thanks for breakfast, I'm just getting a shower."

I watch him take two of his pills and walk down to the bathroom. Going into the closet, I grab a pair of shorts and a t-shirt. I don't have much left here. I make the bed and clean up the kitchen and still Knox is in the shower. Walking down, I knock on the door.

"Hey Knox, you okay? We have to leave soon."

I wait for a few minutes before walking inside finding him sitting on the side of the bath in a towel staring at the floor. Kneeling down in front of him, I bend my head so I can see his face.

"Babe?" It breaks my heart seeing his red eyes and I know this is just the beginning of another meltdown between us. Standing up, I turn around to leave him alone and text Max. Slipping on my shoes, I walk back to him.

"I'm going now. I have to meet your dad in ten minutes."

He stands up and nods walking into the bedroom. He gets dressed and grabs his phone.

"Knox, if you want to stay you can. I texted Max and he is coming here."

"Why? I'm fine let's just get this over with," he says, walking by me and opening the door.

"Knox stay here, I'm not doing this. I told you last night."

Walking out of the apartment, I run down the stairs just as Max walks into the building. "Bailey?" he questions. Shaking my head, I walk to my car and take off without them.

I arrive at the house five minutes late and Richard lets me have it. "Morning Bailey, late for our first appointment."

"Sorry," I mumble, walking to the door. He stops me from opening it and smiles, telling me he is teasing me, but I'm not in the mood for it.

"Okay, show me your new home."

Opening the door I lead him inside and we start in the kitchen. I watch him walk around taking pictures and drawing out each room as it is. When we reach the master bedroom, he smiles at the balcony.

"Wow, this is a surprise."

"Yeah I like it, so I want to keep it," I tell him.

"Of course we're keeping it. I will have to reinforce it though the wood looks a little rotten, maybe I'll stucco it and make it safer for my grandkids."

At his words, I crack, tears pour from eyes and I run into his open arms. "That son of mine," he growls, swaying me in his arms. After a few minutes, I wipe my face and let out a deep sigh.

"Sorry, let's get to work." I force a smile, taking him around the rest of the upstairs. We reach the kitchen and he spreads his sheets across the island.

"Now what are your ideas regarding the bedrooms?" he asks, rearranging the papers for me to see.

"Well, I doubt I'll need six bedrooms, so maybe we can knock down this wall and make a retreat."

He nods as I speak and takes notes, marking weird symbols on the pages. We go through the upstairs and tackle the sitting room. We walk into it and both look around - it is dark and cold.

"We need more light in here. I suggest you take out those windows and put panels in. We can add about four full-length windows across the whole wall and you will get the morning sun in here."

"Yeah, sounds nice," I smile at him, picturing a wall full of windows. We finish this room and the office, then finally the kitchen.

"So what is your idea for here? It's quite a large space, but not very well organized," Richard says looking around at the walls and cupboards.

"Rip it out," I answer, looking around the room.

"Why?" he asks, in disbelief.

"I wanted Knox to decide how he wants it, he is the one who cooks most of the time, so I want to give him free reign," I answer, keeping my face hidden.

"Okay, I'll talk to him about what he wants."

I catch the stern tone of his voice and Richard's double meaning. After I decide on the balcony, I leave him to take his measurements and give him a spare key saying goodbye.

Knox

I have been listening to Max for the last hour going on and on about how much of a dick I am and how I don't deserve Bailey. That she should just leave my ass and go find someone else to love.

"I don't get you."

He says, taking a seat on the sofa. "I mean here you have a fucking amazing woman and you can't even treat her right. She should have never taken you back after the last time."

"Max, shut up, what the fuck would you know?"

"I know a lot more about her than you do!" he shouts at me. "I think you're forgetting she turns to me when you're fucking pushing her away. I listen to her and know about all the shit you give her."

"I don't give her shit!" I shout back at him.

"Don't you? Why the fuck don't you ask her about shit instead of trying to tell her what she is supposed to feel?"

I want to smack him. "You don't get it, Max," I sigh.

"Oh I get it, Knox, it's you who doesn't. What went wrong? How can you go from making everyone around you sick with jealousy to making everyone run for cover?"

"I don't know, Max, I don't know how it happened. All I know is after that last court appearance she changed. She just closed down and all my attempts to help her failed. She didn't want me anywhere near her."

"Knox, she needs you. You have to suck it up and tough it out."

"Seriously, suck it up? What do think I have been doing? She doesn't even let me kiss me anymore! Let alone anything else."

The pain behind my eyes explodes almost blinding me. I can't take this anymore. The more I stress about it, the more I get headaches. Walking into the kitchen I take two more pills, grabbing my phone when it rings.

"Hello?"

"Son, I need you to come up here. Oh and bring me T-square, I forgot mine."

33

"Dad, I have a headache, I'm not going anywhere near her house," I answer, resting my head against the wall.

"I'm not asking Knox. I'll see you in ten."

I hang up the phone. "Motherfucker!"

"What?" Max shouts from the sitting room.

"Not you, dumbass - Dad. Can you drive me up there?"

Max calls dad back to get the address and we arrive after a few minutes. Max whistles when we pull into the driveway. The garden is laid out with flower beds and a water fountain in the middle of the driveway.

"Looks pretentious," I moan, climbing out of the truck. Max rolls his eyes at me walking over to my dad, who is standing by the door.

"Hey kids," he calls, hugging Max and frowning before he hugs me too.

"Dad."

He looks at me and shakes his head before walking into the house. I don't want to go in. I don't want to see where my heart will reside for the rest of my life while my body lives somewhere else.

"Damn, this place is awesome!" Max calls out to me.

Stepping inside, I take a deep breath and follow them into the kitchen. I try my best not to care, but it is a nice house. I can almost picture raising kids here.

"Okay Knox, you have free reign, I was told."

Dad says, waving his arm around the kitchen.

"Free reign for what?" I ask, looking between him and Max.

"The kitchen, son. Bailey said she wants you to design it considering you do most of the cooking."

"Told you, you're a fucking dumbass."

Max is smiling at me while poking around in the cupboards. My dad is watching me and I don't understand what is going on here. Why would she want me to design her kitchen? Does she think we will still be friends if things don't work out? Because that can't happen, I couldn't pretend like that with her. Pretend to be something I'm not when all I want to do is marry her and grow old beside her.

"Knox, the kitchen," my dad says again. "I was thinking about doing the same windows in here as what Bailey decided in the sitting room," he says, talking to me like I am listening.

"Dad, stop, just stop for a minute," I hold up my hand halting him, taking a deep breath I look at him. "Start again, Dad."

He walks us through the house telling us about the designs Bailey has chosen. He shows us the balcony off the master bedroom and I instantly know why she fell in love with this place. You can see the whole lake and the back of Frank's house. Looking over, I see her walking through his back yard to the chairs at the lake. She takes a seat with a book and rests it on her knees.

"Hey bro, get a load of this!" Max shouts.

Turning, I walk back through the room and find him looking out a window at Bailey too. "Yeah, I saw her."

"You need to talk to her, Knox. You know she loves you and you love her. And you are getting a designer kitchen, built by one of the best architects around."

Throwing my arm around his neck, I squeeze and pull him out of the room and back down to the kitchen. Dad smiles at us and tells me his ideas about gutting the kitchen and rebuilding.

"Dad, I know you said free reign, but ripping it all out?"

"That's what your fiancée wanted," he says, showing me the sketches.

"Can I take this and work on it?"

"Sure, I'll start on the front of the house."

Max and I walk around the house again and I can't help but smile, thinking about the kitchen I'll design for Bailey. I know she loves the window seat in her dad's house, so I'll definitely add one. After an hour of talking with my dad, he packs up his sketches and heads home; we agree to go over on Sunday for lunch. Max waves as he climbs into the truck refusing to let me inside.

"Nope, go talk to your woman!" he shouts, then pulls out of the driveway, laughing.

Turning around I take another look at the house and start to walk towards Frank's.

Chapter 5

For the last hour, I have studied hard and finally put my book down. Closing my eyes, I turn up my music and relax in the afternoon sunshine. I spoke with Rachel earlier and things are moving along. The judge requested a further statement from me; luckily I can do it over the phone on Monday.

A shadow falls over me and I open my eyes finding Knox standing there; he is looking at me saying nothing.

"What do you want?"

I am in no mood for this again today, so I close my eyes and settle back against the chair. Knox doesn't answer me, but his shadow is still there. Sighing, I open my eyes again and go to sit up. His hands pin my shoulders against the chair and his lips crash into mine. He kisses me hard and possessively, plunging his tongue into my mouth. Wrapping my arms around his neck, I kiss him back, just as hard as he pulls my legs up, hooking them around his waist and takes a seat on the chair.

His hand grips my hair as he holds me close, refusing to break the kiss. I don't know how long we are kissing and I don't care. I miss this, I miss him.

"I love you darlin'," he whispers against my lips.

"I love you too."

Pulling back he stares at me for a long moment, brushing my hair back with his fingers.

"I miss you darlin'."

"Me too," hanging my head, I feel my heart begin to crack, the walls I have put up to keep everyone out are starting to crumble at my feet.

"Are you okay?" he asks, tracing his fingertips along my collarbone.

"Yeah, I am now. I'm tired, Knox, I'm tired of fighting with you."

"I'm sorry darlin'. I'm so sorry for not being there for you."

I press my lips to his again, not wanting to stop now that I have started again. Knox devours my mouth, taking all of me.

"You kids want to come up for air or dinner?" my dad shouts at us.

Pulling back, I bite my lip trying to hold in my laugh. Knox stands up holding me where I am.

"I can walk, babe."

"I know, but I don't want to let you go," he smiles at me, pecking my lips again.

When we arrive in the kitchen my dad claps and cheers at us. He holds out a beer to Knox and a glass of Jack and Coke for me.

"Thanks, Dad," I smile at him.

Knox finally lets me down and I help Dad with dinner while he talks to Knox about the house. I listen to them chat and hear Knox say he was over there.

"You saw the house?" I ask, looking at him.

"Yeah, my dad gave a tour," he gives me an apologetic look.

"Shouldn't it have been the other way round?" I ask, taking a seat beside him.

"Yeah, it should have," he agrees taking my hand and kissing it.

We have dinner with Dad and decide to walk back over to the house. I bring some flashlights because I don't know if there is any power. Once I open the door, I check the lights, but they are off.

"I need to get the power back on so your dad can work."

"You mean the builders he hires can work," he chuckles from behind me, wrapping his arms around my waist. We walk through the house and out onto the back porch.

"Knox, I need to talk to you."

"Okay."

We sit on the steps and watch the lake in the darkness. Taking his hand, I link my fingers through his.

"I spoke with my attorney today; I have to give another statement to the judge. He says he needs me to give my testimony again because the first time I was so emotional the stenographer put every breath and sob into the transcripts and he thinks it will sway some of the jury."

"Darlin'," Knox wraps his arm around me.

"Yeah I know, it's going to be a pain in the ass but at least I can do it over the phone and it will be recorded."

"When does this happen?"

"Monday, nine am," I sigh.

"Do you want me to be with you?" he asks, kissing my head.

"I'd like you to be with me, but I can't ask you to take time off work."

"Darlin', do you really think your dad will say no?"

Shaking my head, I say no because I know when I tell Dad he will probably insist on it.

"So how about a proper tour?" he asks, looking back at the house.

"Yeah, let's go," I reach for his hand and he pulls me up. We walk around the house with our flashlight. Knox listens as I talk and tell him my ideas. When we get upstairs, we walk into one of the spare rooms.

"I was thinking of making this a guest room."

"Yeah sounds good darlin'. Will you be entertaining many guests?" he teases.

"Not really, probably my Mom or Paige. It's a long list," I laugh.

We walk into another room that faces the front garden. It has an attached bathroom and walk-in closet.

"I was thinking of making this room for Max, but don't tell him. I want to surprise him. I know you will want him close and I'd miss him too if he weren't around."

Knox just shrugs and follows me into the master bedroom. I point the flashlight around the walls.

"What do you think if we put the bed at that wall? Then we can put the TV up on this one and have room over on that wall for pictures."

Knox looks confused. "It's your house darlin'. You can do whatever you want."

"Knox?" I look at him for a minute. "Don't you want to live here?"

He opens and closes his mouth like a fish, then runs his hand through his hair.

"I thought you bought it for you," he says.

"Yes, I did but I'm hardly going to live here alone. What did you think was happening here?"

"I thought you bought it to live alone," he says.

Shaking my head, I laugh at him. Wrapping my arms around his neck, I rest my head on his shoulder. "No, you idiot, I saw it for sale and I thought I'd snap it up before someone else got it. You always tell me that you love my dad's house, so I thought you'd be happy here."

He holds me close to him. "I want to live where ever you are darlin'. I want to marry you and have kids with you. I fought hard for you and I'm not giving you up."

"Knox, I don't want to give you up either. I'm sorry for stressing out and pushing you away. I didn't mean to, I am just so angry…"

He places a soft kiss on my lips, cupping my cheek in his hand. "I know darlin'. I'm sorry too, I'm sorry I wasn't there for you when you needed me."

Looking up at him I nod, he kisses me again, and then picks me up off the floor and twirls me around.

"So you really want me to live with you?" he asks, grinning at me.

"No, I figured we'd get married and I'd live here and you can pitch a tent out back."

Laughing, he pushes his hips into me. "I can damn well pitch a tent darlin'," he says proudly. We laugh so hard we both have tears in our eyes.

"God I missed us," he says leading me down the stairs and out the door. We walk around the lake then go back into my dad's. Knox makes me a drink and we sit on the window seat in the dark.

"Do you want to hear my ideas for the kitchen?"

"No, I want it to be a surprise." I smile at him, "I trust you."

"Really? Maybe you shouldn't darlin', I mean, I have been known to go crazy with my credit card."

I laugh at his sarcasm because we both know he almost breaks out in hives if he has to crack out the plastic. I finally relax, feeling the tension leaving my shoulders and I sigh. All the back and forth with Knox has been hard. I really hope he sticks to his word and stays by my side with this sentencing hearing. I catch him yawning, and pressing the heel of his hand into his eye, rubbing it.

"You still have a headache?"

"Yeah, it doesn't want to go."

I clean up our glasses and we go up to my room; he smiles when he steps inside. Commenting how he hasn't slept here in over a year, it's weird thinking about it. I take a quick shower and throw on a t-shirt. Crawling into bed, I burrow in beside him.

"I love you darlin'."

"Love you too, babe."

I wake up early - my body is wrapped up in Knox, and I feel content. He kisses my shoulder and asks if I am going for a run.

"No babe, not today."

Knox lifts his head and looks down at me. "You feeling okay?" he questions.

"Yes, I take Sunday's off since I started practice again."

"Well it just so happens that I have Sunday's off too," he says, placing soft kisses along my shoulder.

"I know, but why are you awake at this hour?"

"Can't sleep," he whispers, against my neck.

Turning around I face him and frown. "Why can't you sleep?"

"Because I have crazy thoughts running around in my head."

I begin to get worried and check his eyes as best I can in the dim light. They don't look as bad as before. He smirks at me.

"Darlin', not that kind of crazy," he says, pulling me on top of him.

"Oh, that kind," I smile.

"Yeah, that kind."

I hesitate for a minute because it's been a few months since we've had sex and I'm not sure if I want to jump right back in. But then he pulls me down and kisses me softly and all my hesitation flies out the window.

By the time the sun comes up Knox and I are sweating and smiling. I can feel his heart beat against my cheek as I look into his eyes. He traces his fingers up and down my thigh, smiling at me.

"I think it was worth the wait," he announces, settling back against the pillow with his arm behind his head. Shaking my head, I gently bite his chest making him flinch. "Ouch darlin'," he laughs, covering my mouth with his hand. He smooth's my hair off my face, brushing his thumb along my cheekbone.

"What do you want to do today?" I ask.

"Nothing, just stay in bed and turn off our phones and listen to music," he smiles.

"Yeah, sounds like fun. We haven't done that since last Christmas."

I remember last Christmas Eve we did just that, cut ourselves off from the world and stayed in bed all day. We watched movies, listened to music, and made love, and we also ate way too much chocolate. Knox closes his eyes and smiles. I bet he is remembering that day too.

"Come on, we can get breakfast then come back up, but no candy today."

He laughs and agrees, pulling on his jeans he follows me downstairs. After breakfast, we spend the day in my room watching movies and making love. Everything feels like it's getting back to where it belongs.

Chapter 6

After a shower I throw on a tank top and jeans, my heart is pounding in my chest as I walk down to the kitchen. Knox has breakfast waiting for me, but I can't eat, shaking my head I take a seat at the table and place the phone in front of me.

"You okay darlin'?"

Closing my eyes, I take a deep breath and rub my sweaty palms up and down my thighs. After the day spent in bed yesterday, I was able to forget about this morning, but now that's here and I am a nervous wreck. Knox takes a seat beside me and holds my hand. We both just sit in silence as time ticks by. The shrill of the phone ringing makes me jump with fright. Knox gives my hand a squeeze and I pick up the phone.

"Hello?"

"Good morning, Bailey," Rachel says. "I just wanted to go over a few things before we are put through to the court."

"Okay," I answer.

"Okay, just relax, you will be sworn in and then the judge will ask you some questions. Remember this will be recorded as testimony and if I feel something is out of line I will object; otherwise I'll stay quiet, but I will be on the line, okay?"

"Yeah, thanks."

"Okay then, here we go," she says.

I listen to the bailiff swear me in and repeat his words. I can feel my hands begin to shake. Knox grips me a little firmer, letting me know he is with me.

"Good morning, Miss Mortenson, my name is Judge Abraham and I will be asking you some questions."

"Good morning," I croak out.

"In your own words, Miss Mortenson, can you tell me what happened…"

My mind blanks, I can't hear what he is saying and I start to panic. Knox turns my face to his and smiles, mouthing for me to breathe. The Judge calls my name and I snap to attention.

"In your own words please," he says again.

Closing my eyes, I picture myself and my Mom arguing in the car, then me getting out and walking to the graveyard.

"I walked into the graveyard and sat in front of my friend's grave. I was speaking to her, telling her about my life. When I heard a voice behind me, I turned around and saw Ben Miler. He wouldn't let me leave; when I tried to he kept blocking my way. He was taunting me and calling me names. He admitted to sending me the dead roses.

I tried to walk away again, but that's when he hit me across the face. He accused me of turning my best friend against him and blamed me for her killing herself. Then he jumped on me, pulling my hair back so hard I couldn't move. He punched me in the stomach and I knew I had to do something to get away, so I punched him in between the legs.

That's when he grabbed my hair again and began punching me in the face. I tried to fight back. I hit him and scratched him, but I could only see out of one eye. I remember scratching his eyes and he twisted my wrist so hard I felt the bones break. I fell to the ground and he pulled me up by my hair. He smashed my face into the headstone, twice. Then I woke up in the hospital."

The line is quiet for a few minutes before the judge clears his throat. He thanks me for my time then hangs up. Rachel says she will call me later after my testimony has been submitted. I put the phone down on the table and take a few deep breaths. Knox lifts me onto his lap, and I press my face into his neck as my tears fall. To this day, I can feel every punch and kick.

"Knox?"

"Yeah, darlin'?"

"Will you tell me what happened after that?" I ask.

We never spoke about it. It was too painful for both of us. Then life moved on and so did we, for a while anyway. When

43

Knox, Max, and Paige had to give their testimonies in court, the defense attorney argued until I was removed from court, so I never got to hear their sides. That was the day I fired my uncle; he didn't even try to stop me from being thrown out.

We argued on the steps of the courthouse and I fired him. Then in my regular fashion I walked downtown and found myself a new attorney and haven't looked back since.

"Are you sure you want to hear this darlin'?"

"Yes."

Knox takes a deep breath and clears his throat. "After you left with your Mom, I got Max and Paige to walk to that café with me. When we got there, the waitress told us you went up to the graveyard. I wanted to give you some time so Paige got us coffees to go. I don't know why, but I was getting a bad feeling so I started walking that way.

Paige was acting weird, so Max and I walked in front of her. When we got to the graveyard, we heard a scream. I knew it was you, I just knew. I took off running and found some guy beating the shit out of you.

I just crashed into him to get him off you and started punching his face. I don't know how long or how many times, but I just kept going. The next thing I know, Max has me in a bear hug pulling me off the guy I wanted to kill. When I got to you, I tried to lift you up a bit, there was blood everywhere, and your face was so swollen that I could hardly recognize you.

Then, you stopped breathing in my arms. I swear I died right there. I couldn't believe that you left me. I didn't want it to be true. I had to fix it. I had to get you back, so I just started to breathe into your mouth. I remember screaming at Max to help me. The next thing I know some guy is cutting off your clothes and I wanted to kill him too, but Max held me back.

He told me it was the EMT's. You weren't moving, so they put that machine on you. It wasn't working and I was losing it. Max had to physically hold me back. I can't get that voice out of my head. Then when it said it found a pulse, the EMT's had you in the ambulance in about ten seconds and you were gone.

The next thing I know, I'm in handcuffs being dragged away and getting questioned for beating you up."

Although his voice is steady and strong, I feel every one of his hot tears land on my cheek. Pressing myself closer to him I hold on tight. "I love you," I whisper.

"I know," he says, resting his head against mine. "I love you too, darlin', so damn much."

We stay together for a while just holding on to each other. In all my pain and anger, I forgot what he went through too.

"Okay darlin', let's go," he says, helping me to my feet. He rubs his hand across his eyes and down his face drying his tears.

"Where are we going?"

"To the beach. I was supposed to have lunch with Dad yesterday, but we can do it today. You get changed and I'll call him."

I walk up the back stairs to my room, feeling drained. Reliving that nightmare again was painful. Hopefully the next time I deal with this situation it will be the last. I put on my bikini and a sundress and walk back down to Knox. He gives me his megawatt smile and a kiss.

"Ready for a day of fun in the sun?"

"Yeah, so was your dad annoyed about yesterday?"

"Nah, he's cool. We can have lunch with him today. He has to run into the office, but he said he'd be back later."

Knox drives us to his dad's house and when we arrive Richard is already home. He gives me a hug and asks how I'm doing.

"Fine thanks."

"Good, you're a strong woman," he winks at me.

We sit out on the back patio talking about the house for a while. Knox decided to take a photo of us standing by the ocean and text it to Max.

"You're mean."

"I know," he grins, just as his phone rings. He and Max go back and forth with name calling before finally being nice and saying goodbye to each other.

"He said I have to take care of you."

"Yeah? What can I say? All the Porter men love me."

I smile at him, then pull off my dress. We head into the water and splash around for a while, then we act like five-year-

45

olds and jump over the waves. Knox picks me up and throws me over a wave.

"Get back here beautiful," he says, grabbing my hand.

I hook my legs around his waist and whisper, "I love being here."

"I know darlin', me too. It reminds of the night we got engaged."

He looks out over the water, shielding his eyes from the sun. I press a kiss to his cheek and rest my head against his.

"I don't know if I ever thanked you, for saving my life."

"You did darlin' and you don't have too. If I am able to, I will, not that I want to be in a situation where I'd have too."

Turning his face he kisses my nose and we rest our cheeks together again. The sun is warming my skin and the water is lapping over us. Knox is just holding me while we stand and daydream.

"I remember one of the last times I just stood in the ocean. My Mom was having a good day and kept Max and I home from school. We hung out in the ocean all day and just stood here watching the sun go down."

"Sounds like it was a good day," I whisper.

"Yeah," he smiles. "It is one of the best memories I have of her."

Turning around he walks back towards the house, only putting me down when we reach the patio. He hands me a towel and I wrap myself up tight. One of the perks of living in California is always having hot towels at the beach.

"Who's hungry?" Richard asks out the window.

"Yeah Dad," Knox shouts back. "Do you want help?"

Richard declines and Knox relaxes back in his chair. He takes my hand in his, rubbing his thumb across my knuckles methodically. Closing my eyes I relax further into my chair, the sun is keeping me warm and my thoughts turn to the pending court date. Although I try to keep it out of my mind, it tends to creep in when I least expect it. I'm not sure how it's going to go down and I'm not sure why the jury needed another testimony from me. But as long as it gets Ben put away, I'll keep doing it if I have to.

"Darlin'?"

"Yeah," I answer, keeping my eyes closed.

"I think we need to set a date."

Opening my eyes I look over at him, he tilts his face towards mine and smiles at me.

"Is that what you've been thinking about?" I question.

"That's all I think about, darlin'."

I'm actually a little stunned; we agreed to wait until I turned twenty-five and I only just turned twenty-three. I can't find words. I have no idea what to say to him. Yes, the last two days have been great but what if things go back to the way there have been lately. He watches me intently, and I can see his jaw tighten. Just as I am about to open my mouth, Richard walks out calling us for lunch.

"Smells good," I smile at Richard when I sit down. Knox pours me a soda and we dig in to roast beef sandwiches. I can only eat half of it and rub my stomach, groaning. They laugh at me, calling me a light-weight.

"Here you finish it," pushing the plate over to Knox. I nibble on some chips.

"So when is the first game?" Richard asks.

"Oh in a few weeks, just after Thanksgiving."

He smiles and claps his hands. "Can't wait, I'll be there. Just email me so I don't forget."

"Oh, we got new uniforms."

"Oh God, no," Knox groans. "Please tell me they cover more of you."

"No sorry, they are actually tighter and shorter."

"What! They can't get any shorter!"

I nod at him trying to look sorry, but I'm not. I remember my first few games. Knox was like a bull. He couldn't handle all the guys making crude comments about me, and cat calling.

"You don't have to watch, Knox."

"Like hell I don't, those guys are fucking animals," he snorts.

Richard and I both laugh at him knowing full well he can be just like them. I help clean up after lunch and Richard goes back to drawing up the blueprints for my house. Knox and I return to the ocean for a swim.

"Are you for real darlin' or are you just messing with me?"

47

"About?"

"The uniforms," He frowns at me.

"Nope, sorry, there was a vote before I got back on the team and they passed it. We have a photo shoot a few days before the game for our calendar."

Knox hangs his head and sighs. "More ass kicking," he mumbles.

I splash him in the face and swim away screaming as he chases me. After a playful few hours, we finally get out of the water. Knox throws me over his shoulder and walks me back to the house. We sit and watch the sun go down. I am feeling more relaxed than I have in the last two years.

"Thanks, babe."

"What for darlin'?"

"Bringing me here today; I think I really needed it."

He grins at me while drying off his chest with the towel. My eyes rake over his body; he is toned, tanned and God Almighty sexy.

"See something you like, darlin'?" he smirks at me.

"Yes, very much so."

Bending down, I kiss him quickly. Protesting, he pulls me back and nibbles on my lips until I kiss him again, properly this time, shivering as the night air touches my skin. Knox wraps a towel around my shoulders and rubs his hands up and down my back.

"At this rate I'll have a grandchild in a few weeks," Richard comments, out of nowhere.

Knox and I both laugh at him and I leave to get dressed. We say goodnight after a coffee and I drive Knox home. He begs me to stay at the apartment, but I refuse; holding his hands up in surrender he kisses me goodnight and walks backward into the building.

When I arrive home, I take a shower and fill dad in on my day. He asks if I can come to work tomorrow afternoon and I agree. I drag myself to bed just after ten o'clock when my phone rings.

"Hey Max, why are you calling me so late?"

"It's me darlin', did I leave my phone in the car?"

"Let me check. You're lucky you caught me I was about to turn off the light," I yawn.

"Sorry darlin', but I can't find it."

I walk out the garage and check my car, reaching into the door pocket and under the seat. "No babe, let me ring it." I hang up and dial his phone hearing it ring from the trunk.

I call him back. "Hi, it was in the trunk. I'll have Dad bring it in tomorrow."

"Okay thanks, darlin', love you."

"You too, night."

Hanging up, I bring his phone up to my room to charge and get into bed. The minute I hit the pillow I fall asleep.

I am woken up by beeping, and cracking an eye open I see a glow on the wall. Closing my eyes again, I roll over when I hear another beep. Cursing, I get out of bed and grab the phone. I am met with picture texts of naked boobs with captions. Another one comes in this time lower with a crude message written above it.

The number is private, so I don't know who they are from because there is no face, just girly parts. Another message pops up and I almost vomit. I do not want to see some chick with her legs open. I am beyond pissed off now. One, because it's three in the morning and two because this is Knox's phone. I've never snooped in his phone, but I know he has been texting a lot in the last few weeks.

My inner bitch rears her ugly head and I do it, I snoop. I scroll through past messages and phone calls. There is nothing odd on the phone; no other messages like this, but there are a few missed calls from an unknown number, all after midnight. I put the phone down and lie on my bed staring at the ceiling. More message come in and a friend request for his social media page, which I didn't know he had. I click on the link and find Meagan has sent the request; my heart incinerates in my chest.

Scrolling through his profile all I see are girls, lots and lots of girls. He has only about fifty friends and I know most them, but some of the pictures are downright pornographic. Why the fuck do guys do this? Turning the phone off I put it back on the nightstand and get dressed to go run. It's only four in the morning, but it's not like I'll go back to sleep.

Running around the lake does nothing for me, just makes me angrier every time I pass my new house. I think of how my life was supposed to go, how everything seemed okay these last few days, but in all honesty, Knox and I have been hanging by a thread for a while.

When I finally get home, my dad is up and drinking coffee. "Wow sweetheart, you are up earlier than usual."

"Yeah couldn't sleep," I answer, grabbing water from the fridge.

"Try not to let this Ben thing get you down, Bailey. You are moving on, you bought a house, and you and Knox seem to be doing better."

"I know, Dad, I'll be okay."

I kiss his cheek and head up for a shower. Afterward, I grab my bag and drive to the apartment. I know he will only be getting up now. Walking into the apartment I find Max wandering around in his boxers.

"Hey sis, what are you doing here?"

"Hi Max, put some clothes on," I walk into the bedroom finding Knox getting dressed.

"Mornin darlin', this is a nice surprise."

"I bet it is, I got an even nicer one at three this morning."

He frowns at me and tilts his head a little while tying his tie, "What do you mean?"

Taking his phone from my pocket I hand it over, he smiles and says thanks but I don't return his smile. I'm jealous and angry and majorly pissed off.

"Darlin'?"

"You have interesting texts, Knox. Oh and not to forget a social media profile."

"You went through my phone?" he asks, turning it on.

I don't answer because I know I am acting like a teenage girl, but fuck! Who wouldn't after seeing that shit! The phone beeps a few times and he opens the messages, shaking his head he looks at me.

"I don't know who this is," he says, deleting the pictures.

"Well they know you, by name," I answer.

50

"Yeah I know," he sighs, "it's been happening for a while. She just keeps sending me pictures of her."

"Yeah Knox, pull the other fucking leg. You have been texting for months way more than usual."

"Are you kidding me? You think I know this chick?"

Turning, I leave the room and walk into the kitchen, finding Max dressed for work and looking at me puzzled.

"Don't you even stick up for him," I snap.

He holds his hand up and gets up out of the chair. "I love you, but you're fucking way off, sis."

"Sorry Max," I sigh.

He nods and leaves when Knox walks into the kitchen. He looks at me with that same stupid guilty expression. Tears sting my eyes; I'm so angry right now.

"I'm sorry I didn't tell you about the page, but I know how you feel about that site."

"Don't even try to put this on me! If you were even thinking about me, you would have put down that you are in a relationship, not single. And what's with all the fucking porn? Who are these people?"

"I don't know who they are, just some chicks putting stuff up," he answers.

"Yeah well, make a fucking decision, Knox. Either you want what we can have or you can go back to being the single twenty-five-year-old guy in the band."

Grabbing my bag, I walk by him, banging my shoulder off his on my way. He doesn't call me back and I don't turn around. I arrive at college too early. I only have one class today from ten until noon. I find a quiet corner in the café, pulling out my laptop I get to work on my program.

"What are you doing here so early?"

Looking up, I watch Abbey take a seat opposite me with a coffee in hand.

"Bad morning."

She shakes her head and holds up a finger, she gets another coffee and two muffins. Coming back Abbey takes her seat again, handing me a coffee and muffin. "So what has he done?"

I fill her in on my life for the last few days, leaving out some more personal stuff. But I tell her all about Knox's text messages and Facebook page, and her jaw drops.

"I didn't think you guys did the whole social media thing."

"We didn't," I answer, shaking my head. "I don't get it, Abbey, why would he set one up now, and have all those girls on it?"

Grabbing my laptop, she pulls up her own page and finds Knox through Eric. I don't want to look, but I can't help it. We scroll through all the pictures on the wall of skanks. Abbey clicks on Knox's pictures and we see a few of him and Max, the band and some of the beach. There are no pictures of him, and I, and that hurts me even more.

"I don't get it," she sighs, looking up at me.

"Yeah neither do I," closing my computer I sit back down and finish my coffee.

"Come on babe, let's go to class," she says, giving me a sad smile.

Chapter 7

Knox

I drive to the office in silence. Max is listening to music, and I'm freaking out. I thought those texts had stopped. I have no idea who this chick is and I don't know how she got my number. We walk into the office in silence too. I have a feeling Max is pissed at me, but he hasn't even asked for my side.

Sitting at my desk I get to work on my presentation for today. Frank has some buyers and asked me to pitch the project again. I'm not sure if he has spoken to Bailey yet, but I'm sure I'll find out soon enough.

"Hi, Knox," Meagan chirps, as she walks around handing out mini muffins.

"Hey," I reply, turning away from her.

She offers me a muffin and I decline, her bottom lip juts out in a pout, but I don't fall for it. I'm done being nice to chicks; sometimes I get pissed off that I look like I do. I'm not arrogant, I know I'm not an ugly bastard, but still. Sometimes it's annoying when chicks don't leave me alone. I do my best to concentrate and ignore Meagan, praying that she will walk away, but she just stands there, looking at me while sticking her chest out.

"Meagan, I'm busy here."

Another pout and she puts her hand on my arm, leaning in. "Are you okay Knox, you seem a little upset. Did you not sleep well?"

"Meagan, I'm fine. Now please, I'm busy."

"Okay, well if you ever need to talk I'm just over there," she says, pointing to her desk. She turns and hits me in the face with her hair, then says 'oops' and leaves.

"And you wonder why your fiancée is pissed," Max says from behind me.

Turning, I look at him. I'm about to open my mouth when he shocks the shit out of me.

"I never should have served her that night. I should have kicked her underage ass out of the bar."

He walks away from me without another word. Leaving the room, I pace the lobby in front of the elevators. Pulling out my phone I dial and pray that she talks to me.

"Hello."

"Hey Paige, its Knox. Do you have a minute?"

The line is silent for a while before she clears her throat. "Yeah sure, what can I do for you?"

"I need help," I sigh.

"Uh-oh what did you do now?" her voice sounds cautious like she shouldn't be talking to me.

"I need a computer wizard."

"You're engaged to one," she answers quietly.

"Yeah, I know, but I can't ask her."

I tell Paige what has been going on with the text messages and I don't know who they are from. I want them to stop, but the phone company can't help me. I am stuck and I need help.

"Knox, I'm not sure what I can do. I'm a programmer, Bailey is the security expert."

"Fuck, Paige, I don't know what to do and I know she doesn't believe me."

"Okay, leave it with me. Send me all the info you have and forward me the texts."

"They are graphic," I sigh and send them on to her while she waits.

"Knox, no offense but that is some nasty shit. I'm sorry, but seriously."

"I'll send you the less nasty ones and delete the rest again. Thanks, Paige, I appreciate your help."

"Sure, take care and Knox?"

"Yeah?"

"I'm only helping because I don't want my friend hurt again. She's been through enough in the last few years."

Hanging up I'm even more pissed. I know Paige is looking out for Bailey, but so am I. After a few more hours of going over designs, I head to the café, finding Max and I sit down with him. We still don't talk. I know he is stuck in the middle, but he should really let me explain things.

"Hey kids, all set for the presentation?" Frank asks, taking a seat beside us.

"Yes," I answer.

"Fantastic, I'll see you in a few minutes," he pats my shoulder when he leaves and I relax a little; at least Bailey hasn't told him yet.

"You're lucky, Knox. You get the girl, her father likes you, and you have to fuck it all up."

Taking his soda, he walks away from me taking my appetite with him. I see Meagan making her way over to me so I get up and leave. I have no desire to keep entertaining her. When I arrive in Frank's office, we go over the proposal quickly and he says he will meet me in the conference room in five minutes. I have all my boards set up and I'm just going over my speech, a few people are walking into the room.

Lifting my head, I say hello, then take a seat waiting for Frank and the other guys to arrive. Keeping my head down I look over my designs. I love doing this, giving proposals, telling people about my designs. I'm looking forward to the day Max and I can open our own company.

"Sorry we're late everyone, for those of you who don't her, this is my daughter Bailey."

Lifting my head, my stomach hits the floor. She completely ignores me and introduces herself. She sounds so formal, and business-like, once she is finished she walks over to me.

"You're in my seat," she says, banging her bag on the table.

I don't want to make a scene and move out of her way. She grabs my designs and hands them to me without looking, effectively dismissing me. It stings. I would feel better if she had have slapped me.

Frank starts the meeting off as he talks about the design in a general way before nodding for me to take over. I stumble for a minute, but pull myself together and focus on the guy sitting across from me. When I'm done I take a seat and sigh, the tension in the room is obvious, well maybe just to me.

"Hi, I'm Bailey, Assistant Director of Security Programming."

She starts and I have never seen her in action before, but listening to her sell her security software I'm in awe. She gives a flawless pitch and explains everything when asked a question. When the meeting is over she walks by me as if I don't exist. I try to catch her, but Frank corners me in the room.

"Knox, that was a great pitch."

"Thanks, Frank."

"I'm not stupid," his voice takes on a harsh tone, "I know something is going on here and I'm telling you this is the last chance you're getting with my daughter. I love you like a son, but you're not, she's mine and don't think I'd stand by and let her get hurt again."

I swallow hard I can't function right now; pulling out my phone in a desperate move. I show him the pictures and tell him what has been going on. I never in a million years thought I'd be showing my future father in law pictures of a naked chick, but I have to make him understand.

He asks me a million questions and shakes his head in anger, telling me I should have come to him sooner. He tells me he has no one who can access my phone except Bailey. We all know she is the security brains here, but she refuses to accept the title.

"I have someone looking into it," I admit.

"Who?" he snaps.

"Paige, she is good with computers, not as good as Bailey, but at least she knows where to start looking."

Frank paces the room then turns to me. "Go home, son," he says, before walking out the door.

My chest constricts, and walking back to my desk I keep my head down. My hands are shaking as I gather my stuff. I leave the truck for Max and walk home. My head is blank, and I have no idea what the fuck just happened.

Arriving home, I change into jeans and a T-shirt, throw on my boots and grab my helmet. I haven't been on my bike for a while so I drive to my dad's office. It takes me about an hour. Walking in here I get the same shit from the chicks, all smiles and pushing out their chests, touching me when they talk to me. Knocking on his door I walk in.

"Hi son, this is a nice surprise," he beams at me.

The minute I look into his face I crumple, words flow without a filter. Now I'm even showing my own father pictures of some chick. He listens to me while I waffle on. I tell him how much I love Bailey and I thought things were getting sorted between us.

Then I take a deep breath and prepare myself.

"I think Frank just fired me."

My dad looks shocked. I thought I would see anger and disappointment, but after the shock I see sadness.

"It's okay, Knox, you're my son, and I'll take care of you."

He wraps his arm around my shoulders and I feel about six years old again.

"How did it get this messy?" I ask, finally letting the angry tears fall.

I hang out in dad's office for a few hours and then follow him home. We sit across from each other eating dinner. He has a concerned expression on his face and he is watching me closely.

"I think you should get a new phone number and only give it to people you know are not doing this."

"Dad, the only women I have in my phone are the ones I need for work, Bailey, Paige and Peggy next door. I don't give my number to chicks, not after all that shit with Stacey and Lindsey."

My dad shakes his head. "I don't get it, son. You both looked happy yesterday," his voice comes out in a sad whisper.

"We were Dad, then I left my phone in her car."

Dad and I spend the rest of the night going through my phone and trying to figure out who could be sending the messages. We come up empty and I just get angrier. He calls the phone company demanding that they find out who the blocked number belongs too. By midnight, were are both exhausted. I say goodnight to my dad and go to my room to call Max.

"Yeah?" he answers.

"Hey, just letting you know I'm staying with Dad tonight."

"Right, so what happened today, why'd you leave?"

"I didn't leave, I think Frank fired me."

Max is quiet for a while then sighs. "Okay bro, sorry for being a dick, but I don't get you. Seriously Knox, who is the chick?"

"I don't know, Max, I swear. Dad and I have spent that last few hours going through my phone and he called the phone company again."

I'm tired of explaining this to everyone. I only want to tell one person and she totally blanked me today.

"Okay bro, I'll talk to you tomorrow," he says and hangs up. Throwing the offending piece of plastic and glass on the nightstand, I crawl into bed.

Chapter 8

Bailey

We are running drills for practice, Abbey, and Becky are sticking close to me making sure I don't lose it. They don't know that I have managed to build up half a wall around my heart again.

"Come on slackers!"

Ryan shouts at us from the bleachers; he too has been sticking to me like glue. I haven't seen Knox since last Tuesday. Another week of my life fucked up and next week I will be back in Grove, alone.

We practice for another hour. Becky goes easy on me, only knocking me on my ass twice. By the time we are done, I'm sore all over and I just want a bath.

"Okay ladies, milkshakes on me," Ryan calls out as we head into the locker room.

Half an hour later, we walk out to meet him and drag ourselves over to the diner. We take the biggest booth and spread out. I order my shake and close my eyes.

"All set for the game in a few weeks?" Ryan practically shouts at us.

"Dude! Keep it down," I moan, closing my eyes again.

When our shakes arrive I sit up and look around, most people in here have come from practice, so I relax. I know Knox should be working in the bar tonight. Dad said he never came back to work last week and he's worried about him. I suggested he send a picture of a naked chick and ask to meet him. I was told to start acting like a grown up and that his phone is not working.

I have been tempted to call the number to check for myself, but I'm not sure if this is another one of Dad's ways to get Knox and I talking. I listen to my friends talk about the game in a few weeks and nod when I'm supposed to, but I just want to go home.

"Okay folks I'm out, I have a paper to write."

"Liar, liar, liar," Ryan chants. I give him a light slap on the head as I pass.

"I'm not lying, see you all tomorrow."

When I get home, dad is in his office. "Burning the midnight oil, old man?"

"Hi sweetheart, how was practice?"

"Good, the usual, I'm sore. I think I'll take a bath and go to bed."

Walking around the desk, I hug him around his neck and kiss his cheek. He is working on the final proposal alone because Knox hasn't shown up for work.

"I don't know why you didn't just go to the apartment or the bar and ask him what he is playing at."

Dad pats my arm. "Don't worry about it. Are you going to be okay leaving by yourself on Friday?"

"Yeah, Mom is meeting at the airport," I answer.

"Good, at least she will be there."

"Yep, okay I'm going before I can't move in the morning."

My dad stands up and hugs me tight. "You look better sweetheart," he says, letting me go.

"Thanks, Dad. Is that your way of telling me I look fat?" I ask walking out the door.

"No, you look healthy," he calls after me.

"You're such a liar, Frank!" I shout over my shoulder. I hear him laughing as I climb the stairs smiling.

***

Today in class I am swamped. I've decided to hole up in the library and get some work done because I will miss next week.

"I heard a rumor you were back."

Looking up, I smile at Agent Daniels. He insists I call him Matt, but I refuse; he will always be Agent Daniels to me.

"Yep, they took me back."

"Good, I'm glad to hear it. I don't see you signed up for my class."

"No point torturing myself, is there?" I answer.

He gives me a smile. "That doesn't mean you can't take the class. Are you still working with your father?"

"Yes, I like it, but it's not the same. I set out to do something good in my life and ended up ruining it."

"We all make mistakes, Bailey. Just because you can't work for the FBI doesn't mean you can't work locally."

"Nah, I'm good. I write the security programs for Dad's clients and some other small businesses."

Standing up he gives me a wink. "See, landed on your feet," he pats my shoulder as he leaves.

I seriously miss his class, but I fucked that up too; that night I hit Emily at Cara's party. After Ben was arrested, she pressed charges against me and now I have a misdemeanor assault on my record. I can't believe how dumb I was, and that cost me everything I ever wanted. I'm sure Nan and Summer are pissed off with me too.

Maybe that's why Knox and I aren't working. Maybe all the bad I ever did is coming back around on me tenfold. Turning back to my computer I get back to work, managing to write two papers and get some reading done. By the time I leave the library, it's after six and the nights are getting darker earlier. I don't want to be alone tonight so I call Max.

"Yo sis what up?"

"You fool," I laugh. "What are you doing?"

"Xbox, you?"

"You and your video games, are you alone?" I ask, biting my lip.

"Yep, as usual, why you want to hang out?"

"Yeah, if that's cool with you?"

He laughs at me and tells me to get my ass up to the apartment. I use my keys and find him waiting for me, with the game all set up.

"Ah, already waiting for me to kick your ass?" I smile, sitting on the floor beside him.

He gives me a hug and kiss on the cheek. "You wish, Mortenson, you're going down, baby!"

We play video games for a few hours. I'm still crap, but Max lets me play anyway. He never kills me straight away but lets me linger and usually I end up killing myself, by falling off building's or crashing the cars.

"You suck!" he shouts, cupping his mouth.

"Oh shut up!" I slap his head on my way to the kitchen and grab a bottle of water. "Come on bro walk me to my car, I need to get going."

Max grabs a sweater and throws Knox's hoodie at me. I slip it on as I walk out the door. I can smell his cologne and wrap it tighter around myself. Max throws his arm around my shoulders as we walk back to the campus parking.

"What's on the agenda for the weekend, sis?"

"Nothing, hanging out with Mom. I'll probably get a lecture about my weight and my clothes and anything else you can think of," I smile at him.

"Good luck," he groans. "Ah, look your little car all alone."

"Yep, just like the owner. Thanks for walking me," I give him a hug and open the door.

"Are you giving that back?" he points to the hoodie.

I pull the neck closer to my nose and inhale. "Nope," I smile, climbing into the car. Max laughs closing the door for me. I wave to him as I pull away.

I don't have anything left of Knox's in my dad's house, so what if I steal a little ole hoodie. Okay well, it's his favorite one, but I'm taking it anyway and that's weird because he usually wears it to work. I press it to my nose again smelling him in. If I wasn't driving I'd close my eyes and pretend he was holding me.

When I get home, I can't sleep. I have my bags packed and in my car, but I can't settle down. Climbing out of bed I run down to the kitchen and grab the hoodie, wrapping it around myself I crawl back into bed. Picking up my phone I scroll through the pictures. Most of them are old, but I had Knox text me the one he took of us at the beach last week. We look happy and it's been a long time since either of us looked that way.

Steeling myself against the hurt I press his name, putting the phone to my ear I listen, but all I get is a message telling this number is no longer in service. I dial Max and wait.

"Yeah," he mumbles.

"Max, has Knox changed his number?"

"Yeah, he got a new one the other day."

"Oh okay, thanks. Sorry for waking you."

I hang up and lie in bed looking out of the window, time drifts by with the clouds, and I can't take it anymore. Grabbing my phone, I dial the bar.

"Georges Bar."

"Hi Chase, is Knox there?"

"Yep, hang on."

I can hear him yell for Knox and the phone being put on the bar, a few minutes later I hear Knox ask who it is. Chase answers with 'the missus'. "Hey Bailey, hang on, transferring you to the office."

My heart thumps in my chest and now I don't even know why I called.

"Hello," Knox's voice comes over the line. "Hello?" he says again.

"Oh hi, I didn't know you changed your number," I bumble out.

"Yeah, I had too. Why, did you need something?" he asks.

"No, I just couldn't sleep…" I leave the sentence hanging, just like me. Neither, of us, speaks for a few minutes until Chase shouts that it's lights out.

"I have to lock up now," he says.

"Yeah okay, I'll talk to you later. Oh, Dad is worried about you. He is wondering why you haven't shown up for work this week."

"Oh, I guess I'll go see him tomorrow."

"He's gone to DC, he'll be back on Sunday night."

"Right, I'll leave him a message. Okay then, I'm going home to bed, night."

"Night Knox," I answer, hanging up the phone.

***

I arrive in Grove just after noon and my Mom greets me at the airport.

"Hi baby," she smiles and hugs me.

"Hi, Mom."

We drive home listening to the radio, Mom is talking about going shopping, and I agree to go with her. After the whole incident at the hospital, we didn't speak for months. She finally apologized to both Knox and I and we have been getting a little closer each time I have come home for court. When we get home, she makes us lunch and asks how things are going with Knox.

"Shit," I frown.

Taking a seat she looks over at me waiting, and I explain everything to her. It's probably the first time in my life I have actually let her in and confided with her. Once I'm done spilling my guts she gives me a hug.

"It will be okay baby, these things have a way of fixing themselves."

"You think? I'm not so sure, Mom. I acted like a jealous bitch."

"Swing first, ask questions later," she smiles at me.

"God, don't remind me. I know I ruined my life, Mom."

"No, you didn't, you just made a mistake, and unfortunately we all do."

I can't help but scoff at her. Who is this alien inhabiting my mother's body? She laughs at my face and rolls her eyes at me.

Rolls her eyes! My mother!

"I'm just saying, we all make mistakes Bailey, and I didn't literally mean you swing first physically. I'm also talking about emotionally, trust me I know what I'm talking about."

"What do you mean?" I ask, getting up to make us coffee.

"After my father had died, you were only nine years old, but after he had died I was devastated. I couldn't handle the pain of it and I pushed everyone away. My Mom - your father - you. I swore to myself I would never feel that way again and I closed my emotions off, trying to protect myself. But it didn't quite work out that way and I ended up hurting myself, and the people I was trying to protect.

"I know you hated me for a long time and I get it, Bailey, I do. I pushed you to stay with Brad even though I knew you didn't love him. I thought to myself, if you can stay with Brad, you would be happy not emotionally, but you'd make it work and your heart would have been safe from pain. That was wrong of me, and I knew it the minute I saw you and Knox together. You had that magic, that spark that we all want. The mother in me was so happy for you. I was happy that you found someone to take away your pain. But then the more I thought about the pain, the more I knew he could really hurt you. I wanted to protect you again. You went through so much in the last few years, and it hurt me to see you broken. I closed myself off from you for so long that I wasn't able to comfort you when you needed me most. Every time we argued, I kept telling myself that it was better this way. You would get over it and be okay. But again, I was wrong and it took me a while to figure it all out."

She smiles at me and takes my hand in hers, "I love you so much baby, I honestly only wanted to keep you from getting hurt, but I failed, I'm sorry."

I pull her close to me and hug her, for real this time. "I love you, Mom. I'm sorry for being such a horrible daughter."

She laughs at me and kisses my cheek, "You weren't horrible, just intolerable."

We both smile at each other and she hugs me again telling me how much she loves me and misses me.

"All these years I thought you didn't understand me or I wasn't good enough because I wasn't a society girl. But it wasn't me at all; we really are a lot alike aren't we?"

"Too much sometimes," she smiles, getting up she clears our plates. We sit out on the deck for a while talking about the past. Mom gets up when the doorbell rings and I put my feet up on the opposite chair, giggling because I know she will tell me off.

"Hello, Bailey."

Looking up I see Thomas, Mom's boyfriend. "Hi, Thomas, Nice to see you again."

Mom comes back outside and Thomas apologizes for forgetting I was here this weekend.

"Are you supposed to be going on a hot date, Mom?"

"It's okay we can go next week," Mom answers.

"Mom, go I'll be fine. I think I'll just float around the pool for a while anyway."

"It's November," she says, alarmed.

"It's heated," I reply.

"It's California!" Thomas adds and we all start laughing.

After a few more minutes of cajoling, she finally leaves with Thomas for their date. I change into my swimsuit and let the pool heat up while I put some music on. Climbing into the water I hop onto one of the waterbeds and relax. I float around for a while just watching as the sky darkens.

"Cannonball!"

Turning around, I get splashed when the intruder jumps into the pool.

"What are you doing here?" I ask when he surfaces.

"I want to be here for you and to see that motherfucker go down."

"Thanks, so how's married life?" I ask, watching his face split into a shit-eating grin.

"It's actually awesome Bails, you should try it."

"You're an idiot, Roger."

"Yeah but you love me, so it doesn't matter."

He grips the other waterbed and climbs onto it, then reaches out for my hand. Taking his, we float around together.

"So how is Audrey?"

"She's good, eating like a horse."

"I never thought I'd see the day Roger, you married and a baby on the way, in the space of eighteen months."

He grins at me again and I can tell he is really happy.

"Speaking of babies, we found out last week."

"What? Well tell me, come on, you should have called me!" I splash water at him.

"It's a girl," he smiles. "I wanted to ask you something though, well two things actually."

"Okay, what is it?" I ask.

"Well first off, we want you to be Godmother. Second, if you don't have any objections, because I want both my best friends in her life, we are going to use Summer as her middle name," he finishes.

"Really, you want me to be Godmother?"

"Of course, who else would I ask?"

"Yes, I'd love that Roger. Thank you."

Pulling him closer, I crawl onto his floating bed and hug him. We settle down together and I lay my chin on his chest looking up at him.

"I have no objections to you naming her after Summer, why would I?"

"Just thought I'd make sure," he shrugs. "So speaking of weddings and babies, where's the wall of muscle?"

Smirking at his nickname for Knox, I shrug. "Ah, it's just a bump in the road babe," he says.

"Not this time, Roger."

His eyes widen and he shakes his head. "No way, you two are great together."

I just shrug at him in answer and he still looks at me like I just torched his house or something.

"Well then babe, this calls for Nickleback and Jack. Last one dressed is a rotten egg."

He pushes me off the float into the pool and swims to the edge. Laughing, he helps me out. He gets a punch on the arm as I walk over to grab a towel. Roger is still snickering while I dry off.

"So are we getting take out or going out?" He asks.

"I guess take out if you don't mind, I don't feel like going anywhere."

Roger orders the food while I get dressed. I can hear Nickleback playing and walk into the kitchen to a find him with shots of Jack lined up on the counter.

"Oh no, Roger, I haven't had a shot in a year," I complain.

"I don't give a shit, neither have I."

He holds out the glass and I take it, and counting to three we throw them back. We have three shots each before dinner arrives and I can honestly say, I cannot drink like I used too.

"So tell me, are you and special ops getting divorced, for real?"

"What is with all the name calling?" I laugh at him, taking another drink.

He shrugs his shoulders. "Just playing with you, I can tell you still love him."

"I never stopped, Roger, things have just gotten complicated."

"Tell me about it Bails, you are walking complicated, but a sexy one."

I frown at him and he cracks up laughing at me. "Aw babe come on, you've always been that way, but it's what makes us all love you."

"Yeah, I know. Fuck it, I'm complicated, and I don't care who likes it!" I shout out waving my arms in the air. Roger and I are laughing and messing around on the floor.

"Well, you've finally admitted it."

Looking up, I find my mom and Thomas watching us. Roger throws me over onto the floor and lies across me.

"Hey Mom," I barely breathe out.

"Have fun kids."

"Uh, get off me you're heavy."

Roger rolls off me and lies beside me on the floor. "I'm stuffed Bails."

"Me too and my head is spinning. I haven't drunk this much in a long time."

I giggle setting him off too, both of us laugh for a while until I sigh. Taking Roger's hand in mine I give it a squeeze.

"Thanks for being here."

"Anytime babe, you know you just have to pick up the phone and I'll be here."

My mouth moves before I can stop it. I tell him about the texts and the Facebook profile and how Knox changed his phone number and didn't tell me. Roger turns to look at me with disbelief.

"Really, he changed his number and didn't tell you?"

I nod in response. He whistles, then sits up while pulling me with him.

"Come on Bails, it's time to get back out into the world."

He drags me to my feet and into the office. He sits down turning on the computer and pulling up Facebook.

68

"No Roger, I already looked on his page, it's full of skanks."

"I'm not going on his," he announces, telling me to pull up a chair.

I watch him sign into my account. I frown. I forgot he knew my login and password. "Wow Bails, you have 500 messages and thousands of notifications."

"It's been three years, Roger, I didn't think people still saw it."

I tell him to delete the notifications and the emails, but first he skims through them. They are from people I went to school with talking about the case against Ben and making stupid comments about it. Roger pulls up Knox's profile and looks through it, then sends him a friend request from me.

"Roger no! What the hell."

"What? Fuck it. If he wants to be on it, so can you. Besides, look he only has 49 friends; you have 1,276."

"I don't even know that many people Roger."

He laughs clicking through my pictures and sends me to the kitchen for the Jack. I bring a drink each while we look through my pictures, all of them are of Summer and I. Roger grabs his phone and we pose with our drinks.

"New profile pic," he laughs and tags himself in it. "Hanging with my babe."

"Roger, this is silly."

He gives me a look then searches for Max, and Paige, adding them too, and his wife, and his mom.

"Jesus Roger, your mom is on this?"

"Yeah, just to see pictures of Audrey's baby bump."

The computer beeps and he laughs, "Max accepted your request," his phone rings, pulling it out he answers, "Hey wifey."

I laugh at him and he pushes my face away with his hand. He tells Audrey we are having fun and yes it's him on my page. I tune out while talks to her and I pull up the team's page, flicking through the pictures and commenting on Becky's and Abbey's.

Roger hangs up with Audrey and smiles at me. "She was making sure it was you and that I'm keeping you safe."

"Tell her I said thanks."

"Did he respond?" he questions, looking back at the computer.

"Nope, just Max and now Audrey."

My mom walks into the office handing me my phone, "Thanks, Mom."

"Hello?"

"Sis, I just got a request on Facebook."

"Yes, it was us, Max. Roger decided to activate my account again."

"Oh okay, Roger? What are doing in Florida?"

"I'm not, I'm in Grove."

"You sound drunk, Bailey."

"Yep, we are," I laugh.

Max says goodbye because he is working and I hang up.

Roger and I leave the office and head up to bed to watch a movie. I get through a few minutes and feel my eyes getting heavier. Lying down I say goodnight and close my eyes.

Chapter 9

After a weekend of hanging out with Mom, Thomas, and Roger, Monday is here. Sitting at the table I stir my spoon around the bowl, not even able to stomach anything right now.

"Try not to worry, baby," Mom says, putting a coffee down for me and taking my bowl away.

"I know," I sigh. But not worrying is hard. I am praying with all that I have that justice is served today, but who knows what's going to happen.

"It's time to leave, Bailey."

Lifting my head, I see Mom waiting for me by the door. Standing up, I walk out to the car with her. My nerves are shot, and I don't know what to expect. We walk into the courthouse and follow the corridor towards the back. I notice a few familiar faces standing around; some people from school, Meg from café Rouge, Roger and his parents, my cousin Cara, and even my uncle.

Cara hugs me when I get closer to them. "How you holding up?"

"I'm okay, I think."

She nods and gives me a sympathetic smile. Roger and his family hug me too and all stand around me, protecting me from all the people around. Roger grabs my shaking hand and holds it tight. We wait for what feels like hours and then Rachel appears, she smiles at me and asks if I'm okay.

"Yeah, thanks."

"Shouldn't be too much longer now," she announces.

We all turn when we hear heels stomping down the corridor. Emily and her parents arrive, each of them looking like they want to kill me. Rachel takes my arm and leads me into the courtroom. Taking a seat at the prosecutor's side of the courtroom, we leave everyone else to find seats behind us. I can barely think straight, then the side door opens and he walks in, his eyes find mine and I can see the anger in them.

We all stand for the judge, then take a seat after he does. "Good morning," he says.

"Today we will hear the verdict in the case of the state of California –V- Miler. Let me add to the record that further testimony from Bailey Mortenson was recorded into evidence and both the defense and prosecution have had a chance to hear said evidence."

The judge waits a few seconds before asking the bailiff to bring in the jury. I watch them all take a seat.

"Have you reached a verdict?" Judge Abraham asks.

"Yes your Honor, we have."

The bailiff takes the piece of paper to the judge; he reads it and sends it back. I can feel tears sting my eyes, but I can't move; I'm rooted to the chair. Once the bailiff hands the paper back to the jury lady, she opens it and clears her throat.

My heart pounds like a jackhammer and my throat is dry, even though I can feel tears brewing. Rachel turns to me and nods. The judge has asked Ben to stand up and he does but looks at me first. All I can see is anger and hate on his face.

"We the jury," she says. My hands are shaking so badly right now and I think I'm going to vomit. "Find the defendant, Ben Miler, guilty on the charge of harassment." Rachel grips my hand. "We the jury, find the defendant, Ben Miler, guilty, on the charge of menacing phone calls." I take a deep breath and wait for the last charge, clutching Rachel's hand in mine. "We the jury, find the defendant, Ben Miler, guilty of attempted murder in the second degree."

The courtroom erupts in shouting and cheering. The judge bangs the gavel, but no one listens. My body gives out and I land face first on the desk. I can feel tears burn my cheeks and I close my eyes.

"You fucking cunt!" Emily screams from across the courtroom.

The judge gets annoyed and bangs the gavel until everyone shuts up. Once order is restored, he tells Ben to stand.

"Ben Miler, you have been found guilty of all charges and I hereby sentence you to twenty years in state prison without the possibility of parole." He bangs his gavel again and the bailiff handcuffs Ben, taking him out the side door.

"Baby!" Mom cries and grabs me. Thomas wraps his arms around both of us as he sheds some tears too. Pulling back, I wipe my face. Roger hugs me then lets me go. The Milers have already left the room and I'm thankful for that. I don't want to run into them. I follow behind Mom and Thomas keeping my head down. My arm is grabbed from the side and I jump with fright, looking up I'm met with blazing green eyes.

"Darlin'."

Fresh tears fall and I throw myself into his arms. Knox holds me for a long time while I cry on his shoulder. I'm moving, my feet are taking one step at a time, but I refuse to look up. Knox grips me tight as we maneuver around the people and out to the car. Climbing inside I scoot over so he can get in beside me. Mom takes off, driving faster than she ever has before.

When we get home I notice Thomas and the Burke's are here, everyone is in the kitchen drinking coffee and talking about the longest twenty minutes of my life. Taking a seat at the table I watch everyone talk back and forth. Knox stands by the door looking out of place. Mom starts pulling out food to feed the group.

"I'm going to get changed," I tell her, before going to my room.

It's finally over, after all these years it's over. I lie down on my bed and cover my face with my arm, hot tears fall again, but I'm not sad. I'm more relieved that he got what he deserved. I feel the bed dip and can smell Knox's cologne. He rests his hand on my hip, rubbing his thumb across my ribs.

"How are you?" he asks.

I can't answer so I nod. I have too many emotions racing through me right now, and seeing him here has added to the pile.

"I'm not doing this anymore, darlin'."

Biting my lip hard, I nod again. I don't want to see him. I don't want to remember his face on the day he walks away. It's

73

my own fault; Mom was right, I do swing first. My emotional battering ram is always front and center, ready to take down anyone that threatens to hurt my heart. And now, the last piece of the puzzle has finally fallen, taking his beautiful heart and walking away.

"I'm sorry about the phone," I whisper. "I was scared and jealous."

I listen to him breathing, still refusing to look at him. His hand leaves my waist and I feel the chill immediately. Taking my leg in his hands he pulls off my heel, then the other one. Pulling my knees up I roll onto my side, staring out of the window. Knox lets out a deep sigh before climbing in behind me.

"I said I'm not doing this anymore, Bailey. I'm not letting you go off the deep end, then hide away and get lost in that mess," he says, tapping my head gently. "Talk to me, darlin', tell me for once what you're feeling."

He pulls me close, wrapping his arm around my waist and he waits. I don't even know where to start, how can I explain something I have no explanation for. We lie on the bed for a while before he prompts me again.

"Now darlin', I can't wait forever. Start with the phone stuff."

Although his voice is low, I know he is angry, I can hear it in the tone. Swallowing hard, I'm not ready. It's hard admitting how ashamed of yourself you feel.

"I'm sorry, I got jealous and scared and I attacked you before you could hurt me," I whisper.

"Scared of what?"

"Losing you, finally, of you leaving me for some chick who sends naked pictures of herself."

Tears fall, but I ignore them; maybe it will be better if we clear the air. Then at least if I see him on the street, I can hope he won't hate me. He sighs again and I feel the heat of his breath on my neck, closing my eyes I savor it.

"Darlin' turn around, I'm not going to talk to the back of your head."

Turning, I finally look at him. He is the most handsome guy I have ever laid eyes on and he was mine, for three whole

74

years. He brushes his thumb below my eyes wiping my tears away and his hand feels warm against my cheek.

"Do you remember what I said to you on the beach?"

He asks while his eyes are looking all over my face, taking his last look.

"Yes, every word," I answer. He quirks an eyebrow as he waits for me to continue.

"You said that you love me with all that you are and all that you have. You never want to spend another day without me by your side and I'm the love of your life."

I close my eyes forcing back the tears, I can't cry anymore, I don't want him to see me break.

"I meant every word of that, darlin'."

Opening my eyes, I look up at him and nod. "But not anymore," I whisper.

"There you go again, the deep end," he gives me a small smirk. "I still mean it darlin', more now if that's possible. I'm not letting you get away and I'm not letting you treat me like I'm not important to you. When we both know, you are madly in love with me and I'm crazy about you," he brushes his fingers through my hair. "Now please, stop tearing down everything we have built together and kiss me."

He bends down brushing his lips against mine. I can taste the saltiness of my own tears. Knox lifts his head and looks at me.

"Now, I have a few things to say."

"Okay."

He sits up and takes off his suit jacket and tie. He opens the top two buttons of his shirt and climbs back beside me.

"I have no idea who was sending me those pictures. I tried to find out and asked for help, but no one could figure it out. I don't want to see any other naked woman, only you. I wish you would have let me explain things. I wasn't hiding it from you, I just didn't want to add more shit on your plate. I would never cheat on you darlin', ever. I promised you this a long time ago. As for the Facebook stuff…," he shrugs, "it's not anything about you or against you. I didn't mention you on my page because I know that's how that asshole found you the last time when Paige put you on hers."

75

"I'm sorry, Knox. You can have a social media page if you want. I overreacted."

"Yes, you did, but I know why you did and I was actually going to delete it, but then I had a friend request from someone with the same name as my fiancée," he taps the end of my nose and tilts his head.

"It was me, well Roger, we got drunk."

He pulls me close to him and we hug each other. "Okay, are we good darlin'? Because I can't take being away from you. I hate when you don't talk to me and then blow up at me when I have no idea what the hell I've done."

"Yes, I'm so sorry for not talking to you and keeping it all inside. I was trying to protect myself, but I don't know, I went wrong somewhere along the way."

Knox stands up and looks down at me, he reaches down and I take his hand. Standing up beside him, he smooth's my hair over my shoulders and smiles at me. "I mean it beautiful, I don't want to let you go, but I will if I have to."

I nod at him, I understand where he is coming from, and I don't blame him. "Okay," I answer taking a deep breath.

"Darlin'," he chuckles. "I'm never letting you go. I'll just have to beat your ass if you try to leave." He teases.

He squeezes me tight kissing my head. When I step back he is smiling at me then tells me I look like shit.

"Nice to have you back," I comment sarcastically. He swats my ass and tells me to go wash my face because I look like a demented 'it' from the movie. "And the jokes just keep coming."

"Well I'm here for the next three hours," he says, wrapping his arms around my waist.

"Hey, you guys dressed?"

Roger shouts from the other side of the door and Knox grunts, he still hasn't forgiven Roger for giving me stitches. Knox opens the door and looks at him.

"Hey, Knox, good seeing you again," Roger says, strolling by him and into the bathroom with me.

"What's up?" Grabbing the towel, I dry my face.

"Your mom made lunch. Are you coming down to eat?"

"Yeah, I'm just going to change."

"Okay, I see the wall of muscle finally showed up."

He says, motioning with his head to Knox, who is standing by the door with his arms crossed. "Did he get bigger?" Roger asks, smiling at me.

"Yeah, a couple of inches."

We both laugh at the double meaning and Roger pulls me into a hug, "I hope it works out babe," he whispers.

"It will, okay go make me a drink and I'll be down in a sec," I push him out of the bathroom and walk over to my suitcase. Knox closes the door behind Roger and walks over to sit on the bed while I change. I throw on a pair of jeans and t-shirt, Knox reaches into my case and pulls out his hoodie.

"So that's where it went," he smirks at me and I snatch it back.

"I needed it," I confess, holding it to my face and inhaling his smell.

Knox laughs at me, shaking his head. "I'm right here darlin'," he says, pulling me into a hug. "Food time, I'm starving."

"I don't know how you're not huge Knox, you eat like an animal."

"I work out," he says flexing his bicep, "Oh before I forget, you made me a promise three years ago."

Looking at him I frown, he pulls out my ring from his pocket and slides it on my finger. It's still a little big, but I'm happy when I feel it on my finger.

"You promised never to take it off again darlin'."

"Thanks, babe, I missed wearing it."

He snorts at me then opens the door ushering me outside. When we reach, the kitchen everyone is still here. Mom hugs me and asks if I'm okay. I tell her I'm fine and she winks at me. I swear I don't know this woman anymore. We sit down to lunch talking about school, work, and Roger's new bundle of joy. His parents are teasing him about not getting any sleep and how he will be doing midnight runs to the store for weird food cravings.

Knox checks his watch again for the hundredth time in the last hour. He stands up and smiles at me.

77

"I have to leave now, it was nice seeing you all again," he says to everyone, Mom protests telling him he just got here. "I have to work tomorrow," he smiles at her.

"Dad will let you off another day."

I tell him, pulling my phone out of my pocket, but he stops me and shakes his head. After his goodbyes, he gets his jacket and tie from my room.

"Can you drive me back to the hotel?" he asks.

I get my mom's car keys and walk outside to him. "What time are you flying out at?" I ask, feeling a little sad.

"Oh I'm not darlin', I drove."

"What! Why the hell did you do that?" I ask as we get out of the car in the hotel parking lot.

"I needed to think some things through." Taking my hand, we walk through the lobby and take the elevator up to his room.

"When did you arrive?" I ask, helping him to pack his bag.

"About nine last night," he says. "What time is your flight?"

"In the morning, at five."

"Why the hell so early, darlin'?"

"Classes start at ten so I figured I'd have time to get home and grab my stuff."

He looks at me like I'm mad, then offers to have my bag ready at the apartment so I don't have to drive up the hill.

"I don't mind it's only another fifteen minutes, babe," I answer, checking the room one last time before we leave.

"Yeah, that way I'll get the extra time with you in bed beside me. Call me when you land, I'll be waiting."

We stop at the truck and he throws his bag inside, "I don't have your new number."

He groans and pulls out a new phone. I raise my eyebrows at it.

"My dad got it for me, the other is only out of service until I can find out who is sending that shit," he shakes his head.

"Okay, I'll take a look tomorrow night for you."

"Thanks, darlin'," he calls me from the new number and I save it as X so I know it's him. "Okay, I'll see you at home in the morning," he pulls me into a hug and kisses me goodbye. I

78

wave at him as he backs the truck out of the parking stall. "Hey darlin'," he calls out of the window and waves me over.

"Yeah?"

"I love you by the way."

"I love you too," I grin at him, leaning over I kiss him again.

I spend the rest of the night with Mom. Roger is hanging out with his parents too. Mom and I watch some action movies and stuff our faces with popcorn. We talk about Knox and I. I tell her about the house I bought. She said she is proud of me and can't wait to come visit. By ten, I'm in bed after a long shower, I send X a quick text.

Me: Night babe, see you in a few hours.

X: Night darlin', keeping the bed warm.

Me: in bed already?

X: Yeah I just got home after six, I'm tired.

Me: ok night.

X: Night xx

Chapter 10

I walk through the airport yawning, the plane was delayed, and it's already seven o'clock. By the time I get to the apartment, Knox is in the shower getting ready for work. I make coffee and knock on the door before, I walk into the bathroom, he looks out of the shower and smiles.

"Hey darlin', did you get in late?"

I give him a quick kiss and sit on the toilet lid while he finishes. "Yeah, delayed an hour."

Stepping out of the shower he flicks water at me. "You going back to bed?" he asks, drying off. My eyes follow the towel as he rubs it over his chest, he really is hot. "Darlin'," he says, lifting my chin with his finger. "You're drooling," he whispers, smirking at me.

"I'm allowed," I wiggle my ring at him and lean forward to kiss him.

"I suppose," he winks at me. Taking my hand he brings me into the bedroom while he dresses.

"I miss seeing you in jeans and boots."

"Yeah, I miss wearing them," he answers, pulling on a black shirt and silver tie.

"You look kind of GQ babe, not sure if I like you going into the dungeon like that."

He snakes an arm around my waist pulling me closer and his lips brush off mine. Parting my own lips he groans sliding his tongue inside my mouth, his kiss is slow and heart stopping. "Love you," he mumbles against my mouth.

"Love you too," I whisper, as he kisses a hot trail down my neck.

"I have to go," he says, pulling away from me, "Will you be home after class?"

"I'll come back, I need to get a few things from Dad's."

He kisses me again then leaves for work. I watch him walking across the parking lot the same time Max arrives. They climb into the truck and take off, grabbing my bag I head over to campus.

Knox

"So I take it things are better?" Max says, pulling out of the parking lot.

"They're on the right track."

"I figured, you have that stupid grin back on your face," he smirks at me.

I can't help it. I haven't stopped smiling since I came home last night. I talked with Max about the courtroom and what happened. I just hope now that it's over things will finally get back to how they used to be.

"Do you want to grab dinner tonight? I was thinking of heading out to the Italian," Max asks, tapping out a beat on the steering wheel.

"Yeah sounds good. A guy's night out?"

"Sure if you want, we can call Eric and Dave," he asks.

"Yeah, shoot them a text, we can go after work."

We pull into the parking lot and find Meagan standing by her car, looking over at Max he frowns and looks at me.

"Why the hell is she always around?" he asks.

"No idea bro, but maybe you should take her and get her off my back," I laugh, as he pulls a disgusted face.

"Fuck you, Knox, I'm staying far away from that."

We both sit in the truck just pretending that we don't see her. Checking my watch, it's getting close to start time.

"I'll get out first and call you," Max says, hoping out of the truck.

She says hello to him and bends down to get her purse. Shaking my head, I grip my phone as I climb out of the truck.

"Morning Knox," she smiles, falling in step beside me.

"Hello," I nod at her and pray that Max calls me. When my phone rings, I answer it without looking at the caller ID.

"Hi son, how did everything go yesterday?" My dad asks.

"Hey Dad," I answer, slowing down my pace. Meagan slows down too and I freak out. When we reach the elevator, a few other employees arrive, being the gentleman that I am, I step back and let them on then quickly turn around and walk away.

"It was good, we talked," I tell my dad as I hit the stairs.

"Good, that's good son. How did the verdict go?"

Sighing, I laugh at little just from relief, "He got twenty years."

"Great, I'm glad that little shit got sent down. How's my future daughter doing, is she okay?"

I smile at my dad's words. He started calling Bailey, his daughter last year; he seriously treats her better than Max and I.

"She's okay. I didn't get to spend too much time with her, but I have her all to myself tonight."

I push through the office door and find Max waiting for me shaking his phone and lifting his hands. I mouth Dad and he nods.

"Right Dad, I'm in the office I'll call you on my lunch."

Max tells me the guys are down for dinner and asks how I got away from Meagan. Laughing, I tell him I took the stairs. When she walks into the room, she looks down at me and I quickly lower my head pretending I'm busy. My phone beeps with a text, lifting it up I find a picture of the quad, with the sun starting to fill it up and Bailey's eye. I laugh at her text.

I C U xxx

I miss my own phone, this one is old, and crap but hopefully soon Paige can figure out what is happening. I decide to give her a call, picking up the phone on my desk I dial her number.

"Hello?"

"Hey Paige, just checking in. Seeing if you have anything for me."

She groans and I hear her tapping on the keyboard. "Sorry, it's so fucking cold here and my hands are numb," she says, and I forward Bailey's text to her.

"Hey, I sent you a gift."

I hear her phone beep in the background. "You're an asshole," she laughs. I wait for her to do whatever it is she is doing.

"You know I keep getting a block, I can't go further than I have. All I can get is the carrier and the location of the phone when the messages were sent."

"Okay, thanks for trying. I'll just have blue eyes try tonight."

"So things are going better?" she asks.

"So far, I just hope it continues," I sigh.

"Me too Knox, me too. Anyway, I better go. I have a meeting in an hour and I'm frozen."

"Okay, thanks for trying, Paige. Talk to you soon."

Hanging up I sit back in my chair running my hands through my hair. I watch Max chat away to Alison. She is the only female engineer here and we have been trying for about three months to get Frank to ask her out, but he refuses; he said it's against company policy to date employees. When I asked him about Bailey and I, he just waved me off. Throwing my phone on the desk I head over to them.

"Morning Ali," I smile at her.

"Morning handsome," she answers, "the handsome other half and I are going to get breakfast. You in?"

"Yep, lead the way."

The three of us head out to the employee café.

Bailey

After classes, I drive to the office. Dad called and asked to meet me for lunch. Arriving in his office, I give him a big hug.

"Hi, sweetheart."

"Dad." I kiss his cheek. We decided to go to a new café down the block for lunch. On our way out, we end up in the elevator with Knox, Max, and two other employees. Knox grins when he sees me and I turn my back to him. Only a few people here know we are together and we want to keep it that way. I feel his hand rest on my hip and he squeezes. I take a small step back getting closer to him so I can feel his breath stir my hair. Max chuckles and I smirk over at him. When the elevator stops, Max holds the door for Dad and the others, then he steps out. Knox turns me and plants a kiss on my lips, then winks letting me go.

I step out first and walk away with Dad as if I didn't really know them. Dad laughs at me. "I take it things are better?"

"Yes," I smile, linking my hand through his arm. We walk down the block and have a seat, ordering our food. I tell Dad about the hearing and he looks relieved.

"Was I that much of pain?"

"No, I'm just happy it's over. Now we can all move on and get our lives back."

"Dad, you know I think I love you."

He laughs at me then tells me it's good to see me getting back to my old self. He missed my jokes.

"Dad," I ask, getting serious.

"Yes," his tone is cautious, which he usually reserves for times when I want to dip into my trust fund.

"Knox asked me to set a date the other week."

"Oh," he says, taking up his water, "and what is it you want?"

"I'm not sure I want to get married, but I also want us to be in a better place."

"Maybe you should take some time and see how things go for the next few months, then go from there," he tells me.

"Yeah, do you think I'm too young?"

"No, it's your life sweetheart. You're my little girl, so there is a part of me that never wants you to grow up, but you have too. I just want to see you happy Bailey; that's all we want for our kids."

I smile at him, "Thanks, Dad."

We enjoy our lunch then walk back to the office. We have been gone for two hours and Dad blames me. He jokes with his assistant not to let me disturb him for the rest of the day. She never liked me, so I am sure she took it literally. I make way down to the dungeon breezing past nosy Meagan.

"Hi, babe."

"Darlin'," he says, without looking up. I watch him finish a drawing then he looks up at me. "How can I help you, Miss Mortenson?"

"I need your phone, the other one," I nod at the one on his desk. He opens the drawer and hands it to me.

"Are you doing that now?"

"No, I'm bringing it home," I answer.

"Oh okay, are you leaving now?"

"Yeah, see you later."

He tells me to wait in my office and he will come up in a few minutes to walk me out. I walk out of the dungeon and up to my office. Dad's assistant gives me one of her looks as I walk past her and into his office.

"I'm taking off, Dad. See you later."

He gives me a hug and says he will be late. "Oh, I'll be staying in the apartment tonight," I say goodbye when his phone rings and leave the office. When I walk around to my own, Knox is waiting for me.

"Ready?"

I nod, grabbing my bag and lock my door. Knox takes my hand as we walk out to my car. "I'm going out with the guys after work tonight, what time are coming home?"

"Oh, I was going to grab some stuff from dad's and head there now. I'll do my assignment and get started on the phone. I'll probably go for a run too."

"Okay darlin', I should be home about seven anyway, I'm not staying out late."

"Okay."

He presses my back up against my car and kisses me tenderly, "Maybe I'll be home at six," he says.

"No babe, hang out with the guys. I'll have you all night."

He raises his eyebrows at me. "That so?" he growls at me, sliding his hands under my shirt.

"Yes, so maybe you should fill up on some calories."

I wink, kissing him again. I get a beautiful smile from him as I pull out of the parking stall. When I get home, I take a walk over to my new house, finding Richard and some other men all talking around the kitchen island.

"Hello," Richard calls out wrapping his arm around me. He introduces me to the foreman and another architect from his firm, who will be helping when Richard has to leave town. We go over the ideas again and we decide to replace all the windows because a lot of them are older and starting to rot. I decide to change one of the upstairs rooms too.

"Can we take out the closet and make the room bigger?" I ask, looking at Richard.

"Of course, you can do what you want."

I tell him my idea for what I want and he smiles at me. "You're a good person Bailey," he says, hugging me.

After another walk around I head across the lake to Dad's house. Gathering some clothes and my school stuff, I drive back to the apartment. Setting up my laptop on the kitchen table, I plug in Knox's phone and run the program I developed for one of Dad's clients. I know it takes about an hour to work through the phone so I take off for my run.

When I get back to the apartment, I have a quick shower then get to work. My phone rings.

"Hi."

"Hey Bailey, listen I have a confession."

"Okay, do we need to hide a body?" I laugh.

"No, haha. Knox called me last week and asked me to help him with something."

"I know Paige, I'm just about to start digging through it," I answer, sighing.

"Yeah I got stuck, I could only get the carrier and a ping tower."

"That's because you're not me," I laugh at her.

"Yeah, yeah miss smarty pants."

We talk for another thirty minutes. She tells me that she is fed up in New York and needs a holiday. We agree, to organize a girls' weekend away in the new year. I hear the door opening, both Knox, and Max are home, so I say goodbye.

"Hey darlin'," Knox smiles, when he sees me and gives me a sloppy kiss on the cheek.

"You drunk babe?" I question, squinting my eyes at him.

"No, darlin' I only had two beers. Any luck with the phone?"

"I haven't started babe, just about to."

He and Max go play video games while I scour through the phone. It takes me about another hour to sort through the data and figure out who is who and where they usually call from. I curse Knox for deleting the pictures because I only have one to go on now. I run another program when I come up empty and take a breath. Walking into the sitting room, I sit on the sofa.

"Giving up already super spy?" Max jokes.

"Nope, just working a different angle," I answer.

Knox turns around to me and gives my knee a squeeze, asking if I have eaten yet. I tell him no and he goes to make me dinner.

"Hey darlin', the computer is beeping."

He shouts and I jump up, running into the kitchen. I type in some codes that Agent Daniels gave me and I am able to get an account number from where the pictures are sent. Grabbing my phone I call Paige back, "Hey Paige, which carrier did you get? And where did it ping from?"

She gives me the information, telling me the FBI are fools for not taking me. After we hang up, I do some more digging, then end up tracing back to Mortenson Engineering. When I find the name, I am pissed off; more than pissed off in fact.

"Hello sweetheart," Dad says when he answers.

"Hi, Dad. I found out who the phone belongs too."

"Oh?"

"Yeah it's an employee, I'll fill you in tomorrow. I'll meet you in the office."

After I hang up both Knox and Max are looking at me expectantly, "Sorry I can't tell you."

"What! Why? She's been harassing me and caused my relationship to fall apart," Knox says, sounding hurt.

"Babe," I wrap my arms around his neck. "I have to tell Dad first and clean out your phone before I can give it back to you. I don't want you picturing her when you find out who it is."

"Fine, fine as long as it stops and I get my phone back. All my pictures are on it," he pouts at me.

"Fuck me, you sound like a chick," Max says, leaving the room.

Knox and I laugh at him. " Seriously though darlin', all our pictures are on it."

"I'll save them for you, babe, don't worry."

Chapter 11

I find myself weirdly calm as I walk into the building. I have never really pictured it as a business, well, I know it is, but it's my dad's so I think the personal aspect of it always clouded that point for me.

Today though, as I walk into the building, I feel like a boss. I know everyone knows who I am and some are still uncertain about what I actually do here. Though most of them know it's some kind of security. I actually do a lot for my dad behind the scenes but only he and I know about that stuff, not even Knox knows about it.

"Hi, Dad."

"Hi sweetheart," he sighs. No doubt, bracing himself for my news.

"So, before we get started I want to say, I'm pissed off, no – I beyond pissed off."

I hand him the paperwork I printed out from the program scan. He reads over it and sighs.

"I don't want to get any further involved Dad, it's too personal for me. I think you and personnel should handle it from here on out."

"Yeah, I know sweetheart."

He grabs his phone and telling his assistant to organize a meeting with the head of personnel in his office, now.

"Okay, I'll see you later I have class today and practice tonight."

Standing up, I give him a hug and kiss before leaving. On my way out I pass Mr. Henry, the personnel manager. He looks a little scared when he sees me come out of Dad's office. I give him a smile and nod as I pass him.

After classes I go straight to practice; the girls and I have fun. We don't hold back and I can feel the bruise already forming on my elbow from when I hit the field hard. Once we are done, I'm still pumped so I stay out on the pitch and decided to run a few laps. Becky and Abbey try to coax me for a milkshake, but I refuse.

Running around the track, I almost feel at a loose end. Although I know I am safe from Ben now, part of me still feels as though he is out there watching me. I'm not sure if I'll get over what he did to me because it's always in the back of my mind. I can't just wipe away that day. I've tried, but it refuses to leave my subconscious.

After running for a while I get tired and head back to the gym to grab my bag. On my way back out I find Knox, leaning against the wall with his arms crossed over his chest.

"Hi, what are you doing here?" I ask, reaching up to kiss him.

"It's late darlin' and I'm walking you home."

He takes my bag and throws his arm around my shoulders, kissing my temple. We walk back to the apartment and I notice for the first time how dark it is. I was too caught up in my mood to notice the floodlights weren't the sun. When we get home, Knox turns on the shower for me and says he will make me something to eat.

"Knox."

"Yeah darlin'?" he stops, at the door of the bedroom, his hands resting on the frame as he leans back to look at me.

"Thanks," I smile. A big grin breaks out on his face and winks before walking away.

After my shower I put on my pajamas and one of Knox's BRU sweaters, walking into the kitchen he smiles when he sees me.

"You look tiny in that."

"I know but I like wearing your stuff," I shrug, grabbing a water from the fridge.

"I like you wearing my stuff, darlin'."

Sitting down, I start to eat my dinner. Knox sits opposite me tapping on the table, "What's up?" I ask, looking at him.

90

"So did you talk to Frank?" I nod in response. "Are you going to tell me who was sending those pictures?"

"Nope."

He looks at me like he doesn't know me. His brows knit together and he takes a deep breath, "Aren't you annoyed?"

"Yes, I'm more than annoyed," I answer, trying to keep my tone civil.

"You don't look it, in fact, you kind of look like you don't care."

His eyes give him away. They look hurt, as he tries to keep his face blank of emotion. I smirk at him, pointing my fork I say, "I do care, Knox, that's why I'm trying to not think about it, otherwise..." I shrug not finishing.

"You'll go beat her ass?" he asks and I give him my biggest smile.

He lets the subject drop while I eat my food. I know it's late and I shouldn't be eating, but I'm starving. After I'm done I head off to bed crashing the minute I hit the pillow.

"Hey darlin'," Knox calls and shakes my body, cracking open an eye I look at him.

"What?" I mumble into my pillow, he smirks at me before brushing my hair off my face.

"It's time to get up."

Lifting myself up, I look around the room confused, I only just got into bed. But I see the sun is shining and he is dressed for work.

"Sorry, did I really sleep all night?" I wonder out loud.

"Yes, you were out of it when I came to bed. I had my wicked way with you of course..." he shrugs.

"I'd believe it too," I smile, teasing him back. He tells me he has to go and gives me a kiss on the cheek. His movements seem hesitant like he is waiting for me to do or say something.

"Okay babe, see you later, don't forget I have that photo shoot tonight so I'll be late."

He nods before sliding off the bed. Grabbing his hand, I pull him back to me and kiss him properly. "Now we can both have a good day." He nods and grins at me before walking out the door.

After a shower, I decided to blow off my lecture today and spend the day working on my paper. By two, o'clock I'm finished and my eyes hurt. Becky and Abbey have been texting all morning reminding me about the shoot. I pack my uniform in my bag and make my way to campus parking, where we are meeting.

"Hey, where were you today?" Abbey asks when I walk up to them.

"Studying at home."

I reply climbing onto the bus. I take a seat behind Becky and flick her hair. "Hey, Bex." She waves at me while keeping her nose in her book. I sit beside our quarterback, Georgia and the four of us joke around all the way to the hotel. Once we get there, we are lead to a conference room, where the photo shoot is set up. We take our group pictures, then the individual ones for our website and the calendar. It's so much fun, everyone is messing around and doing different poses, some of us are using props and a very sexy Santa.

"Holy crap!" Abbey whispers.

"Damn," is all I can manage when I see the hot guy dressed in Santa pants and nothing else. We all stare as he takes his position standing in front of the camera, he looks over and smiles at us, and I swear we all melt just a bit. Coach calls everyone over to stand around him and I have never seen a bunch of girls move as fast. It is almost like a stampede.

I can't help laughing as Becky and one of the other girls jockey for a position at his side. "What's so funny Mortenson?" Coach yells at me.

"Nothing," I clear my throat.

"You down front."

She says pointing at me. I shake my head no and step back a little until she yells at me again. I run to stand in front of sexy Santa, not knowing what to do, and look around.

"Get down on one knee," the photographer hisses and asks for another girl to kneel opposite me. We hold our helmets under our arms and he takes the shot. He makes Santa flex his muscles a few times and we all drool.

Once it's over, I walk over to coach to see if I pissed her off. She laughs at me and says no, that she was having fun.

92

"Not funny," I smile at her.

"Of course it was, you should have seen your face."

I swear this lady is evil. "You do know my fiancé is bigger and hotter."

She laughs at me and pats my shoulder before walking away. I pack my uniform again and sling my bag over my shoulder. When we are back on campus, we are warned about the game on Saturday and not to be late.

"You coming over to the diner?" Abbey asks.

"Nah, I'm going home to hang out with Knox."

Walking across to the apartment I spot Max heading to the bar and wave at him. It seems they work far more hours at the bar now since they bought their uncle out last year. He wanted to retire and Richard offered to buy the bar for them, but they wanted to do it alone. Unfortunately, the bank didn't give them the full amount so I dipped into my trust fund and became a third owner; although I chose to be a silent partner.

Dad wasn't happy about it, but because of all the Ben shit he found a way for me to sign my money over to him. Once Ben lost that battle, Dad gave me back twenty-five percent of my money and put the rest back into my trust fund. I was able to help Knox and Max with the bar, buy my house, and I still have enough to live on for quite a few years.

I also used some of it to fund my computer program, with Paige's help. She is one of America's top one hundred entrepreneurs under twenty-five. She gave me some good advice about starting my own business, but I'm waiting for a few more years before I decide to do it.

"I'm home," I yell when I walk into the apartment but don't get a response. Dropping my bag, I kick off my shoes. I then hear the sounds of guitar coming from the room and walk slowly over. I stand outside the closed door and listen for a few minutes. I can hear Knox singing softly and smile, reaching out I open the door finding him sitting on the stool with his guitar and his headphones on. He strums away while in his own world. I honestly missed this. We used to sit in here for hours while he played and sang. I would just listen and get lost in the lyrics. He lets out a deep sigh and changes songs, this one is a soft, sad, melody, and he closes his eyes as he plays.

Resting my head against the doorframe I listen to him, the tune is almost tragic. He begins to hum along while his eyes are closed. I don't recognize the song so I watch him. His face is too sad as he gets caught up in the melody and I wonder what is going on inside his head. I have to swallow hard to stop tears from spilling down my face. He always gives off the impression of a tough guy, someone not to be messed with, which is true. But seeing him look like this like his heart is breaking is really getting to me.

Walking inside, I rest my hand on his shoulder and his eyes spring open, his face breaks into one of his huge smiles when he sees me.

"Hey darlin'," he says, taking off his headphones.

"Hi," I whisper, then clear my throat.

He gives me a puzzled look then pulls me onto his lap, wrapping me in his arms.

"What's with the sad face?"

"Nothing, I was just listening to you play," I smile at him.

He kisses my lips softly, "How long were you standing there?"

"A few minutes."

He smiles at me and kisses me again, telling me how much he missed me today. His lips make their way down my neck and along my collarbone. A soft moan escapes from my lips and Knox stands up, taking me into our bed. He gently pulls off my t-shirt before laying me down. His mouth tastes every part of me, leaving a trail of hot wet kisses behind.

His hands slowly peel off my jeans tracing back up my bare legs. Reaching out, I open his belt and zipper, trying to push his jeans off. He helps me out and pushes them to the floor along with his boxers. At the sight of him I am almost purring, needing to feel him inside me. I hook my legs around him and pull him close with my heels, my hands pull off his t-shirt and glide down his hard chest and abs.

He sucks a breath in through his teeth at my touch and closes his eyes briefly.

"I missed this," I whisper.

Knox slides his hand under my legs and lifts up slightly as he pushes inside me, we both groan as he fills me up. Our

94

bodies move together slowly at first, building into a wild dance. He kisses me hard then softly, biting my lower lip. My hands grip his shoulders pulling him closer, deeper. I want him so badly. I want every part of him to touch me.

I let out a deep moan as my body soars with each thrust. Knox slides a hand over my hip, gripping me tight. I feel like I'm flying, my body comes apart as I grip Knox to me. With another hard thrust he groans, collapsing on top of me. Our bodies are slick with sweat and Knox presses a soft kiss just below my ear.

"I love you darlin'."

"I love you too," I cling on to him, refusing to let him climb off me.

"Hey, you okay?" He asks, looking into my eyes.

Nodding my head, I loosen my hold, and he rolls onto the bed but pulls me into his arms.

"Spill it blue eyes," he says, tilting my chin up with is thumb and forefinger.

"Spill what?"

"The reason why you look sad darlin'."

"No reason, I'm not sad. I'm happy," I reply, earning a raised eyebrow and skeptical look.

"I was wondering what that song was you were playing."

"Oh," he frowns, "it's something I wrote a few months ago."

Turing my face, I look up at him. "It was really sad."

He shrugs and places a kiss on the tip of my nose. "I was sad when I wrote it."

My heart constricts and a wave of guilt washes over me, obviously I was making him sad. But that song was really, really sad, like the way I felt after Summer died.

"Hey, what are you looking like that for?" he asks.

"No reason," turning around I press my back into his chest. Although we were having a hard time, I never once thought that Knox had that kind of pain in his heart. Silent tears fall from my eyes and I feel such guilt for causing him to hurt so much.

"Okay darlin', I'll make dinner then we can head over to the bar and have a drink," he says kissing my shoulder, as he climbs out of bed. I can't answer him for fear of my voice betraying me. Knox pulls on his jeans and stops, he bends down so that we are eye level. When he sees my tears, he frowns wiping them away.

"Hey, hey what's this darlin'?"

He lifts me up into his arms pressing my head against his chest. I can feel his heart beat slow and steady as he rocks me gently.

"Why are you crying darlin'? Did I hurt you?" his warm lips brush off the tip of my ear. I shake my head no. "Tell me then, why are you upset?"

"Just hearing that song and now I know that you wrote it," I blubber against his chest.

"Darlin', you don't even know the words," he says, kissing my temple and squeezing me.

"I know, but it sounded so sad and if you wrote it that means that you were sad and only I could have made you like that."

He pushes me back so I can see his face. He is smiling at me and I don't get it. I'm not sure how a song so sad can have anyone smiling like that.

"It is not about how you made me feel darlin', it's about how I was making you feel."

I'm confused and he chuckles when he sees my face.

"I'll sing it to you sometime. Now get out of bed and dry that beautiful face we have fun to be had."

After a quick shower and dinner, we are walking across to the bar. My mood is somber and I can't seem to pull myself out of it. Knox is talking about work and I'm not even listening to him. He holds my hand in his as we walk into the bar, it's full again, and Max looks overwhelmed. Taking a seat at the end of the bar I wait for Knox to bring me a drink, he talks with Max for a few minutes before walking back over to me.

"Hey darlin'," he pouts, leaning his elbow on the bar and resting his chin in his palm.

"Yes?"

"Chase can't make it tonight and Max needs help," he says, looking apologetic.

96

"Okay, that's fine I have a game tomorrow anyway," I shrug, taking my drink from him.

"You do? You never said," he says, tracing my lips with his finger.

"I know it's just a friendly one, no big deal."

"All your games are a big deal darlin', tell me when and where, and I'll be there." Leaning closer he kisses me. I just nod and smile. He looks at me sadly for a minute then gets to work. I listen to the band that's playing. The music is good, but I much prefer to hear Knox singing.

I can't seem to pull myself out this funk even when Amber starts her usual back and forth joking with me. I zone out while everyone laughs, dances, and makes out all around me. Checking my watch I frown at the time, it's only ten o'clock. I thought it was later. Finishing my drink, I wave Knox over, he strolls to me with a sexy smile.

"Yes, darlin'?"

"I'm going home."

He looks puzzled, "Why? I'm sorry our date night got ruined, but we can hang out in a few minutes."

"It's okay I'm tired anyway," I give him a kiss and leave.

Chapter 12

Knox

"What's up with her?" Max asks when he sees Bailey leave.

"Nothing," I shake my head and get back to work. The rest of the night goes by fast and we are closing before I even realize I hadn't taken a break. We clear out the bar, and I start sweeping the floor, leaving Max to restock the fridges. We work in silence until three in the morning.

"Let's get out of here, bro," I call out to Max. He walks through the beads with his jacket on and flips off the lights. I lock the door and we set off home. Neither of us talks for a few minutes.

"So what's up with Bailey?" Max asks, watching me.

"I don't know, Max, she was fine earlier."

"What did you do?" he questions, sounding just as puzzled as I am.

"I was just hanging out after you left, then when she came home we had sex and then she was upset about a song I was singing."

Max stops walking and I turn back to look at him. His face breaks into a huge grin and I shake my head. He starts to laugh at me and gives me shit about my bedroom prowess.

"Oh fuck!" he chokes, bending over holding his stomach.

"Get up you douche."

I grab his neck and pull him along the sidewalk not letting him go. "Okay, okay, I'm sorry. I'm sure you're a stud in the sack," he laughs.

"I'm a fucking machine, asshole," I push him away and laugh. "Are you coming to her game tomorrow?" I ask him.

"I didn't know she was playing, but I'm down. Are you telling Dad?"

"Don't know, wasn't planning on it, she only told me about it before she left."

Max hooks his arm around my shoulders and gives me a pat. "She'll be okay bro, just stick with it."

"I don't plan on leaving Max, she's it for me and we all know it."

When I get home, I find her fast asleep in bed with the TV on. Taking off my clothes I grab a quick shower to try wind down, by the time I climb into bed it's after four in the morning.

When I wake up, I'm alone and I feel all those feelings rush back, the ones that plagued me all last year. Climbing out of bed I walk towards the kitchen, but she's not there. I check the sitting room finding her on the sofa typing away on the computer.

"Mornin darlin'."

She gives me a smile and says hello. Resting my arm above my head on the doorframe I watch her. She has her head down again and continues to type.

"What time is the game?" I ask.

"Two."

"Did you eat yet?"

"No not hungry."

"Okay," I mutter, turning I head for the kitchen, I stop and look around. It looks a mess. Sighing, I pile the dishes in the washer and turn it on. I clean up the food that was left out on the counter and frown at the dirt on the coffee maker. I walk back into the sitting room.

"What happened in the kitchen?"

"Huh, oh sorry, I'll clean it in a minute."

Her fingers fly over the keyboard again and I get annoyed. Walking over I slam the laptop closed, only in my annoyance I catch two of her fingers. "What the fuck!" she shouts at me. Getting up I can see she is crying again and I follow her to the bathroom.

"I'm sorry I didn't mean to catch your fingers," I explain when I reach her.

She tells me to fuck off and leave her alone. Walking back into the bedroom I fall back on the bed and stare at the ceiling. A few minutes later she walks in with a band- aid on each finger, now I really feel like a dick.

"I'm sorry, I didn't mean to do that."

I watch her pull on her clothes and shoes and she scowls at me then, shakes her head.

"Darlin' where are you going?" I don't bother to raise my voice or look at her.

"I'm going to get breakfast with the team, I was going to invite you but never mind."

She walks out the door and I feel like I traveled back in time, this is just like last year and I know it's my fault. Getting off the bed I have a shower and shave and get dressed. On my way past the sitting room I notice she left her laptop on the sofa. The temptation to look at what had her attention is overwhelming.

Shaking my head I make some breakfast and turn on the TV, after an hour she's still not back and the computer is fucking sitting right there. "Knox you're being an asshole," I scold myself, but I open the computer anyway. When the screen comes to life all I find is bullshit, or as she calls it computer code.

I run my hands over my face and rest my head back against the sofa. I'm about to close it down when a message pops up, from a Derek. Opening it I find a group chat with her, Becky, Abbey and some Derek dude. I read through the messages finding nothing but football chatter but then at the end Derek asks if Bailey is dating anyone. My anger simmers and I want to fucking smash the computer off the wall.

I scroll through the messages again and see they went to the diner in town. I grab my keys and head out. Walking down the street I am not paying attention and almost pass the place, I walk inside to a full house. It looks like most of the team and their families are here, and I feel like a bit of douche now.

Scanning the room, I don't see her. I know the messages said here so I look again, finding her in the back with some guy and the two troublemakers she hangs out with. Walking over I pull up a chair and sit at the edge of the table.

"Mornin," I smile at them.

Abbey says hello and Becky nods at me. I seriously don't get why she acts like a dude. The guy nods to me, and Bailey raises an eyebrow causing me to lift mine in answer. I order a coffee and just hang out. I can't leave now because I made such a show of getting here.

"So Bailey, how do like being the wider receiver?" Derek, the douche asks.

She gives him a polite answer and sips her coffee. I just sit back and enjoy the show. He makes more talk about football, but he sounds like he hasn't got a clue about the game. Pulling out my phone I silence it and type her a text.

Me: How do you like being a wide receiver?
Bailey: fuck off.

I sip my coffee without looking up, I hear him try again.

"What are you doing after the game? Maybe we can take a walk on the beach."

I almost choke on my coffee and look at them at least she looks uncomfortable.

Me: The beach huh? He's really going all out.
Bailey: Fuck off.

"I mean we can grab dinner first if you want to," he says to her.

"Thanks, but I have to meet my dad tonight," she says.

"Oh okay, then perhaps we can hook up after, hit a club or something."

Me: Hook up? In a club! Damn smooth.
Bailey: Fuck off.
Me: I can hook you up, right now on the table.

Lifting my eyes, I see her blush a little then she types back.

Bailey: No, and fuck off.

101

Me: damn darlin', you say fuck a lot. I'm kinda getting hard sitting here.
Bailey: Then fuck yourself.

I smile at her answer and listen in, as Derek goes for it again. He moves a little closer and I sit up straighter, keeping an eye on his hands.

"How about you wear that new uniform tonight and we can have our own game at my place?"

Me: what the fuck!
Bailey: ☺

"Sorry Derek, I only wear my uniform on special occasions."

"Yeah well, we can make it special."

He answers and his finger brushes down her neck. Pushing back my chair so hard it scraps off the floor I stand up. Derek gives me a dismissive look and I ball my fists. Bailey looks at me, she is waiting to see what I do. Reaching over the back of the booth I pull her up into my arms and kiss her hard. She wraps her legs around my waist but breaks the kiss.

"You're still an asshole," she says, sounding sad rather than pissed off.

"I know darlin', but you love me," I smile, then press a kiss to her temple. "I'm sorry baby I didn't mean to hurt your fingers."

"I know," she pouts, holding them up. Taking her hand in mine I kiss each finger.

"What time do you leave?" I ask.

"Noon."

Checking my watch, it's already after eleven, dropping her to the floor I grip her hand. I turn to the douche watching us and pat his shoulder.

"Sorry bro, sometimes you just have to take charge and let them know who the boss is."

Pulling Bailey behind me I hear her giggle, usually I hate that shit but not from her. She never really does it and she sounds pretty fucking adorable. Once we are outside I race down the street to the bar. She gives me an odd look when I open the door and push her inside. I lock the door behind me and push her up against it kissing her hard.

"Taking control, huh?"

"Yes, darlin'."

I kiss her again, walking her back towards one of the booths, opening her jeans as I go.

"What are you doing?" she whispers, when I slide my hand inside her panties and slip my fingers inside her. "Oh okay," she breathes.

I kiss down her throat as I build her up. I can feel her legs start to shake, so I pull my hand out and push her jeans down. Flipping her around, I push her over the table then open my own jeans. I want to be inside her so fucking bad, lowering myself over her I press my lips against the back of her neck. She lets out a soft moan and arches her hips.

"Now Knox," she growls, reaching back and gripping my hair.

I fucking love this chick, grabbing her hips I push into her. She moans and grabs the sides of the table, my body is on fire, and I begin to move. My hips push forward and she pushes her ass back into me.

"Jesus fuck," I whisper, as we push against each other. I reach around and use my fingers, making her cry out, and I feel her lose it, a few more thrusts and I'm done. Collapsing on top of her, I pant out that I love her.

"Fuck off," she whispers and laughs.

I walk her over to the bus on campus and agree to meet her at the game. I text my dad as I walk back to the apartment and tell him about her game. He replies that he will meet us there. When I get home, Max is waiting for me.

"Hey, where did you go?" he asks.

"Out with Bailey."

He shrugs and goes back to Xbox, and I have to laugh at him. He has Paige's old apartment, but he spends all his time here. I kick his leg, then sit beside him grabbing the other controller. After an hour, we hit the road, arriving at the game just before kickoff.

"Shit bro she'll kill us."

Max laughs as we run through the stands to find my dad. I see him sitting behind her team and curse his ass. We fall through the people and say sorry or excuse me a million times before reaching him.

"Hey Dad," I'm breathless and he laughs at me.

"Boys, a little late."

"Fuck no we're on time," Max laughs, pushing against me.

We stand up and shout when the team runs on the field. I know at first I was afraid for her, but seeing her play is fucking awesome. The uniforms make me choke and my dad frown.

"Did they shrink the uniforms?" he asks, looking worried.

"Yeah," I grind out. Max is having a feast looking all the ass cheeks hanging out. We cheer and shout during the game. Our team loses by two points and the girls are walking off with their heads down. All I want to do is run down and grab Bailey and make her feel better.

Bailey

In the locker room, we are all down. We played our asses off but still lost.

"Next time ladies," Coach says, as we file onto the bus.

All the way home we are quiet. Most girls have their headphones on and some are sleeping. I stare out of the window thinking about Knox and him taking control. I can't help the grin on my face. I want to spend tonight alone with him.

When we arrive back at campus I find him waiting for me, he gives me a sad smile holding out his arms. I smile back as I walk straight into him and get wrapped up in a hug.

"Sorry you guys lost darlin'," he kisses me.

"Thanks, but it's only a game," I shrug.

He takes my bag from me and leads me home. "I was thinking we could stay in tonight, get a pizza, and watch some action movies."

"Sorry darlin', Chase has the flu or some shit so he is out and I can't ask Max to do it again. It's not fair."

"Okay, that's fine. I'll come over and hang out, maybe even get drunk."

"Hey now, that's enough of that talk," he teases.

After dinner I follow Knox over to the bar, it's full and he is run off his feet. I offer to help, but he refuses and hands me a Jack and Coke, telling me to relax and have fun. I watch the customers sing and laugh when they are bad, even though I'm alone I still manage to feel good. At the end of the night, I help clean up the glasses while Amber stocks the fridges and Knox counts the cash.

"Night Amber," I call when she leaves.

Knox wraps his arms around me and kisses me. "You look tired, Knox."

"I am darlin'," he sighs.

We walk home wrapped around each other against the chill in the air and although I still feel guilty about that song, I'm happy that we are us again. I stop walking and he yawns as he looks down at me.

"Everything alright?" He asks.

"Yes," I wrap my arms around his neck and press my lips to his. "I just wanted to say that I love you, really, really love you."

"Yeah?" he smirks.

Nodding my head I kiss him again gently, "Yeah."

***

105

Chapter 13

Christmas Eve

Standing in the crowd, I shuffle my feet again against the ache that is starting. I'm anxious and I just want to get the hell out of here. Finally I spot her and wave, running towards her we clash in a hug.

"Oh my god, it's so good to be home."

Walking outside the sun is shining and I watch Paige stop and spread her arms and close her eyes, tilting her face towards the sky.

"Sunshine, how I've missed you."

"Get in the car Paige, have you seen the traffic?" I push her along the walkway and she grumbles at me.

"It's good to have you back though," I smile at her. We climb into my car and pull out into the already building traffic; at this rate it will take us at least an hour to get home.

"So I was thinking," she says, staring out of the window.

"About?"

Sighing, she shrugs her shoulders and bites on her thumbnail. "I was thinking of coming home," she whispers.

"What! For real?" I ask shocked because as far as I know, she loves New York.

"Yeah, it's time," she nods, more to herself than me.

"You know, you have never told me why you left in the first place."

She looks at me and pulls a face. "There were many reasons, really. My family, this town, Max."

"This town? It's hardly a small town Paige."

"I know, but growing up here and never leaving was claustrophobic. My parents were driving me insane and my brother. They kept trying to tell me what to do and how Max wasn't good enough for me. I think after I lost the baby, I finally snapped. I wanted to stay with him, but I couldn't do it. I didn't want him to look at me and wonder, what if."

"How do you feel now though? I mean it's been two years since you've seen or spoken to him and he was in a really bad way after you left."

"Yeah I know. I dialed his number a few times but forced myself to hang up. I couldn't hurt him any more than I already have. Jesus…" she groans.

"What?" I ask, glancing at her.

"Its fucking Christmas and I'm having a pity party. We need booze!"

I pull up to the apartment just after eight. I told Knox that Paige was coming home. He was torn between protecting Max and seeing me have some fun with my friend. We put her cases in the spare room and sit on the sofa.

"So is Knox avoiding me?"

"No, they are playing in the bar tonight."

I watch her face and see one emotion after another chase across her features.

"Can we go over?" her voice is shaky and she looks at me, begging me to help her in some way.

"Sure, it's usually packed when they play so we can blend in."

Getting dressed up is fun, it's been a long time since I did it and I miss it. Paige is in and out of my room every two minutes with something different to wear, asking 'what about this?' Finally she decided on some satin shorts and a loose pink blouse, her hair is a little longer now and she has highlights in it.

"Ready?" I ask, tying up my boots.

"I guess," she says, then bites her lip nervously.

We walk through campus and she admits to missing it and our lunch on the quad. She is rambling by the time we arrive, then scoffs at the doorman. "For real?" she says. Laughing, I nod and pull open the door. The body heat smacks us in the face, and we have to press our way through the crowd.

Reaching the end of the bar, I find a very annoyed looking Amber.

"Hey you, what's up?" I ask her.

"Some fucking loser tipped my tray," she answers, before turning to hug me hello. She screams when she recognizes Paige and grabs her in a hug. "Holy shit! You came back."

"Yeah for the holidays," Paige answers.

We take a seat and harass Chase like we used too, but he still loves it. We get a drink and a shot each for old times. Paige begins to tap my arm like she is having some kind of attack.

"What! Are you okay?" I ask, a little freaked out, maybe she can't do this after all.

"Are you seeing what I'm seeing?" she asks, smirking.

"Huh?"

"Holy shit, Bailey, there two of them," her eyes glint and I crack up laughing.

"Yeah I see it, so which one are you taking?" I ask.

She shrugs her shoulders and grabs another shot. "I'll let you know in a while, but now I want to dance."

We head to the dance floor and now I'm panicking, Max will freak out when he sees her and I feel bad for not warning him.

"Hey, you never told me what happened with that phone shit," she shouts, over the music.

"Oh, it was Meagan, an assistant. I never told Knox so don't say anything. I'd rather forget her face and her boobs."

We both laugh as we arrive on the dance floor. We are a little squashed, but it's just like how it used to be. We dance together having fun not paying any attention to anyone else. When the band stops, so do we, both of us are sweaty, but I feel great. Walking back to the bar Paige stays behind me, holding my hand.

"What if he screams at me, Bailey?" she asks, pulling me to a stop.

"I don't know Paige, scream back," I shrug.

When we arrive at the bar, Knox spots me, and smiles, he sees Paige hiding behind me and glances at Max, who is talking to some other girl.

"Hi darlin'," he gives me a kiss. "Paige," he says and gives her a hug too.

"Hi Knox, Merry Christmas."

He smiles at her and then gets us a drink. I perch myself between Knox's legs while, he sits on the stool. Paige is nervous and she keeps glancing at Max. I take her hand giving it a squeeze. Nodding, she takes a deep breath trying to relax. Max says goodbye to the girl he was talking to and heads our way. When he arrives, he says hello to me and grabs his beer. We are all quiet watching him.

"What the fuck is up with you two?" he asks, frowning at Knox and I. Then he turns his head to look around and finally sees Paige. The beer bottle stops halfway to his mouth, which is now open as he stares at her.

"Hi, Max, Merry Christmas."

She looks so small and scared, nothing like her usual self at all. Max just stands there until Knox kicks his foot bringing him back to the here and now.

"Oh, yeah, you too," he looks at me and I swear I see pain in his eyes and hurt. He excuses himself and walks away.

"Shit," Knox mutters.

"I'll go, babe," I tell him following Max into the office.

"Max," I ask, as I enter and close the door behind me. "I'm sorry I didn't tell you she was coming, but she asked me not to."

He is sitting behind the desk just staring at the wall, "Max?"

"I'm fine sis, just a little shocked."

Rounding the desk I hug him to me, "I'm sorry bro."

"It's okay, Bailey, I'm a big boy I can handle it."

"I know, but I still feel bad. We weren't supposed to come here, but I guess we miss you guys playing."

He smiles at me and hugs me again. "I know you do. I miss playing too." Letting me go he sits in the chair, "So what should I do?" he asks, looking up at me.

"I'm not sure. I know some of her side, and I know how you were after she left. I honestly feel bad for both of you."

"Yeah? So does she have a boyfriend or is she married now?" he asks, scratching his head and blowing out a breath. He and Knox are seriously so much alike it's scary sometimes.

"As far as I know she is single, but she hasn't mentioned anything in a few weeks."

"Okay thanks, sis, I suppose I should go out there and face her, huh?"

"That's up to you, Max. You could always hide out here like a pussy."

I shrug grinning at him. He laughs, gripping me in a headlock as he opens the door. He keeps me like this until we reach the bar then relinquishes me to Knox.

"She," he points at me, "has a dirty, dirty mouth," he says, looking at Knox.

Knox laughs passing Max a beer. "Yeah I know," he answers, wrapping his arm around my waist.

"So, Merry Christmas," Max says, raising his beer. We all do the same and clink glasses. Max watches Paige for a minute then gives her a nod. I can see her blush and can't help but smile at her. Knox lifts me up off his lap and places a line of kisses down my neck to my shoulder.

"We'll finish that later," he whispers.

"Don't threaten me," I wink, as he steps out from my side. He laughs at me pulling me in for another kiss. I watch him walk back to the stage and gives Max a nod. He just shrugs picking up his guitar and throws the strap over his shoulder.

"He's pissed?" Paige says.

"No, just shocked," I reply. "Hey, are you dating anyone? You haven't talked about a guy in a while."

"Ha! No, I'm single and have been for about ten months. No one compared," she answers, turning to look over at Max again.

I can tell things are going to get a little messy over the next two weeks. Ordering another drink, I turn on my stool and watch Knox. He is singing a slow song with just his guitar. A few couples are on the dance floor and the sight of him brings me back to that song I heard him sing.

I watch the muscles in his arms flex as he strums, the veins pop out with each movement. His eyes are downcast as he gets lost in the song. His voice is smooth and curls around me like a secret lover.

I am getting lost in him just watching.

"You okay?" Paige asks, nudging me.

"Huh, yeah, fine."

She grins at me giving me a knowing look and sometimes I wonder how Knox even fell for me. Did he want to run a mile when he knew how fucked up I was? Or did he see me as a challenge or perhaps a girl who needed saving? I know he loves me with all his heart and I love him just as much, but I can't get over the pain and sadness of that song.

"Hey we need to dance," Paige grabs my arm pulling me up.

We get to the dance floor and the music picks up, we rock out for another hour or so until Max sings the last song. Paige's dance moves falter a little before she recovers fast and continues.

"This is for two very special ladies."

Max announces glancing at us. He sings Hero and I can tell by Paige's face that the song just pummeled her heart.

"You good?" I ask.

"Yeah, awesome."

She smiles back me as we dance. Once the band leaves the stage, we make our way over to the bar. Knox asks if I'm having fun and I nod, waving my hand in front of my face to cool down.

"I love watching you dance, darlin'."

"Yeah?"

He nods his head while hooking his fingers in the waistband of my jeans and pulling me closer to him. "I love every move your body makes," he whispers, sending a shiver down my spine. His lips gently brush off mine, like the touch of a butterfly's wings before he steps away from me. My body hums from the kiss and the feel of his thumbs tracing circles on my hips.

"Wow, you look a little undone," Paige whispers.

"Yeah, I guess I do."

111

I watch Knox move around behind the bar. His movements are fluid as he steps around Chase. Walking back to us he takes a seat beside me cracking open his beer.

"You look tired, babe."

"I am, I just want to go to bed."

He gives me his megawatt smile and his eyes shine like emeralds. I can't resist, reaching up to trace my fingers along his jaw, pressing my hand to his lips he places a soft kiss on my palm. After what seems like hours, the bar is finally empty and the four of us are walking home in awkward silence.

Max keeps looking at Paige, who keeps looking at him while Knox and I glance at each other trying not to giggle like schoolgirls. When we get to the apartment Max crashes on the sofa while Paige takes the guest room. Knox and I fall into bed and he wraps his arms around me.

"Just put it in. No, I don't need you to put oil on it. Jesus Christ, would you listen to me and shove it in."

Waking up to this monolog I'm a little confused. Lifting my head, I brush my hair off my face and turn around finding Knox, with his face in his palm shaking his head. Scratching my head, I push myself up further and move over to him, noticing for the first time the phone pressed against his ear. His back is against the wall and he gives me a smile.

"Dad, can you just listen to me, put the turkey in the oven and walk away from it."

Feeling a little devious, I start placing light kisses along his toned stomach. My lips travel lower meeting with the stirrings of his arousal. Snickering, I lick the length of him while he talks to his dad. He clears his throat and resumes his semi-argument with Richard. Gripping him in my hand, I take him into my mouth slowly. His body tenses and his hand tangles in my hair.

"Okay, Dad, look just put it in the oven and I'll get there early. Yeah…okay …bye," Knox hangs up on his father throwing his phone onto the bed with a thud. His right-hand grips the side of the bed as I move my mouth up and down.

"Jesus …fuck!"

112

He pants as I move faster and faster. I can see his stomach muscles tighten and he tells me to move back. Lifting my mouth, I finish him with my hand feeling the warm liquid spill out of him. Gently I kiss my way up his stomach to his neck, placing small kisses under his chin. His head is back against the wall and he has a smile on his face. Placing my lips over his, I whisper, "Merry Christmas," earning a chuckle from him.

"Merry Christmas, darlin'."

Finally opening his eyes he looks at me, my heart thumps in my chest when I see all the love in them.

"You're the best present ever," he jokes gripping my hair, he brings my lips to his and kisses me thoroughly. Knox lifts me up so that I can straddle him, slowly he lowers me on his already hard shaft. Sinking down, I let out a soft moan into his mouth. Sex with Knox Porter is one of the most amazing experiences I ever had and in all the time we've been together I have never wanted to experience it with another man.

My body shudders with release and Knox wraps me in his arms holding me close. We just stay like this for a while and when he pulls out I feel empty, almost disconnected from the place I'm meant to be.

"Hey," he whispers. "Why do you look so sad darlin'?" his face scrunches with confusion.

"I'm not," I answer, shaking my head with embarrassment.

"Yes, you had a funny look on your beautiful face and your eyes looked sad."

He tilts his forehead against mine and pulls the sheet up to cover my back and shoulders.

"I was just thinking about us and sex." I can feel my cheeks burn. I don't know why I am getting embarrassed, but it's almost too personal to explain. Knox furrows his brows and pulls me against his chest.

"Tell me darlin', did I hurt you? Or did you not like it?"

His voice sounds a little scared and desperate.

"No, nothing like that. I was just thinking that I love having sex with you and I've never even thought about wanting another guy."

He lifts me back by the shoulders. "And that's why you got embarrassed?" he says, still confused. Shaking my head no, I bury my face into his neck, "Then why?"

"It's stupid, never mind," shaking my head I snuggle into him, but he won't let it go. He pesters me and tries to tickle it out of me until finally I give in.

"Okay, okay you big meanie. I sometimes feel weird after we have sex," I start, but his look of horror has me laughing, "Not that kind of weird."

"Well, what do you mean exactly because a guy can seriously get worried over here."

"I'm just saying sometimes after sex I wish we could stay connected. It feels horrible when you leave my body," I shrug, feeling completely out of myself, and stupid for even saying it out loud.

"Ah," he says, scooting lower in the bed so he is lying down and I'm still on top of him. "I get it darlin', I get that too, it's almost like a part of you has been taken away."

Lifting my head I look at him and he smiles at me. "What, you thought guys don't feel like that? That we are all horny bastards who just want to fuck?"

"Yeah, pretty much."

He laughs at me squeezing me to him and kissing my head, "Don't get me wrong darlin'. I love a good fuck, but I much prefer to make love to my beautiful fiancée."

I stay wrapped in his arms for a while refusing to move, even though I can hear Max banging around the kitchen. Knox rolls over landing on top of me and giving me his amazing megawatt smile.

"Love you darlin', Merry Christmas."

Climbing out of bed he pulls me up telling me to be in the kitchen in five minutes. When I walk in I, find Max and Knox making breakfast while Paige drinks coffee.

"Merry Christmas," Paige smiles at me.

Taking a seat I give her a hug, "You too." Knox brings over French toast, scrambled eggs, bacon, and sausage. Then pours us coffee, we eat in silence before I decided to break the awkwardness.

"What time are you going to your parents?" I ask Paige.

114

"Oh, I'm not, they don't know I'm home."

I'm a little shocked and I look at the guys. "Oh, how come?"

"I can't deal with them or my brother and his freaking girlfriend, she bugs the piss out of me. I'm just going to crash on the sofa and watch old movies if you don't mind," she says.

"Why don't you come to the beach with us?" Max says.

"Oh no, I'm not imposing myself on your family time," Paige shakes her head.

"You won't be. I'm sure Knox has more than enough food on the menu and Dad won't care," he shrugs.

Knox and I look at each other. He clears his throat and tells Paige she is more than welcome to come with us. After each of us shower and gets dressed we load up the truck with gifts and set out. I text my dad making sure he is still joining us, he replies by telling me not to worry that he and Richard are already hitting the eggnog. Laughing out loud I read his text to Knox.

"Fucking alcoholics," he laughs.

We arrive just before one o'clock. Max and I pile the gifts under the tree while Knox takes control of the kitchen. Paige says hello to my dad and Richard; they give her a hug and hand her a drink.

"Wow Dad, it's not even five o'clock and you're on the sauce already," I tease, giving him a hug.

"It's Christmas," he scoffs and wanders off to get another.

I send my mom a text and ask her how her Hawaiian vacation is going. Thomas took her away as part of her present. I'm happy for her. It's nice to see her smiling again and after our talk, I can understand her a little more than I used to.

Knox snakes his arm around my waist pulling me back into his chest while I text my mom. His warm breath brushes along my neck, giving me goose bumps.

"What would you like to drink darlin'?"

"Oh, coffee or juice," I answer, turning my head a little so I can see him.

"What? No, Jack?"

"No, maybe later," I answer, kissing his cheek. I love feeling the smoothness of his jaw after he shaves - it's like a babies butt.

We sit around the table out on the patio while watching the ocean. California Christmas is like no other. It's about seventy degrees and the sun is shining. A clear contrast to what the rest of the world envisions Christmas to be like. Knox is back and forth checking on dinner while Richard talks to Paige about her time in New York. Closing my eyes, I tilt my head towards the sky, allowing the sun to warm my face.

I love days like today, warm but not hot, a light breeze blowing across my skin and the warmth of Knox's body, as he gets close to me before pressing a kiss to my lips.

"I want to marry you," he whispers, in my ear and a smile breaks out on my face.

I want to marry him too, but I want to get the house finished and graduate first so he has another year at least to wait. Keeping my eyes closed and my face tilted upward, I tune out all the background noise. Knox slips his hand in mine but doesn't interrupt me. My mind wanders to the last fun Christmas I had with Summer; it really was a blast. Life was fun and silly then; no Ben to mess it up, but I don't want to recall him so I switch my memory over to Summer only. I miss my friend. But time has helped, the wounds are still raw and sometimes I break down and have a cry, but mostly I'm dealing.

It's hard to believe so many years have passed and yet it feels like yesterday. Knox has been so good to me over the years and has helped me through a lot, especially the cry-fests. He never judges me or makes me feel foolish; he just holds me until I'm done then fills me up with white chocolate and kisses.

Turning my head, I open my eyes allowing the day to filter back into my mind. Knox is chatting with Dad and they are both having a glass of beer and laughing. Max, Paige, and Richard are still talking about New York and I feel blessed that I have these people in my life. Summer left a gaping hole in my heart and soul, but I can't live in the past. I like to remember the good times because we had plenty of those and keep moving forward. I know she would want me to.

Lifting Knox's hand I place a kiss on the back of it drawing his attention to me. I receive a smile and wink from him knowing by the look on his face that he knew where my thoughts had drifted.

"Love you, babe," I whisper.

After our afternoon in the sun, I help Knox dish up the dinner. He gives Max and I direction and we move around following his orders, both of us calling him Chef Ramsey. He takes it all in good fun but threatens us every few minutes. Max and I have the table set and the side dishes ready out on the table.

"Come on sis."

He grabs me around the waist and we dance to a Christmas song playing through the speakers. Both of us move through the dining room into the kitchen and circle around Knox. He rolls his eyes and laughs at us, slapping my ass when I pass him. He has gotten used to Max and I acting like kids and usually ignores us.

"Come on you two, time to eat," he says, lifting the turkey and walking into the dining room. Max and I waltz in behind him and take our seats.

"You two at it again?" My dad shakes his head while smiling at me, he knows how Max and I carry on too.

"One day they will grow out of it," Knox says, smirking at me.

"Hell No!" Max scoffs and we high five.

"At least Max lets me play video games with him."

"So do I," Knox looks really offended.

"Yeah but I don't kill her after five minutes," Max laughs at Knox.

"Okay kids," Richard smiles at us, reaching for his drink. He proposes a toast to us all and then we start to eat.

Taking a bite of my turkey I can't help but laugh. Knox questions me with his eyes sending me into a fit of giggles. Everyone looks at us, and he shrugs not knowing what is up with me.

"So Richard," I start, "were you able to follow Knox's instruction okay for the turkey," I ask, innocently.

117

Knox chokes on his beer spilling some of it down his chin. Reaching over, I wipe it off with a concerned look.

"Yes I did, it was easy enough to understand what was going on," Richard says, chuckling at me.

Knox's eyes widen and he looks like he wants to die right there. I must admit Richard got me with that one, but I just laugh with him. Knox squeezes my knee under the table and he squints his eyes at me, letting me know I am in trouble later.

After dinner, Paige and I clean up the dishes and leftovers. Max floats into us, helping here and there. Once we are done, we decided to open gifts. I feel bad for Paige because no one knew she would be here so they didn't have anything for her. I got her a pair of boots she picked out about two months ago when we were on the phone and browsing the Cosmo website.

"Holy hell, Bailey!" she squeals, jumping up she hugs me and thanks me about fifty times.

Max hands her an envelope, "This is from Knox and me, sorry it was last minute."

Taking it from him she smiles and opens it, pulling out a piece of paper. Peeking over her shoulder, I see it's a gift voucher to one of her favorite stores in the mall.

"Wow thanks, guys," she gives both of them a hug then sits down by the tree. She passes us a small envelope each and I question her with my eyes, she already got me some clothes. Waving her hand she says it's something small and not to worry about it. Max almost chokes when he takes out the paper. He looks up at her and frowns, turning I look over to Knox, who is frowning too, so I rip open my envelope. Pulling out the small card I read it. She has given us a first class round trip ticket to New York for next week.

"What's this for?" I ask, not rudely, but I don't get it.

"Well, I'm moving home and I was wondering if you wanted to spend my last New Year's Eve in New York with me in Times Square."

She chews her lip nervously as her eyes dart between the three of us. Knox shrugs at me, Max is in shock, and I jump up.

"Yes! Of course we will."

I grab her in a hug and we both laugh, Dad and Richard are smiling at us while they take in the scene. We pass out the rest of the gifts. I got Knox a set of handlebar grips for his Harley, and Max wanted new motorcycle boots. Dad and Richard told us not to get them anything, but I still got them some shirts and ties. Max passes me a box and by the look and feel of it, I'm guessing it's a DVD, opening it I laugh at him. He gave me part two of a video game we play and my own purple controller.

"Thanks, bro," I hug him and give him a kiss on the cheek.

Knox laughs at us then hands me a small box, ripping open the wrapper I open the velvet box finding a gold chain bracelet. I'm a little confused to say the least he then passes another one to me. Opening it I find a small charm of a car.

"You look confused," he says

"A little."

Smiling, he leans forward resting his elbows on his knees. "The first time I saw you, you were hiding behind your car," he hands me another box and I open it.

"A cocktail glass?" I ask.

"The first time you actually spoke to me in the bar."

My smiles grows and I get another box, he keeps bringing them out each containing a small charm representing a time in our lives so far. A motorcycle, for our first time on his. A stiletto for when we went clubbing. A key, to his heart and a bed for when we moved in together, an infinity symbol, to represent his love for me, and how unbreakable it is. A tree of life, for me fighting for mine, and winning. A seashell for when Knox proposed.

By the time he has each one hanging from the bracelet I'm in tears, he gently brushes my eyes with his thumbs.

"Thank you," I whisper. I want to say more, but my voice is stuck.

Taking my hand, he excuses us and brings me out to the beach. We walk down to the water and he turns to me.

"You okay darlin'? I didn't mean to make you cry."

"I'm fine, they're happy tears," I reply, fingering the charms on my wrist.

"Do you like it?"

"Yes, oh my god, yes. I love it," throwing my arms around his neck I squeeze him.

119

"We're not done darlin'."

Stepping back, I look at his outstretched hand and then back up to him, "This is a special one I found."

Taking the box, I wipe my eyes not knowing if my heart can take anymore. Lifting the lid I stare at the beautiful rose charm, it has pink stones encrusted on it and a gold stem. I know roses are a symbol of love so I guess it's for love. Looking up at him I smile and say thank you. He snorts at me taking the rose from the box and lifting my wrist.

"This one darlin' has nothing to do with me," he says, fastening it to a part of the bracelet. "This one is for the past, I know how much you still miss Summer and I remember you telling me pink roses were her favorite. When I saw this I knew I was meant to get it. It was the only one in the store and so this one is for you, to know that she remembers you and I'm pretty sure she is keeping an eye on my beautiful girl for me."

Tears stream down my cheeks ruining my makeup completely. I have no words to say to him to describe what a beautiful gift it is. He winks at me, lifting the bottom of his shirt he wipes my face.

"I don't know what to say," I blink, away more tears.

"You don't have to say anything darlin', I know."

He pulls me into him holding me close whispers soft words to me, "I love you, Knox Porter."

"Yeah? I love you Bailey Mortenson, more than I could ever say."

Chapter 14

New Year's Eve
Max

We arrived in New York about an hour ago and I'm starting to question myself. Why did I come here? Do I want to know what she has been doing for the last couple of years? Do I want to meet her friends?

Because I'm an idiot – yes – and yes.

When the cab pulls up outside of a brownstone, I am quickly reminded how successful and rich Paige is. I'm not holding it against her, but I actually forgot there for a minute. Paying the cabbie, I climb out stretching my legs. Paige and Bailey climb out of the other cab while Knox and I grab our bags. Two days, I should be good – it will be okay. We agreed to spend tonight in Times Square and then help Paige pack up her stuff tomorrow before she moves back to the West coast.

"Fuck, my balls are frozen."

Knox says stopping beside me. I hadn't even noticed the cold until he mentioned it.

"You okay?" his voice is concerned as he throws his arm over my shoulders.

"Yeah I guess," looking at him he nods, understanding that I'm not okay, but I don't want to talk about it right now.

"Come on you two!"

Bailey calls out, waving at us from the top of the steps. Knox gives me a reassuring squeeze and we head up to the door. I honestly don't know what to do, if it weren't for him I probably would be freaking out even more. We follow Bailey through the door into a pretty house. The floor is carpeted with a thick, deep burgundy carpet and the walls are painted a cream color.

I walk into the kitchen surprised that it's quite large. The floor is wooden and it has a small center island with four chairs. There is no table, which seems odd, but there are plenty of pictures on the far wall. I don't want to look at them. I don't want to see her in the arms of another guy even if it was a long time ago.

"So anyone for a drink?" Paige asks, opening the massive fridge.

Looking over at Knox, I bust out laughing. He looks like he just saw a hot naked chick. "You just creamed yourself didn't you?"

"Fuck off," he says, staring at the subzero.

"Darlin' we're getting one."

He says to Bailey while pointing at the fridge. We take our beers and sit around the island. Paige opts to stand on the other side so she can talk to us. She tells us we are meeting her friends tonight for dinner then we can all head to watch the ball drop. I really don't know if I want to go, my feelings for her never went away and now I am being assaulted left and right.

"Do you mind if we shower first?" I ask, needing to just say something and get away at the same time.

"Oh, yeah let me show you. I have one guest shower so if you guys want that Bailey can use mine," she says.

I follow her up the narrow stairs watching her ass sway, taking a deep breath I force my eyes off of her and stare at the end of her hair instead.

"Here you go," she pushes open a door to a bathroom then the one across from it. "This is where you can sleep, so just throw your stuff in here."

"Thanks," I mumble, stepping into the room, she nods then leaves me alone. I want to reach out and pull her back, but I can't, I won't. The room is a weird grayish cream color, it's not ugly or anything just something unusual. Opening my bag, I pull out my clothes for tonight and wash bag. Kicking off my shoes and socks, I pull off my t-shirt and toss it on the floor too. Grabbing my bag, I open the door and run smack into her. Her face hits my bare chest and she stumbles back a little.

122

"Shit, are you okay?"

"Yeah sorry, my fault I was just getting extra towels for you," she points to the bundle sitting on top of the toilet.

"Oh, thanks."

Stepping around her, I quickly close the door and run my hands through my hair. Fuck! Why did she have to touch me? All I want now is to feel her hands all over me. Stripping down I turn on the shower and have a quick shave, then hop into the cool water, memories of us together flood my mind.

"Fucking traitor."

I moan looking down at my rock hard dick, gripping it in my hand I get to work relieving myself of the stress and torment being around her causes. When I'm done picturing her fucking me, I cum hard and almost shout out. Leaning my head against the wall while I ride the wave, I bite down on my fist. My breathing is shallow and I'm so annoyed at myself, it's been months since I allowed myself the pleasure of her memory.

I even tried to date someone last year. I never told Knox or Bailey though. Amanda was nice, she was opposite to Paige, and I was happy about that. She loved sex, like really loved it, every time we decided to go out I'd pick her up at her house, but we never made it on our dates. We would just fuck in every room and drink afterward. It helped numb the pain, but after about the tenth 'date' I never went back.

"Hey, you almost done?"

Knox's shouting startles me and I turn off the now cold water. Wrapping a towel around myself I pull open the door. Knox takes one look at me and frowns pushing my chest until I step back inside and he closes the door.

"Are you sure you're going to be okay?"

He looks really concerned and I nod trying to make a joke of it. He tells me to stop acting like that and I cave.

"No, I don't think so bro, it's hard, harder than I thought it would be."

Sighing, I grab another towel and dry off my chest and arms. "I want to fucking scream. How am I going to deal with her friends?"

"You have me, Max, you don't have to deal with anyone."

"I know, thanks. I'll be fine it's just tonight and tomorrow," I tell myself. We walk back into the bedroom and Knox gets ready for his shower.

"Why are you in here?" I ask, dropping my towel and grabbing my boxers.

"We have to share the room bro, just like old times," he grins at me, kicking off his own clothes.

"Where is Bailey sleeping?"

"With Paige, she only has this room other than her own," he answers.

"Cool, I guess we are having a threesome tonight," I joke, getting a punch on the arm.

"Never fucker."

Knox laughs on his way out. I'm always busting his balls about us and Bailey. Getting dressed in my new black jeans and blue shirt, I slip on my new boots Bailey got me for Christmas and head downstairs to wait. I can hear the girls laughing as I pass by another door, taking note that it's Paige's bedroom.

Taking a seat in the kitchen I look around. I have no clue what to do with myself so I grab a beer from the fridge. The fridge is stocked with food, which makes no sense considering she is leaving tomorrow or the next day. Taking a swallow, I walk over to the pictures on the wall, from afar it looks like a jumbled mess but the closer I get I start to recognize some of them.

There are some of us all in the bar, the band, Bailey. Paige and Bailey. Paige and some other chicks, Paige and some dude. Clenching my jaw, I take in every detail of the picture, trying to read what it means. They look like they are laughing with arms slung around each other, both of them are turned towards the camera, but their bodies are pressed together. Moving on I scan the rest and notice he is in a few of them, fuck! What am I doing?

Walking away from the wall of horror, I sit at the island and Knox joins me. After about fifteen minutes, we hear the girls laughing as they walk down the stairs. Bailey enters first and I have to say she is a beautiful looking chick, her dress is short and black, and my brother is fucked. Shaking my head I

124

chuckle at him, she never lets him down when they are going out. I know she loves dressing up for him and misses it.

Paige follows her and I almost lose my own shit. Her hair is pulled back off her face, and falling over her shoulder in big curls. It matches her eyes, a honey color with streaks of caramel that make you want to sink into them. Her dress is a little longer than Bailey's but not by much and her long legs are capped with sparkly shoes. I quickly gulp down the last of my beer almost choking myself.

"Ready? We can walk to the restaurant, it's only two blocks," she says.

Following her out, we walk down the cold ass streets of New York. Knox is holding Bailey tight and I have to admit I'm fucking jealous as fuck. Paige shivers a little so I move closer at least she can have some of my body heat.

"Thanks," she smiles at me. We stop at a crosswalk and she links her arm through mine to cross the road. I don't say anything to her when she doesn't let me go. We walk into a nice place the dining room is full and we wait for about five minutes before we are seated. The table is set for eight people, I sit down beside Knox, and Paige takes a seat beside Bailey so we are across from each other.

A few minutes later a waiter takes our drink order and two people join us. Paige introduces them as Claire and John. They sit down beside her, leaving the two seats beside me free.

"Andy and Trevor are running late, you know what traffic is like today," Claire tells Paige. She nods and sips her wine and the girls start talking. Knox turns to me.

"You good?" he whispers.

"Yeah so far," I answer, just, as the seat beside me gets taken.

Turning my head I notice a raven-haired beauty situating herself beside me, her eyes are huge like a puppy dog and she smiles at me. The dude who sits next to her looks at me, it's the fucker from the picture, and I instantly dislike him. The chick crosses her bare legs. I notice she is wearing a very revealing skirt and top. Her eyes meet mine and she slowly draws them down the length of my body and back up to my eyes.

"Well, Paige, where were you hiding this one?"

She asks, with a British accent. Her lips are full and pouty and my dick twitches just thinking of sliding in between them.

"I wasn't," Paige snaps, drawing my attention to her. I swear I see a look of hurt cross her face before she turns away.

"So I'm Andie, with an *ie* and this is my brother Trevor," she says, holding out her hand. Taking it, I shake it.

"Max, my brother Knox and his fiancée Bailey."

Andie smiles at them then turns her full attention to me. She shifts her body so that I can see right down her low cut top and force myself to keep my eyes up. The waiter brings her a drink and she sips it while watching me. She is one of the sexiest chicks I have ever met and I bet she knows it.

"So how's work, Andie?" Paige asks.

I can hear the slight annoyance in her tone, but if Andie notices she doesn't let on.

"It was okay, a little boring without my helper," she smiles at Paige. I get the feeling we are missing something here.

"I'm hardly your helper," Paige replies sounding bored.

"Come on girls, not tonight."

Trevor finally opens his mouth. Paige glares at him and I know that look all too well. My girl is getting ready to fight, and I, for one am loving it.

My girl? What the fuck am I saying? The meal is a little weird; Knox keeps glancing at me and me, him. Once it's done, Paige pays for us all and it rubs me the wrong way; none of these fuckers even offered to pay. On the way out I take her elbow and stop her.

"Why did you pay? I thought we were paying for ourselves."

"Oh it's okay, don't worry about it," she smiles at me.

We walk outside into the biting wind and she quickly squeals. Laughing, I am about to wrap my arm around her when douchebag does it. Trevor the fucker, his sister grips my arm and attaches herself to my side as we walk to a bar down the block. I can't help but notice that these places are pretty high end and I'm wondering why we are going to them. Paige knows we don't give a shit about this type of stuff considering the type of bar we own.

126

We walk into the place, which is jammed. Paige offers to get the first round and it pisses me off. I am about to step in, but Bailey beats me to it.

"I'll get it, you got dinner," she says, over the noise.

We order the drinks, finding a table near the back we let the girls sit down. Andie turns around so she is facing me and makes sure I notice her.

"So how do you know Paige?" she asks, keeping her eyes locked on mine.

"How do you?" I ask, not wanting to get into history here.

"Oh she and my brother," she nods over to Trevor the fucker.

"Oh right, I thought you worked together."

"Ha! No silly, they work together, but I work in the same building." She shrugs.

"What do you do? Computers too?"

She laughs at me, throwing back her head back like I just cracked the funniest joke ever. Her hand trails down my arm and she smiles again.

"I'm a model, my agency is housed in the building with the nerds."

I nod in understanding, well pretending to. I know the kind of chick she is, a man- eater, and someone who wants what she can't have. My eyes are drawn to Paige, who looks uncomfortable with Trevor's arm around her shoulder. Finishing my drink, I put the bottle down on the table and make my way around to her.

"You okay angel?"

I ask, cursing myself for that slip of the tongue. Her eyes light up when she looks up at me and smiles.

"I'm okay."

"You want another?" I nod to her drink and she says yes offering to come to the bar with me.

"You and Andie seem to be getting along."

Looking down at her I notice she is fidgeting with her hands, she is totally different now. She seems almost shy and hidden away when she is out with these 'friends.'

"She's alright, I guess."

I order our drinks and check the time, it's almost nine, and I'm wondering when we're leaving this place. Paige takes her drink from me and walks back to the table with me behind her. Once we get back, Trevor claims her shoulders again, and I swear I see her slump under the weight.

"I see you are on someone's radar tonight," Knox says, nodding at the now empty seat.

"Fuck that!" I answer and we both laugh. "Not happening bro, she is a piece of work."

"Yeah I can tell and I swear she is doing it on purpose. When Bailey went to the restroom, she tried to hit on me."

My eyes widen and I laugh at Knox. He shakes his head telling me he doesn't need this hassle and he wishes we were at home.

"Yeah me too. Does Paige seem different to you?" I ask.

"Kind of," he sighs, "I don't know her all that well but she seems a little depressed or something."

I agree and we leave it at that, after another hour of this place we finally head off to Times Square. It's so fucking cold my teeth are chattering and I seriously feel for the girls, wearing those skimpy dresses. I watch Trevor rub his hands up and down Paige's arms and she steps back a little. When she doesn't know it, I catch the look of annoyance cross her face and the eye roll she gives him.

We stand in the cold for two hours until the countdown finally starts, the crowd cheers and screams and the ball finally drops. Knox and Bailey dive on each other while the other couple, have a little peck on the lips. Trevor hugs his crazy sister and I look at Paige. This time three years ago we were wrapped up together, then life changed so much that night. I still remember the look on her face when she told me we made a baby, she was scared and so was I, but I wanted it, after the shock I wanted it.

Looking at her now, her eyes are filled with pain and sorrow. I move through the small crowd and take her in my arms.

"Happy New Year, angel."

Her arms lock around my waist and she holds me tight, she whispers back to me and I swear she said sorry. I step back and instantly miss her in my arms. Trevor the fucker grabs her planting a kiss on her lips. Her body goes rigid as he kisses her, I can't take it, I need to get the fuck out of here. I'm about to walk away when Bailey grabs me and hugs the crap out of me.

"Love you Max."

"Love you too, thanks."

I know she is watching out for me and I love her for it. She really is the sister I never had. I catch Knox rubbing his eyes and start getting worried.

"You okay, Knox?"

He nods telling me he is starting to get a headache, which is happening a lot lately and honestly it frightens me a bit. My mom used to have headaches too, then she got cancer and I seriously get scared every time he gets one.

"Let's get out of here."

I call out grabbing his sleeve and pulling him. He grabs Bailey, who gets Paige. We make a human chain down the street until the crowd is scarce and we can walk side by side.

"Did you take your meds?" I ask, looking at my brother.

"I forgot them, I'll be good probably just need water."

My heart beats a little faster knowing his medication is across the fucking country. I have never told him how scared I get. I don't want to seem like a pussy but still, he is all I have and I don't want to lose him.

When we get back to Paige's, Knox and Bailey take the room and I offer to take the sofa. I make him some tea and knock on the door before I walk inside.

"Hey you okay bro?"

He nods his head but keeps his eyes covered with the wet cloth, "I made you some tea and I have some Advil, that's all Paige has."

"Thanks, Max, I'll be okay," he takes the medicine and I leave him with Bailey.

"How is he?" Paige asks.

"Okay I guess, he forgot his medication," I shake my head, frustrated with him.

Paige places a cup of tea in front of me, smiling.

"Thanks," I say, sitting down I take off my jacket. I can't help but think back over the night and her friends. "So how are you friends with that lot?"

"Long story," she smirks at me.

"I've got a few hours," I reply.

"Well, I met Claire when I first got here. We hit it off in NYU and got an apartment together. When I started working, I met Trevor and Andie. They seemed really cool and fun. We had hung out for about a year before Trevor asked me out and I said yes," she shrugs.

"Then?" I question.

"Then I dated him for a while, we worked together and it was easy enough. We'd have lunch together, and then I'd come home to study and he went out with his friends. I'd go on weekends to the bar with them but after a while it got a little stale. They were kind of boring and then Andie shows up one night and things got weird. She would make comments about other girls and how Trevor should try for this one or that one.

She would target guys who looked like they had money and I figured out they were both just using people. I distanced myself from them when I broke up with him, but Trevor and Claire are friends too so I never said anything about it. We would all hang out in a group and I would ignore him and he me, until tonight."

"Yeah, he looked like he was your boyfriend."

Shaking her head she lets out a deep sigh and pulls the pins from her hair. I watch her run her finger through it and I'm hard already.

"I don't know what game they were playing tonight, but they were up to something," she continues. "He was way too touchy-feely and she was trying to hook you," her eyes meet mine and she looks sad.

"Max, I'm sorry for hurting you the way I did. You didn't deserve to get the brunt of all my shit, not that you'd believe me, but it was really hard to leave you."

"Didn't feel that way, it seemed to me like you were okay with it," I answer, feeling hurt and betrayed all over again.

"I know, I'm sorry but honestly, it was the hardest thing I did. I wanted to run back to you at the airport, but I knew I

130

couldn't. I just had to get out of there. Away from everyone and all the memories that were hurting me."

"They were hurting me too Paige, every day. Every damn day when I looked at you and your stomach was flat when it should have been big and round." I wipe my eyes quickly and clear my throat, trying not to go back to that time.

Reaching over she rests her hand on mine. "I'm so very sorry Max, so sorry," she squeezes my hand then gets up to leave.

"Angel," I whisper, just needing to say it again.

"I miss that," she says, "I miss you every day, Max."

I watch her walk out of the room and hear her footsteps on the stairs and her door closing. Rinsing the cup, I make myself comfortable on the sofa and close my eyes.

Chapter 15

The next morning I wake to the smell of coffee, dragging myself into the kitchen I see Bailey.

"Hey, sis."

Turning she smiles at me. "Morning, you look like you got about as much sleep as me," she says sounding tired.

"Is Knox okay?"

"Yeah he was awake most of the night though, but he finally fell asleep about an hour ago."

"Fuck, let's get this shit packed, he needs to get home and so do I."

Just as the words leave my mouth Paige walks in behind me, she looks hurt and I feel like a douche now. I make coffee and down it then hit the shower. The three of us pack up as much as we can, the sitting room, kitchen, and her office. By four, o'clock we have nearly all of the stuff done.

"Our flight is at seven sis, you need to wake him up."

Bailey nods and leaves to wake up Knox, taking this opportunity I try explain myself to Paige.

"I am worried about my brother. I didn't mean that I wanted to leave because of you or anything."

"Yeah I know, I get it," She answers, moving away from me.

"Paige."

"I get it, Max," she snaps at me leaving the room.

Fucking hell, I can't take this shit anymore. I march up to the room and wake Knox up.

"Come on bro get up."

I lift him up and he winces, but I don't care I need to get him the fuck out of here and on that plane. Once I have him up, I make him shower, with Bailey's help. When he is dressed, he takes two more Advil and has some water, by five-thirty we are calling a cab and I swear it can't come fast enough. Saying goodbye to Paige is harder than I thought it would be, giving her a hug she stiffens in my arms.

"See you guys in a few days," she says, waving to us.

I know she was supposed to come home with us now, but I guess I fucked that up too. Once we land back in California, I feel like a complete asshole. I had dad meet us at the airport with my brother's medication. Dad actually looks pissed at Knox and it's been a while since I've seen that look on his face. Bailey drives him home to bed and I go to hang out with my dad.

"When will that boy learn?" Dad asks, shaking his head.

"I know Dad, he just forgot them. Go easy on him."

"Max," he sighs, "I don't know how he forgets them. He knows how important they are."

"I know Dad," I don't want to tell him that my brother's headaches are getting worse. And it's freaking me out because it will freak him out too and I need him right now even if he doesn't know it.

"I swear if I get another call from a hospital about one of you, I'll fucking lose it."

I almost laugh at him for swearing, but I know how upset he is over this.

"So tell me, how was your New Year?"

I do laugh now and shake my head, "Same, a load of shit."

He smiles at me and we both end up laughing. When we get home, I order pizza and crack open a beer for each of us. I talk to him about Knox and then about Paige, I really need advice on this.

"Son, life is hard. Like I told your brother, if she is the one, then do everything you can, to get her back, because it hurts like a bitch when they leave."

"Dad, Mom, didn't leave," I whisper.

"I know, not by choice, but as I said it hurts Max."

I can still see the pain on his face from my mother's death; it's has been nine years already.

"Dad?"

Turning he looks at me with a question in his eyes.

133

"Do you think Knox is okay?"

"Yeah, why do you ask? Do you know something I don't?"

"No, no I'm just wondering."

He gives me his stern look and I curse, causing him to sit up in the chair.

"I'm just scared, Dad. Mom had headaches then she died. I don't want to lose my brother too."

Dad relaxes a little and pats my arm, "You won't Max, no more than I'll lose one of my son's. Mom had migraines too, sometimes they were so bad she was in bed for days, the cancer was separate."

My mind is all over the place right now and I say goodnight needing to finally get some sleep. My dad gives me a sad smile and I know I have made him worry and I feel yet another weight on my shoulders.

***

Bailey

Getting Knox into bed was a little harder than usual, he mumbled an 'I love you,' then crashed. Texting my dad, I let him know we are home and set up the video game Max got me. I actually never play alone, but I have no one to hang out with, so I set it up and get my zombie warriors killed within two minutes. I play for an hour until I can't take it anymore. Turning off the game, I make myself a cup of hot chocolate and grab my iPad.

Flipping on some random movie I begin to read a book, getting through half of it before my eyes get heavy. Making my way into bed I snuggle against Knox. I hate when he is down like this, I wish I could take his pain away. By six in the morning I am up ready for my run, Knox is still sleeping and I kiss him before I leave. I run around campus and the track before heading home. When I get back, I shower and dress in my shorts, and t-shirt and work on my program.

Max arrives about two in the afternoon with cookies and donuts.

134

"Hi, Max."

"Sis," he says, ruffling my hair and putting down the goodies.

"Ooh yummy," I open the box and pull out a warm donut. We both eat in silence savoring the sweet goodness.

We hear a noise from down the hall and look around to find a very disheveled Knox walk into the room. He scratches his face and takes a seat beside me.

"How long was I out?" he asks, taking a donut.

"Just a day, babe."

He nods then bites into it groaning. I make him a coffee and watch as he eats another one.

"Okay fatty," I tease, pinching his side. "Real food." I make him some eggs and toast and a large glass of juice.

"I was thinking of getting some more ink, you down?" Max asks Knox.

"Yeah, what were you thinking?"

"Not sure, I just want another one."

"Aren't you guys running out of space?" I ask, getting a look from both that basically says I'm nuts.

"No way sis, we have loads left," Max grins at me.

They discuss tattoos while I lay on the sofa reading my book. Knox lifts my legs gently and rubs them. Max brings in the cookies and I frown at him.

"You develop a new sweet tooth, Max?"

"No, just feel like a little today. I'll burn it off in the gym tomorrow."

I watch the two of them stuff their faces with cookies, more donuts, and lots of juice and water. I don't know how either of them don't hit a wall from the sugar rush then crash. They watch some action movie and I get a funny feeling Max is keeping an eye on Knox. By ten, o'clock I have a shower and crawl into bed, Knox joins me soon after.

"How are you feeling, babe?"

"Okay darlin', don't worry about me," he wraps me in his arms and kisses me.

He is asleep within minutes again leaving me staring at the ceiling. By two in the morning, I am still awake. Getting out of bed I walk to the kitchen grabbing some warm milk. I can hear

Max shuffling around so I make him one too and bring it into him.

"Can't sleep either?" I ask, walking into his dark room.

"No, just thinking about stuff. What about you?"

"Same, I made you a drink. I bet you're on a sugar high," I smirk, crawling on top of his bed.

"No, they were for Knox. I figured out years ago that after one of his bad headaches, junk food kind of helps so I just kept doing it. It's probably all in my head but still."

"You're a good brother, Max," leaning over I kiss his cheek.

"Thanks, sis."

"I take it things in New York didn't work out for you," I ask, looking at him.

"Not really, I'm just more confused," he sighs.

We talk for a while about Paige and Knox. He talks about finding a new tattoo and tries to get me to have another one done too. Yawning, I close my eyes and rest my head against his arm.

"What the fuck is this?"

The voice booming in my ear makes me shoot up clutching my chest against the fright. Looking around I find Knox standing at the door with his arms crossed and his expression is livid. At first I don't get it, but looking around I realize I'm still in Max's room. Turning, I find Max out cold with his arm around my waist. Shit.

"We were talking babe and I must have fallen asleep."

Knox shakes his head and slams the door on his way out causing the window to rattle and Max to jump up.

"Earthquake?" he stares at me a little panicked.

"Knox," I sigh, climbing off the bed.

I have a shower and get dressed, ready to go to my dad's when Max emerges from his room. He gives me a nod then frowns turning his head towards the sitting room. The noise of the video game is quite loud even with the door closed.

"What's up with him?" Max asks.

"He saw us asleep this morning."

"Oh, so," he looks perplexed.

136

"Yeah, anyway I'm off now I have to work on something with Dad, see you later."

I twist my wet hair up into a bun as I race down to my car. The streets are quiet this time of year and I make it up the hill in ten minutes. When I walk into the house though, Dad is not here.

"Hey, Dad. where are you?" I ask when he answers his phone.

"Oh sorry sweetheart I forgot I had a meeting today, I left the files on my desk."

After a brief conversation to which I got no information, I get to work in Dad's office. The files are sensitive, so I have to make up a security program for the company to keep their designs away from the public eye. I get to work, reading and coding and trying to figure out what I'm doing with only half paragraphs and lines here and there.

After a few hours, I take a walk around the lake and into my house. I find a lot of the walls are marked off with spray paint and some of the pipes have been marked too. I can't believe this is my house, my own home, where one day I'll raise a family. Well, that's if I don't kill Knox first for his stupid behavior. Smiling, I finger the charms on my bracelet remembering each story. That man drives me insane, but I love him like crazy. After another walk around the house, I go back to Dad's and decided to quit working.

Driving back to the apartment I stop to get take out. When I park my car, I notice the bikes are gone. Pulling out my phone, I text my wall of muscle.

Me: Hey babe I got take out, are you coming back soon?

Shoving my phone into my pocket I grab the food and head upstairs and put it in the oven to stay warm. After thirty minutes I give up, dishing out my dinner, I sit down to eat. After dinner, I watch a movie. I have no classes for another week and so I have nothing much to do. I watch the clock as well as the movie, by eight o'clock I haven't heard back from Knox. Taking out my phone I call him. He is probably still

137

ignoring me, but both bikes are gone so maybe he and Max talked.

Getting no answer I call Max, still nothing. Throwing my phone down, I surf the tv for an hour, then decide to head over to the bar. It's dead when I arrive. There are about ten people and Chase.

"Hey," he greets me, looking relieved.

"Busy night, huh?"

He grins at me as he pours a drink, placing it down in front of me, "Thanks, Chase."

"So how was your holiday?" he asks, leaning his forearms on the bar.

"It was good, New York was freezing I don't know how Paige can take that nonsense."

"Yeah sounds like it was fun," he smiles.

Chase and I hang out until closing. I help him clean up and he counts the cash. I still haven't heard from Knox or Max and I'm a little pissed off. Chase locks the bar and I walk across the street towards the apartment. I declined his offer to walk me home. Still no bikes when I cross the parking lot, so I call Richard to check. He answers, with a groggy, 'hello,' considering it's almost one in the morning.

"Hi Richard, are Knox and Max staying with you?"

"No, I haven't seen them today, why?"

"Neither have I since this morning and they aren't answering me."

He tells me not to worry that they probably took off and lost track of time. I hang up with him, then get ready for bed trying Knox again. It's not like him to ignore me this long, he usually texts me, but even Max is not responding. Turning off the light, I try to sleep.

Chapter 16

Opening my eyes I reach out for Knox, but he is not there. Shooting up, I check the apartment and out of the window, but still no bikes or no fiancé. Pulling on jeans and a sweater, I grab my phone and start dialing. No answer from either of them and now I am seriously worried. I call the hospital and my dad, but no luck with either, my hands are shaking, and I can feel a panic attack coming on.

Pulling off the sweater, I sit on the floor with my bare back against the wall trying to control my breathing, after a while I can finally take a deep breath. I count ten breaths then, stand up. Walking into the bathroom I splash my face with cold water. After a few more minutes, I call Paige.

"Hey, I was just about to call you," she answers.

"Oh, why?"

"Because I arrive home tonight and I was wondering if you wanted to go for dinner?" she says.

"Oh, oh sorry, I forgot you were coming home, listen, Paige, I haven't seen or heard from Knox and Max since yesterday morning. I'm getting worried."

"What? How's that possible?"

I fill her in on all the details and she sighs. Telling me the way Max and I act together can sometimes come across wrong and that was one of the issues she had with us. I'm a little pissed off at her because she knows I would never hurt Knox like that and now he is gone and I'm panicking. Paige tells me that she will change her flight and see me soon.

Hanging up, I call Richard and tell him that I'm worried now, for the first time ever I hear him get upset. He says he will call hospitals in the area and let me know if he hears anything. This is turning out to be a shit new year, again!

Pacing the apartment, I grip my phone so tight my hand is aching.

"Hello," I answer, after one ring.

"Hi Bailey, they're not in any hospital so I don't know what is going on. Did they go camping or something?" Richard asks, a little panicked.

"No, not that I know of. There was no note when I got back yesterday."

After a few minutes, I hang up with Richard wanting to keep my phone free. I don't get this, why aren't they calling me. I spend my day pacing and checking in with Richard. At four thirty, Paige arrives.

"Hi, any news?"

"No, nothing. I don't get this Paige."

She gives me a hug before setting out to make coffee. We sit in the kitchen in silence for a while, drinking coffee, and eating donuts. I help Paige settle back into her apartment and then we both camp out on my sofa. The tv is on, but we are not watching it. I'm trying not to cry, but the urge to do so is getting the better of me.

"Don't cry, I'm sure they're fine," she says, but her voice sounds worried.

Swiping at the escapee tear, I am getting angrier by the minute. I dial Knox again and still don't get an answer. I make Paige call Max, but she gets voicemail too. We sit in the room for a few hours finally we decide to go to bed. It's just after midnight and I tell Paige we are going driving around the whole town and mountains tomorrow.

Crawling into bed I hug Knox's pillow, smelling his cologne and sending up a prayer for him to come home safe. I can't sleep, tossing and turning I kick the covers off me and open the window slightly. I lie back down and wait for sleep, but I don't get it. Instead, I get an almost heart attack when I hear the roar of motorcycles coming into the parking lot. Jumping out of bed I scramble to the window and watch them walk towards the building.

When I open my door, Paige is already standing outside of it. We rush to the front door and I swing it open just as Knox raises his key. When I see his face I am shocked, he has scratches along his cheekbone and his eye is black. Looking at his hand I see his knuckles are swollen and scraped.

"What the fuck happened?" I ask as he pushes past me.

Max follows inside with his head down, but he too has a cut lip and busted knuckles. Paige grabs Max, startling him and pulls him into her room. Closing the door, I find Knox in the bedroom taking off his boots.

"What happened, Knox? I was so worried. Your dad and I were calling hospitals for fuck sake!"

Lifting his head he just looks at me, "Aren't you going to say something? Where were you?"

"Don't worry about it, I'm alive and so is Max."

"I can see that, but what the hell happened? Did you two fight?"

I am appalled that they would even hit each other, I can't understand it.

"I said I'm alive, now I'm going for a shower."

He brushes past me and I snap, pushing him up against the wall, I slap his already beaten face. My hand stings and I instantly regret it. Angry tears spring from eyes as we stare at each other.

"Don't you think I deserved a call or a text to say you were okay?"

I scream at him, he frowns at me opening his mouth to speak, but I leave the room. I'm so annoyed at him and my hand fucking hurts. I run it under the cold water in the kitchen when Paige walks in.

"You okay?"

"Yeah," I nod, then, shake my head no. She gives me a hug and tells me it's okay. "No, it's not," walking back to my room I grab my bag and start packing my clothes. My anger is simmering very close to the top and I am about to blow. I can't take it anymore, marching into the bathroom I slam the door behind me. Knox looks at me then rolls his eyes.

"We're done, Knox," I pull off my ring slapping it into his hand. "How dare you do this to me? You had me worried and for what! Because you decided you don't trust me with your brother? Well you're an asshole and I am not like you," I shout at him, completely losing myself.

"This, obviously didn't mean shit to you did it?" I ask, shaking my bracelet at him.

He runs his hands through his wet hair and sighs, "Darlin', I'm sore and tired."

"I don't care, I'm fucking tired and worried, I haven't slept in two days."

Shaking my head I pull open the door smacking it off the wall, Knox grabs my arm pulling me back against his chest. He holds me tight and I can't move, I can hardly breathe.

"Let me go Knox I'm done this time, I really am," I whisper, against his chest.

"Darlin' just stop," he whispers, "Stop shouting."

After a few minutes, he loosens his grip on me asking me to just wait for him. He grabs his clothes and we go into our room, when he sees my bag he grabs it off the bed and throws it into the closet.

"You're not leaving, Bailey. This is not over, we already had this argument. I meant every word when I gave you that," he points to my wrist, "Can we not fight? I'm tired."

"Knox, what the hell happened?"

I'm almost too tired to listen and climb up onto the bed, resting my head against the wall.

"Max and I went for a drive up to the mountains. We talked, we fought, and now we're all good. I'm sorry I didn't call you back, I lost my phone. We spent a few hours looking for it. It's over now, so please let it go darlin'."

"That's not good enough."

"I know it's not, but that's all you're getting; the rest is between my brother and me."

His answer is final, turning he hands me back my ring and looks disappointed doing it.

"You know, you made me a promise that you would never take this off, but you've done it twice already. Correct me if I'm wrong, but I get the feeling you don't really want to marry me."

Getting up off the bed he walks out of the room bringing his pillow with him. Putting my ring back on, I groan kicking my feet in frustration. After a while the apartment is quiet and dark, the clock says four thirty now and my eyes hurt from lack of sleep. Climbing off the bed I put on my running gear and head out. I run around the campus track until my legs ache and turn to jelly, letting me know I pushed myself too hard.

I lie down on the grass and stare up at the sky, wishing I could fly up there. My music is off and I clear my mind of all the clutter and bullshit, everything is out of control. Hot angry, frustrated tears drip from my eyes down my temples. I watch the sun rise from my spot on the grass, and watch it move towards the arts building. Once it passes behind the metal and glass structure, I begin to walk back home.

My steps are slow, not from the aching muscles but because I am weighted down again, with worry, with anger and with sheer disappointment. When I arrive home, I hear laughter from the kitchen, shaking my head I run a bath, locking myself in the bathroom. Sinking down into the water I try to block out the fun being had in the other room, maybe being an only child I just don't get it.

Maybe I don't understand the dynamics of brothers, let alone twins. Supposedly twins are closer than normal siblings, but how would I know what they feel on a deeper level. A knock at the door draws my attention, Paige asks if I'm okay and I tell her yes. She leaves me alone to stay in my bath until the water runs cold. I don't bother moving, then either.

"Hey Darlin', can I come in?"

"No."

"Please?"

I don't answer him again, the door is locked, and I'm not moving to open it. Paige says goodbye sometime later, telling me that she and Max are going for lunch. When the front door closes, Knox gently knocks on the door again.

"Baby, you okay in there?"

Silence.

"If you don't answer I'll have to break down the door and then the landlord will be up my ass and you will be mad," he says.

Sighing, I sit up making the water slosh around, reaching for the plug I let the water drain and climb out. Wrapping a towel around myself I open the door and walk into my room getting followed by him.

"Darlin', your lips are turning blue, what the hell?"

He reaches for me, but I duck out of the way, resting his hands on his hips he sighs.

"Can you leave while I dress?"

"What for, I've seen you naked millions of times."

"I don't want you in here right now."

"You don't want me seeing something I've had my mouth all over?" he smirks at me.

I turn away to hide my smile because it's true he has kissed every inch of my body, his warm hands circle my waist. He holds me for a few minutes allowing his body heat to penetrate me, warming up my whole body. He starts kissing the back of my neck and down my shoulder.

"I'm not having sex with you."

Stepping away from him, I pull some clothes from the drawers. Knox takes my hands and places them on his shoulders.

"I don't want to have sex with you darlin'."

He grabs my thighs and lifts me up onto his waist. I lock my ankles together and he just holds me, running his hands up and down my back while his head rests on my chest.

"I'm sorry darlin'..."

"Stop, I don't want to hear that word anymore."

He nods his head, kissing me at the base of my throat. His tongue dips into the hollow point as he tastes my skin.

"Darlin', I love you more than anything in the world, you know that right?"

"Yes, Knox I do but I don't like you fighting with Max about our friendship," I sigh, trying to get down but he holds me tighter.

"We weren't fighting about you darlin'. Well at first it was, but afterward we went out for a ride, we're good."

Shrugging my shoulders, I nod, accepting his statement, finally deciding that I don't get it because I don't have a brother or sister. Knox carries me into the kitchen placing me on the chair. He makes me some lunch taking the seat beside me. I don't get his one- eighty mood swing but I'll just go with it for now.

Chapter 17

Knox

Watching Bailey stew in annoyance about Max and I is killing me, but I made him promise he wouldn't say anything to her about the accident. I'll admit, when I saw them in bed like that I was pissed but after a few minutes of killing zombies I realized what a dick I was being. Even thinking they would do anything together is funny. I know they are close, but it really is more like a brother-sister thing.

We eat in silence and she keeps looking down at the charms on her wrist. I hope she doesn't think I was anything but truthful when I told her what they were. My face fucking hurts like hell and my back. I don't think I could even have sex if I wanted to right now. Getting up, I grab my medicine and some Advil for my pain and swallow them fast so she won't see. Max said he would call Dad and let him know we are okay. I never thought she would start calling hospitals or my dad.

We only have today and tomorrow off before I go back to work, so I want to hang out with her alone. Prove I'm not the asshole she said I was, and that slap; fuck did that hurt, she is way stronger than she thinks. It actually started my headache again it was so hard.

"Do you want to go see a movie darlin'?" I ask, wanting to get out of here with her. She sighs while she thinks for a few minutes then finally agrees. I hide my smile behind my hand because I know she doesn't want to be mad at me but is trying to keep up the show.

"Okay, I'll wait for you to get dressed while I check out what's on."

She leaves the room and I clean up our dishes and wait for her, the only thing playing is some chick flick and a Christmas ghost movie. When she comes back, I can't help the smile I give her. She is so fucking beautiful, her jeans hug her ass, and the sweater is clinging to every beautiful part of her. Her hair brushes off the top of that amazing ass and I want to reach out to wrap it around my hand.

Standing, I take her hand and we leave the apartment. I actually love holding her hand. It's tiny inside mine, her delicate fingers thread through mine as we walk down the street. I love this, I love that such a simple act can tell the world that she is mine and I am hers and nobody is breaking us apart.

When we arrive at the cinema I get us tickets and she gets the popcorn and all the other junk food she buys when we come here. I watch her wait in line and check her out. I can see a few guys doing the same, and while it used to bother me it doesn't anymore. Unless they put their hand on her, then, of course, they will be fucking sorry.

"Can you grab these?"

She asks, trying not to drop the bag of candy between her teeth, taking it out of her mouth I swoop in and kiss her. I get a beautiful smile in return and a view of her perfect ass as she walks in front of me. We take a seat up the very top and settle in to watch this ghost thing. The movie is a little weird, suspenseful but Bailey seems to like it so far. Her hand is crushing my arm and I laugh at her.

"What?" she asks.

"Nothing darlin', you scared?" I tease. She shakes her head no while looking at the screen.

"Oh, no don't go in there," she says. "He's in there…oh, look in the corner!"

I'm laughing at her shouting at the girl in the movie, then she turns to me.

"Did you see that?" she asks, shaking her head in disbelief.

"No sorry, I missed it."

She lets out a sigh then rests her head on my shoulder grumbling about the girl in the movie. Kissing her head, I pull her closer to me and relax back, the movie ends with the girl getting away from the creep. Bailey stands up and stretches, her sweater rises up and I get a glimpse of her stomach, leaning forward I place a kiss on it.

"What was that for?" she smiles, down at me.

"No reason," taking her hand I follow her out. We walk down the street with me pulling her closer to me.

"Am I forgiven?"

"What for?" she asks.

"For being a douche."

"You're always a douche," she laughs, trying to pull away from me.

"That so?" I tickle her ribs making her squirm against me. "So I was thinking," I start and she bursts out laughing, stopping I look down at her.

"Did it hurt babe?" she grins up at me and I just shake my head at her.

"You're mean spirited darlin', I had something really important to say."

I pout for good measure and she frowns at me. I know I have her now, but I wait a little bit.

"I'm sorry babe I was just teasing," her face falls a little and I grin at her. She threatens me bodily harm and punches me on the arm.

"Okay, okay, seriously…" I start and pull her close to me again, "I was thinking of a June wedding."

My heart speeds up a little just throwing it out there like that, but I want to marry this girl. I want to see her walking towards me in a white dress. I want her to know that she is everything to me and always will be.

"June, of this year?"

She looks a horrified when she tilts her head to me and my heart has just crash- landed in my stomach.

"Yeah," I sigh, "you graduate in May, and you said you wanted to wait until after that and you have a job already. You practically own Mortenson Engineering, so what are you waiting for?"

"It's kind of soon, no?"

She chews on her bottom lip while she contemplates. I want to scream it from the rooftops, I want to marry her and yes this June.

"Not really darlin', I mean if you don't want to marry me..." she cuts off my sentence with an elbow to my gut.

"I never said I don't want to marry you, but I don't know. I mean I'm only twenty-three."

"So, I'm only twenty-five," I reply.

My heart begins to pick up speed again, she hasn't flat out said no and I can see she is thinking it over. I begin chanting in my head, please say yes, please say yes. She stays silent as we walk further down the street and I'm not above begging, I'll get down on my knees right here, right now, if I have too.

"It doesn't matter," I mumble.

"Don't be like that Knox, I love you, and you know it."

Yeah, I do, but I want to marry you! I shout in my head. She takes my hands in hers and looks down at our rings. I even went as far as wearing a black-banded ring to show that I am taken, not that it stopped some chicks. My heart is still beating fast and I know my eyes are pleading with her when she finally looks up at me.

"You seriously want to marry me? That badly?" Her question is full of disbelief and surprise.

"Yes, darlin' I do, I'd marry you right now if I could. I want to make you Mrs. Bailey Porter."

She gives me her cute smile, the one I get when she is thinking about how much she loves me. Leaning forward I give her a light kiss on the lips while holding her hands against my chest.

"You're really serious about this, huh?"

I nod my head resting my forehead against hers. "Okay then, this June it is," she smiles.

"Yeah? You're sure?"

She nods at me and I pick her up twirling her around the street. "I love you darlin'."

"I know, now take me home and show me what our honeymoon will be like."

She smiles at me and her blue eyes sparkle, taking her hand we walk very fast up the street. Glancing over at her she gives me a quick look from under her lashes.

How the fuck did I get so lucky?

Chapter 18

After our honeymoon escapade, Knox and I start looking online at wedding venues. I'm terrified and nervous, but also really happy.

"How about Edgewater?"

I type in the hotel name and wait for the site to open. Knox sits beside me as it appears. He whistles low and his eyes shine.

"It's beautiful darlin', but it's kind of expensive."

"We can check out the prices and they have a coordinator to help."

He purses his lips as we flick through the pictures of the ocean view terrace and the ballroom, the dining hall and best of all, the bridal suite. He scratches his face and looks at me.

"Is this what you want?" He asks, slipping his arm around the back of my chair.

"It's just an option," I shrug, in answer.

"If you want it, then go get it darlin', just send me the bill."

"Babe, if we are doing this, then it's fifty-fifty okay?"

He gives me his stern face, but I roll my eyes at it and kiss him instead. After some back and forth about the cost, he finally caves and agrees to let me pay for half.

"I should call and see if they have any dates available, it is kind of soon."

"Okay, I'm going for a shower and I have to call my dad anyway."

He kisses me once more and leaves. Grabbing my phone I call the hotel and keep my fingers crossed. The coordinator tells me June is fully booked, but she just got a cancelation for the end of July, without thinking I agree. We set up a meeting for next Saturday morning so Knox and I can go view the room and pick our menu. We have to choose next week because of the time frame.

I dial my dad and leave him a message to call me back. Walking down to the bedroom I school my face and pout a little. Knox is still on the phone, so I climb onto the bed beside him. He gives me a questioning look and I just pout more, while my inner kid giggles and dances around.

"Okay what's going on?" he asks, when he hangs up.

"June of this year is all booked up. You have to book at least a year in advance," I tell him sighing for emphasis.

"Shit, sorry darlin'. I didn't mean to get your hopes up. We will do it next year then."

Lifting my head, I look into his emerald eyes. "Why next year when we got the end of July?"

It takes him a minute to catch up and they he grabs me crushing my bones in his arms. He kisses all over my face, climbing off the bed, he swings me around again.

"This is fantastic," he breathes, letting me down.

"Yes, it is," I tell him about the appointment for next week and we have to organize dresses and tuxedos.

"You're going to be beautiful darlin'," he smiles at me with that look of love in his eyes. He traces the side of my face with his finger and over my lips, "I can't wait," he whispers.

"Me neither."

Honestly I can't, I've been thinking of reason after reason to put it off, but now that we have the hotel semi-booked I am starting to get excited. Knox heads off for a shower and I stare out of the window. It's crazy to think that a few weeks ago it felt like everything was falling apart, but now it seems to be falling into place. My eyes drift over the parking lot, stopping on Max and Paige. They look like they are talking and laughing. Wow, I'm not sure if I'm more shocked or worried, for both of them.

Knox finishes his shower and walks back into the room. When I turn around I frown at the marks on his face, they seem much more pronounced now.

"Don't worry darlin', everything is good."

"I know, I just don't like seeing you, and Max be angry with each other. It goes against the laws of nature."

He chuckles at me. "The laws of nature huh, well then be pleased to know all is well," he winks pulling on a pair of black jeans and black t-shirt.

"Where are you going?"

"I have to open the bar darlin', it's my night."

I forgot all about that, the night sharing of the bar. Sometimes, I wish it were like the old days. Sighing I join him on the bed as he pulls on his boots. I run my fingers through his wet hair and get a soft groan from him.

"How's the head babe?"

"It's okay, I think I'll take a trip to the doctor though, see if I can different medication."

"Okay, I can come with you if you like."

Turning, he kisses me quickly then knocks me back onto the bed for a more passionate kiss.

"I can't wait to make you my wife."

His smile reaches his eyes and he kisses me again, all over my face and neck while tickling me.

"Okay, stop babe," I laugh, trying to push him up, "please or I won't come over to visit you tonight."

He stops tickling me and helps me up, we kiss all the way to the front door where we find Max standing on the other side. They greet each other as usual then Knox leaves for work. Max gives me his cheeky grin as he passes me and I follow him to the sitting room.

"What's the smile for mister?"

"Can't a guy smile at his brother's girl?"

"Eh, no, spill it, Max."

He laughs at me and shrugs his shoulders, "Nothing to tell sis. just had a good day is all."

"Oh and would this good day be involving a certain someone?" I ask, taking a seat beside him.

Max grins at me, "We're just friends Bailey, at least we are talking and not killing each other."

"True, so are you going to tell me what happened with you and your brother?"

"Nope, sorry," he answers, slapping my leg on his way up off the couch.

153

I've decided not to push the issue and leave them at it if they want to tell me they will. Max and I have dinner before I go over to the bar, when I arrive it's fairly quiet.

"Hey, babe."

Knox gives me a smile from behind the bar as he watches me move around it and towards him. I kiss him, then hand over his dinner.

"Thanks, darlin'. I'm starving."

I man the bar while he eats, the most I can do is open a beer and pour a simple mixed drink but I never really have to. When Knox is finished, he joins me back behind the bar.

"So what type of food are we thinking about?"

My eyebrows furrow at him and he laughs, "For the wedding."

"Oh, okay, I'm not sure babe. We will have to wait and see what they can do for us."

Knox rests his hands on the bar behind him and looks at me thoughtfully for a few minutes. He stands up abruptly and makes me a drink, putting it down on the bar he leans down on one elbow so he can look out over the room.

"What do you want to do about music?"

"Don't know babe, I haven't even thought that far ahead," I give him a smile and get one in return.

"We're really doing this, right?" he looks at me slightly worried.

"Yes Knox, we really are," leaning closer I kiss his cheek.

With nothing else to do tonight, I hang out in the bar with Knox, a few more people have come in so he is moving around now. After ten, Max and Paige walk through the door. Knox smirks at Max and says hello to them.

"Hey," Paige greets me with a hug.

"Hey, what are you two doing in here?" I ask, looking between them.

"Just fancied a drink," she answers.

Max strolls behind the bar and has a few words with Knox. He makes himself, and Paige a drink. Knox pulls me out back after a few minutes and asks if we can tell them. I laugh at him and agree, when we come back, I sit down and wink at him.

"Okay," he starts and rubs his hands together, "Bailey and I have some news…"

Max chokes on his beer and looks at me with huge eyes, laughing I shake my head no and Knox continues.

"No dumbass, she's not pregnant. We set a date for the wedding."

He smiles proudly at me. Max grabs him in a hug and they have a brotherly few minutes while Paige grips my arm so hard her nails leave indentations.

"Oh My God! That is awesome, when?" she screams.

I fill them in on the details so far and Knox asks Max to be his best man. I swear I saw a tear roll down Max's cheek. We have a toast to celebrate and my eyes find Knox's. He is looking at me in that way he does, the way that makes my heart race and my legs turn to jelly. I can feel myself turn to mush under his stare, but I don't care. I love being this way with him.

In two strides, he is beside me cupping my face in his hands telling me he loves me with such determination that I can't fathom ever doubting him.

"I love you too, Knox."

My words are barely a whisper as they pass my lips before he takes them with his own. I'm lost in his kiss, the world my brain travels to, has no gravity. I'm floating – I'm flying and I don't want to come down. Knox breaks the kiss leaving me crashing back to earth, my chest rises with each breath, and our eyes stay locked.

Knox brushes his thumb over my bottom lip and his green eyes shine. "Is it closing time yet?" he asks, with a husky voice.

"No," I smile at him.

"Damn it," he says, smirking. His warm hand leaves my face and I feel the chill.

Turning around, I find Paige and Max staring at us, their eyebrows are raised and Paige's mouth is open.

"You do know you're in public?" Max asks, looking between us.

Knox laughs at him and says he doesn't care. Max winks at me then calls out to Knox to bring us some shots.

"Hey, you're working tomorrow," I scold.

"And? Frank loves me," Max answers, gripping the shot in his hand.

We slam the shots back and I shake my head with disgust. Looking over at Knox he laughs at me.

"What was that?"

I have a bitter taste in my mouth now. Knox strolls over to me holding out another one. "No way, that was nasty Knox." He laughs again, telling me this one will be better. I don't believe him, but Max takes his and smiles, lifting the shot I'm a little dubious, but I throw back while Knox watches me. When I swallow this one, I get a sweet taste and smile too.

"See darlin', you have to do both for full effect."

"Yeah, you could have said that first."

"And miss you make that face?" he smiles at me.

"Well I think you're trying to kill me, so I may as well go home."

"No, no, no," Knox grabs my hand. "Stay with me baby," he pouts.

"Oh my god, you're such a girl!" shaking my head, I sit back down and switch to water because I can feel myself get a little buzzed. Max walks Paige home while Knox cleans up the bar. I want to help him, but I can I feel my wonderful world tilting a little.

"Hey, babe."

"Yeah," he calls over his shoulder.

"Knox, I don't feel good."

He crosses to me looking concerned as he takes my arms, he scrutinizes my face, and eyes.

"Are you going to be sick?" he asks.

"No, I just feel really yuk."

He smiles wrapping his arms around me apologizing for giving me the shots. He admits they were top shelf liquor. Letting me go, he runs out back to grab his hoodie and makes me put it on.

"Come on darlin', let's get you to bed."

"That was your plan all along," I tease, but it sounds more like a grumble.

He laughs at me again. "Isn't that always the plan?"

156

Knox holds me close as we walk home. I sip on water and the cool night air is helping. Once we are home, Knox puts me to bed with a kiss and I drift off.

Chapter 19

After nursing a serious hangover all day I climb into my car and drive up to my dad's house. Walking through the door, I find him snoozing on the sofa.

"Hey Dad," I whisper, lowering myself down beside him. He opens one eye then smiles and wraps his arm around me.

"How's my favorite daughter?"

"Hung over," I grumble resting my head on his shoulder, he gives me a squeeze and we both relax in silence.

"Did you talk to Knox today?" I ask, after a few minutes.

"No, I was out most of the day, why?"

"We set a date."

My dad moves to sit up forcing me with him. He takes a look at me, and smiles then hugs me tight.

"That's great sweetheart, when and where is it?"

"Edgewater, they had a cancelation for the end of July so we took that."

"Wow Edgewater, that's fancy sweetheart, show me what you got."

We leave the comfort of the sofa and traipse into his office. Turning on the computer I flick through the hotel website and show him the area we have in mind. I take a quick glance over my shoulder and notice his eyes are brimming with tears.

"Dad?"

He smiles at me and pats my shoulder. Standing, I pull him into a hug, "I love you, Dad."

"I know, I love you too sweetheart. I'm happy for you, you deserve this."

"Thanks, Dad."

I hang out with him for a few hours just sitting by the lake and relaxing. We talk about work and my house before I leave him to go back to the apartment.

"Love you, Dad, see you later."

"Love you too, sweetheart."

Climbing into my car I drive slowly down the hill, my head hurts and I just want to sleep. I find Knox and Max eating dinner while watching tv. Taking a seat beside Knox, I steal one of his fries.

"Hey darlin', I thought you were staying up with Frank."

"No, I was there all day with him."

"I didn't make you anything to eat," he says, passing his food to me.

"No thanks I'm not hungry, I'm still hung over."

Knox smiles at me before wrapping his arm around my shoulders. "Sorry," he whispers.

"I'm okay just a headache, maybe I can take one of your pills?"

He shakes his head no and tells me they are prescription so I'm stuck with regular over the counter medicine and lots of love from him. After dinner, Max leaves us alone and heads out. Knox brings my pillow to me and makes me lie on the sofa so he can watch me.

"Oh we got a new assistant today, did you know?" he asks, turning down the volume on the tv.

"Really, I didn't know," I answer.

"Wonder why Meagan left, she seemed to like the place." He says.

"Who knows," I sigh.

Knox taps my leg, so I turn to face him. He is looking at me with an expression that says he knows I'm lying.

"You do know why, but you don't want to tell me, I get it. I'm not in the Mortenson circle," he smiles at me.

"No, you're not, so what's this new person like?"

"She's nice, smoking hot and she has long hair like you," he answers looking off into space.

"Oh really?"

"Yeah, I never saw her name though. I mean who cares when she has huge…"

159

I kick his leg as he holds his hands in front of his chest demonstrating just how big her boobs are.

"I get the picture babe."

He smiles at me again and watches me for a few minutes, "What?" I ask.

"I'm just kidding, she's not that hot."

He laughs when I kick his leg again before throwing himself on top of me and teasing me with his lips.

"Seriously though, do you know what happened with Meagan?" he asks.

"Why, do you miss her?" I reply.

"No, but I kind of have a feeling something is going on," he says, brushing his lips off mine.

"Yeah, there was if you think hard enough you will figure it out."

I watch his face for a few minutes while he thinks it over, he frowns a few times and then gives up.

"Ah who cares. I just asked because she looked pissed when she left like it was my fault or something."

Running my hand through his hair I sigh, "It was your fault babe."

"What! How? What the fuck did I do?" he asks, getting defensive.

"You told me and I told my dad, who fired her for sexual harassment."

"What do you mean told you? I didn't tell you anything about her. I hardly talked to her, mostly I tried to avoid her."

"Knox, think about it," I answer, kissing his lips.

"I can't, I have a headache," he moans, allowing his body to fall onto mine, crushing me. I run my fingers through his hair again and give him a head massage. He settles himself on top of me and slides his arm under by back. "That feels so good darlin'."

"I know babe," I whisper, kissing his temple. My fingers work for a few minutes rubbing his scalp and trying to relieve his pain.

"My dad wants to pay for the wedding."

"What, no," he mumbles against my shoulder, where his mouth is crushed. Snorting a laugh I ask him if he wants to go fight about it with my dad, he declines. After a few more minutes, he lifts his head and smiles at me.

"Thanks, darlin'," he pecks my lips, then climbs off of me. I watch him stretch and get a glimpse of his abs when his shirt rises up. "See something you like darlin'?" he asks, with a cocky grin. Rolling my eyes, I stand up and grab him around the neck.

"No, I see something I love," I whisper, before kissing him hard.

Knox wraps his arms around me crushing my hips into his. After a few minutes, he pulls away though, leaving me hot and horny. "I think I'll go to bed darlin', my head hurts."

"Yeah, it probably didn't help that you and Max beat the shit out of each other," I answer, frowning at the scratches on his face.

"Come on," he says, grabbing my hand and pulling me behind him. After a shower I climb in beside him, his eyes devour my face. "It was Meagan, wasn't it?"

"Huh?" I ask.

"She was the dirty texter."

"Babe, just forget it and get some sleep," I answer, throwing my leg over his.

He nods in agreement and pulls me closer to him. His body heat almost smothers me, but I press myself closer to him.

Knox

I wake up to an empty bed, but this time I don't freak out. Things are good again between Bailey and me, so I know she is probably just out running. Climbing out of bed, I check my watch and stroll into the kitchen to grab something to eat. I find a note on the table telling me that Bailey and Paige went shopping. I can't help but smile, I love her so damn much. I check my phone to make sure my appointment is still at ten and have my breakfast.

Just before ten I arrive at the doctor's office. I feel weird coming back here. Once I check in, I sit in the waiting room and get eyeballed by the mother of a kid, who is coughing up a

161

lung. After a few minutes, the kid extracts himself from his mother and walks over to me. He stops in front of me and just stares. I'm getting a little freaked out.

"Hey, kid."

"Hey," he answers, watching me.

"So you sick?" I ask because really what the fuck do you say to a weird kid who is staring at you?

"Yeah, I have a cough. Are you sick?" he asks.

"Yeah, I have a pain in my head," I answer and his mother moves closer to us.

"Me too, sometimes I can't open my eyes because it hurts," he says.

"Me too," I smile and so does he.

"I like your ink," he nods at my arm and I smile. This kid is about eight years old.

"Thanks, I have a few," lifting up my t-shirt sleeve I show him my tattoos. He jokes telling me he is getting one and he wants to know the best place to go. I tell him where I got mine and I begin to get into the conversation when I get called. I say goodbye to him and follow the nurse. I can't help but smile at that kid, he seemed weird but actually I think he just wanted to talk to someone.

Entering the room, the nurse instructs me to take off my clothes and put on the gown. Frowning I shake my head, "I'm just here for my head."

"You missed your last check up," she says, consulting her notes. "The doctor wants to do your annual physical." Nodding at the gown on the bed, she leaves closing the door with a smile.

"Fuckin place," I moan, stripping off and putting on this stupid gown that doesn't cover shit. After a few minutes of waiting in this cold room, the doctor finally walks in.

"Hello Knox, it's been a while," she says, smiling at me.

"Yeah, sorry I got busy," I answer. I just didn't bother my ass to come before, and now I'm regretting it. I watch her read through the notes.

"So tell me, how have you been? It's been two years since I last saw you."

I have been coming to her since I was a kid and I got my first migraine. She treated my mom too, so it was easy for me to stick with her. I tell her about getting engaged and soon to be married. She asks about my dad and Max and then gently pushes my shoulder, so I lie down on the bed. She listens to my heart and lungs while I talk about shit. Once she is done, I sit up.

"So how are the headaches?" she questions.

"They are getting worse actually, that's why I came today."

She nods and looks in that damn file again. "Your last scan was almost four years ago. I thought we agreed you would get them every two years?" her tone is just like my mothers and I feel like a kid again.

"Yeah, sorry things just got busy," I say again because I really have no excuse. She frowns at me.

"I'm guessing you still haven't told your father or brother."

"No, there's nothing to tell," I reply, fidgeting on the bed.

"Okay, well you need another scan, so why don't you get dressed and we can make the appointment."

Once she leaves the room, I jump off the bed and pull on my clothes and boots. Exiting the room, I find her by the desk talking with the nurse. She hands me an appointment card for a CAT scan for tomorrow morning and points to her office. I follow her inside and take a seat.

"Don't miss that appointment, Knox," she says, sternly pointing to the card in my hand.

"Okay, I won't but can I get something stronger for the pain?" I ask, shoving the card into my wallet.

"No sorry," she sighs. "You are on the highest dose I can give you Knox."

Nodding I let out a sigh myself. She reminds me not to miss the appointment tomorrow as I'm leaving. Once outside, I straddle my Harley. I'm not looking forward to this shit and I have to take another day off work. Starting the engine, I decide to drive up the lake and meet my dad at Bailey's house.

Chapter 20

Paige and I have spent all day at the mall, my feet are aching, but we had so much fun.

"I can't wait to come see you play."

"Ha, yeah in a few weeks the season starts, we just had a friendly at Thanksgiving," I answer, as we haul our bags up to the apartment. Opening the door, I drop my stuff in the hallway and walk into the kitchen.

"I'm still coming though," Paige says. She takes a seat at the table as I make the coffee.

"Yeah, I don't mind. I have gotten used to people in the stands cheering for me," I laugh, as I sit down.

"Wow conceited much?" she laughs at me. "What time are the guys due back from work?"

"About four, why?"

"Do you want to come out for dinner? I have been dying to have Little Italy for ages," she answers.

"Yeah I'll just text Knox and let him know, we can meet them there."

Pulling out my phone I send him a text.

Me: dinner at Italian tonight xx
Knox: okay
Me: meet you guys there after work.

I put my phone down when he doesn't respond and show Paige, the hotel's website. We look through all their pictures and talk ideas about the wedding. Knox walks into the apartment after two and puts his helmet on the chair.

"Hi, babe. I thought you were at work?"

"No, I'm here, with you," he smiles, wrapping his arms around me and kissing me. Paige clears her throat and I laugh. Knox excuses himself and leaves us to it.

"Is he okay?" Paige asks.

"Yeah, just his headaches are getting to him."

Paige grabs her shopping bags. As she stands to leave, we agree to meet downstairs at four o'clock to go for dinner. Walking back into the apartment, I slip into the bathroom and sit on the toilet lid. I can hear Knox chuckling because he knows I'm in here.

"So how did the doctors go?" I ask.

"Okay darlin', I have to get my eyes tested in the morning," he answers.

"Yeah? I think I'd like you in glasses," I answer, picturing him. "I think you'd look great in those black frames, and you can put them on when out get out of the shower. With your hair all wet and dripping onto your face…" I drift off as I picture him in my mind looking sexy as hell.

"You're a little pervert," he laughs, as he steps out of the shower. My eyes rake over his body, enjoying the way the water beads on his skin and his hair, just as I described, it hangs over his forehead and drips onto his face. Knox quirks an eyebrow at me, but he doesn't reach for the towel. Standing, I move closer to him and run my fingertips from the hollow of his neck all the way down until I grip him firmly in my hand.

"I'm your pervert," I grin at him as I move my hand up and down, stroking him. He sucks in a breath between his teeth and closes his eyes briefly.

"Just the way I like you," he whispers, pulling my hair tie out and letting my ponytail loose. His fingers brush through my hair as his lips meet mine. My hand moves again, stroking him slowly, teasing him. He grips my thighs and lifts me onto his waist as he carries me to bed. My clothes are swiftly pulled off while his lips devour me.

"I love you darlin'."

He whispers in my ear as he nudges my legs apart with his knee, "I love you too babe." My breath catches when he pushes inside of me and our bodies move together. Dancing in sync, I grip his shoulders pulling him closer as my lips find his. Knox slides his hand under the small of my back, holding me as he rocks his hips into me. Our bodies push and pull as we lose ourselves in each other, shaking as we come apart at the same time.

Knox rests on his forearms while breathing hard. He kisses a slow path from my shoulder to my earlobe, nibbling on it when he reaches it, "I love you, Bailey."

"You too babe," I reply, looking into his eyes. He never really uses my name and when he does, it sets off alarm bells. "You okay?" I ask as he rolls onto the bed beside me.

"Yeah darlin', I'm good. Actually I'm great now," he grins at me.

"Okay," I smile rolling on top of him. His hands slide up my back and back down, resting on my ass. "We should get ready for dinner and text Max too."

"Yeah in a minute," he answers, turning me over onto my back. He just lies on top of me, staring into my eyes.

"Are you sure you're okay?"

"Yes darlin', I'm perfect," climbing up off me he pulls me up too. I watch him dress, through the mirror, noticing him rub his head a few times. I watch, as he send a text to Max and I can clearly see his face is full of pain.

"Knox."

Lifting his head he smiles at me, "Yeah darlin'?"

"Are you sure you're okay?" I ask again, walking toward him.

"Yeah, I'm fine. Let's go eat." I take his outstretched and follow him through the apartment. We meet Paige in the parking lot and walk to the restaurant, where Max is waiting for us. He says hello to us while looking at Knox. I know by his face he is wondering what is going on too.

"Hey you missed a good day today," Max says to Knox. Knox smirks at him and I punch his arm.

"You better not be going on about this new assistant," I warn.

They both laugh at me and Knox pulls me close, kissing my head "No darlin', never."

"Liar," I elbow him playfully in the stomach.

166

Paige and I take a seat at the table opposite to the guys. Knox frowns at me, but I ignore him. All throughout dinner he is watching me with a questioning expression. Max keeps us entertained with jokes and stories from work. He and Paige are getting along far better than I ever would have imagined.

"So who is having dessert?" Paige asks, browsing the menu.

"I'll have the chocolate lava cake," I answer.

"You don't usually get dessert," Knox says.

"Well I feel like a change," I smile at him. He shrugs in reply and watches me as I eat my cake licking melted chocolate from my lips. He smirks at me and I can tell by his eyes that I am getting him worked up. After my cake, I excuse myself to the bathroom and pull out my phone.

Me: Did you enjoy that?

Knox: Yes, you know you're in trouble now, right?

Me: I'm counting on it.

Knox: open the door.

I reread his last text and then open the door to the single restroom, finding him leaning against the wall with that sexy smirk on his lips. He looks around before pushing through the door and crashing his lips to mine. My heart pounds in my chest and legs tremble, his hands are gripping my ass so hard, I swear he will leave bruises.

"Darlin', that was wrong," he mumbles against my neck.

"No, it was right, so right," I pant, as he pushes my bra aside and latching on to my nipple. We both jump when someone pounds on the door and Knox's phone beeps at that same time. He laughs telling me Max is outside and the manager is coming. We quickly exit the bathroom and Max laughs at us.

"You two are fucking crazy," he says, as we leave the restaurant. He grabs Knox around the shoulders and pulls him back so they can talk.

"So you and Max seem to be getting along," I say, to Paige as we walk towards the bar.

"Yeah we are friends again, but that's it. I think it will be good if we stay that way," she answers, but I can tell she is not too happy about it.

"Is that what you both decided or him?"

"Both," she smiles at me, "we haven't taken the whole dating thing off the table, but we just want to be friends for now."

"That's good, I hope it works out for you," I say, in all honesty.

When we enter the bar Paige and I sit in a booth, it's not busy tonight so Knox and Max can relax. Knox places our drinks down and takes a seat beside me, resting his hand on my leg.

"Are you not drinking babe?" I ask, noticing his soda.

"No, I don't want to be hung over doing my eye test tomorrow," he grins at me.

"Maybe you should, just so you can get those glasses."

"You just want to live out your fantasy," he replies leaning over to kiss me.

"Oh I live that one out daily," I whisper.

Knox rests his forehead against my temple and sighs. His hand flexes on my leg and he rubs it up and down. "I love you so much darlin', I can't wait to marry you."

"I love you too Knox. Are you sure you're okay?" I am starting to get worried by his behavior now, but he kisses me quickly and moves back telling me he is fine. After about an hour, Knox climbs out of the booth and turns to me with his hand out.

"Wanna dance darlin'?"

Smiling, I grip his hand as he helps me onto the dance floor. He wraps his arms around me and we sway to the song. Knox sings along and twirls me around; we end up dancing to a few songs before he yawns.

"I think someone needs a nap," I tease.

"Yeah, I do."

Grabbing my purse from the seat I say goodnight to Paige and Max.

"Oh Max, I'll be in the office in the morning you want to ride in with me?"

168

"Can I drive your car?" he asks.

Rolling my eyes, I sigh and agree to let him drive. He gives me a hug and a kiss on the cheek.

Knox and I walk slowly back to the apartment our hands holding tightly together. He keeps checking me out and I pretend not to notice.

"You're beautiful, you know that?" he says.

"Really? I didn't know that," I tease.

He smiles and shakes his head, wrapping his arm around me and kissing my cheek.

"I love you darlin'," he sighs.

Chapter 21

Knox

I watch Bailey get ready for work. She tells me that she will be done by noon, and we can hang out after if I want. I agree and tell her I'll be waiting by the door. My heart is thrashing in my chest as I ride to the hospital. I am barely paying attention to the traffic around me, but I finally make it.

Parking my bike I make my way inside and up to the third floor. Being here brings back memories I don't want to think of right now. I had spent six months back and forth from this place before my mom died. Her room was number 402 and even without walking into the room, I can picture every detail of it. I know that there was a small crack in the bottom left corner of the window. If you looked straight down you can see the front entrance of the hospital and I know, many times, when I looked out I wished, I was somewhere else.

After checking in at the nurse's station, I take a seat in the small but open waiting area. I have my phone turned off because I know one text from Bailey and I'd be out of here. I'm scared, for the first time in my life. I am actually scared for myself. I have so much to lose now, it's not just me anymore. I have a beautiful woman who will soon be my wife, but what if things are worse than I thought? What if I get the news I have always dreaded?

"Mr. Porter?"

Looking up I find a nurse looking at me. Standing, I nod at her and she smiles.

"This way."

Following her down the hallway, I swallow hard. My heart is about to burst right out of my chest and I can feel the hunger pains in my stomach.

"The doctor will be in soon. Here is your gown, please remove all clothing."

She says, and blushes when she looks at me. I just nod and turn away from her. If I were another person, Max, I'd give her a flirty answer but I'm not in the mood for anyone right now. Once she leaves the room, I slowly begin to undress and slip on another too small gown. I fold my clothes neatly just to keep busy and climb into the bed, covering my manhood.

"Good morning, Knox," my doctor says when she barges through the door. She is consulting a file again and I get even more worried. "Have you fasted for twelve hours?" she asks.

"Yes," I croak out and clear my throat.

"Good, you are next in line for the scan so sit tight."

She pats my leg then leaves me alone. I hate this, really fucking hate being here. My mind drifts to when Bailey was in hospital, that night when I snuck in to see her. She looked so goddamn bad, I wanted to hunt down Ben and murder him. Just thinking about it is giving me a headache, so I take a few deep breaths to calm down.

Focusing on the small stain on the ceiling I count, I don't know why but I do. It keeps all other thoughts out of my mind and the simple act of saying one number after another helps slow my heart rate. When I count up to three thousand, two hundred and six, the door to my room opens. Looking over, I nod at the male nurse as he reads my chart. He tells me he will bring me down to the room for my scan. Once we are sitting outside the room, I am trying everything I can, to keep my modesty, the wheelchair is not helping. This stupid gown is not staying put and I have to keep adjusting myself, for fear of flashing the other patients around me.

After another lengthy wait in the hallway, I am finally brought into the room. My nerves are frayed and I am pissed off too. This fucking gown is annoying the fuck out of me. They guy tells me to lie down as he adjusts the bed I am on, and reminds me to relax before leaving. When the machine begins to hum, I close my eyes and think of Bailey. The way her hair tips the top of her ass. The way she smiles at me when she catches me watching her, her eyes. So blue you could drown in them and her smile, that amazing smile that captured my heart over three years ago.

I loved meeting her and getting to know her, not the tough-chick persona she sometimes displays, but the deeper more fragile part of her. The haunted girl that lay under that exterior; she reminded me so much of myself. But she is tough too, it takes a special person to get through what she did and I know she can pretty much get through anything life throws at her.

The machine stops and I breathe a sigh of relief. When I am back in my room, I quickly dress and feel way more comfortable. Turning on my phone I have a text from Max making sure I am okay and one from Bailey asking if I will be Clark Kent or Superman tonight. I laugh at her text but don't reply. I don't trust myself right now not to tell her the truth.

Lying down on the bed I close my eyes for a bit. I am tired from not sleeping last night and my head is hurting. I don't know how long I slept for, but my doctor wakes me up with a rough shake.

"Oh sorry," I say, sitting up and rubbing my face. She looks neutral, I don't know how or why, but she looks different than the normal happy smiling face.

"I have bad news, Knox," she starts and I blink my eyes a few times because I am taken off guard by her words.

"Okay," I say and prepare myself for what she is about to say.

Leaving the hospital, I call my dad and ask if he is home. He tells me he is at the lake house but will be home by three. I text Max to meet me at dad's after work and make my way there. I have a couple of hours to kill so I change into my swim trunks and grab Max's surfboard. I'm not too good on it, but I just need something to hold on to, something tangible to keep me afloat.

Sitting on the board I just stare at the horizon, my mother consumes my thoughts again. I keep remembering those last six months, the last time she had fun with us. The last day of her life; a day that ripped me in half. I remember walking into the hospital, that awful smell of disinfectant assaulting me. My steps, though steady were unsure because I knew what I was walking into. On some deeper level, I knew I was going to say goodbye to her that day.

"Hey, what are you doing?"

Turning around, I spot Max with his hands out by his side standing in the sand in his suit. He is smiling at me as I paddle back toward him.

"Hey, what's up? No specs?" he asks, laughing at me, taking the surfboard from my hands. We walk into the house and I see my dad sitting at that table drinking coffee. I go dry off and change back into my clothes. Once I join them in the kitchen, I take a deep breath.

"You okay bro?" Max asks, noticing my stiff posture.

"Yeah, I just need to talk to you both."

They exchange looks as Max sits at the table with a soda. He passes one to me, but my stomach is in knots and I can't bring myself to sip it.

"So what's going on?" My dad asks.

"Okay, so my headaches are getting worse," I begin, Max instantly leans forward resting his elbows on the table. "I just need to say this, so I'm going to say it, but you are sworn to secrecy." My dad and Max both arch an eyebrow in question, but I have to continue quickly.

"I wasn't getting my eyes tested today, I was at the hospital getting a brain scan. I have a lump on my brain that has gotten bigger. It was small for years, so I never bothered about it and that is why I get headaches. But over the last two years it has grown and now I have to get an operation to have it removed. I don't know if I will though because there is a chance I may not survive."

Swallowing hard I look up at them, both are pale and staring at me.

"What do you mean years?" My dad asks.

"I found out after Mom died; I didn't want you to worry so I said nothing," I answer.

"That was almost ten years ago," my dad says looking shocked.

I nod my head and take a gulp of the soda Max gave me. I look over at him and he is pissed. I can see anger in his eyes, mixed with tears.

"Fuck you," he whispers. "Fuck you Knox!" he screams at me. Standing he knocks the chair over with force. He clamps his hands on top of his head and paces the room. "You're an asshole you know that! I fucking knew, I knew," he says, more to himself.

"Max…" I start.

"No! No, don't you dare 'Max' me. You're a selfish bastard, Knox, you should have told me!" he shouts at me again as tears fall from his eyes. "After everything we've been through together, don't you think I deserved to know?"

"Max, please just listen to me," I beg, standing up to meet him.

"No, I don't want to know, go die for all I care! I hate you, I fucking hate you."

He storms over to the sliding glass door, pushing it so hard it bounces back to hit his shoulder. After a fight with the door, he storms off to the beach. I am about to go after him and explain, but my dad tells me to sit down and leave him alone.

"You should have told us, son," his voice is low and hoarse from unshed tears.

"I'm sorry, Dad. Mom just died and I found out, I didn't want to add to the grief."

He shakes his head and clears his throat. "You should have told me, Knox," he whispers, finally shedding the tears he has been trying to hold back.

"I'm sorry Dad, I am, but it was the right thing to do at the time."

He wipes his eyes and nods at me, without warning he grabs me into a hug. I am trying so hard to be strong here, but I finally lose it. My tears come hard and fast and I sob onto my father's shoulder.

"We'll get through this son, we will, I promise. I'm not losing you," he whispers. Nodding, I bury my head against his shoulder. Everything is in my grasp, but it could all be gone in a heartbeat. Dad and I separate, he excuses himself for a minute and I take a seat out on the patio. I scan the beach for my brother, but I don't see him. I'm worried about him. After a few minutes I start down the beach, I make my way to the rocks way down the end. I can see him sitting on top with his legs hanging over. We used to sit here for hours after my mom died. Climbing up beside him, I take a seat, he ignores, me and looks the other way. I wait in silence with him, as the waves crash off the rocks. Finally, he turns to me.

"I'm sorry. I don't hate you," he says.

"I know you don't, I'm too good looking to hate."

He snorts and shakes his head, "Not the time for jokes, bro."

Smiling I wrap my arm around his shoulders and we just sit there watching the sun descend. "What are you going to do?" he asks.

"I'm not sure," I answer.

"This is shit Knox, I knew something wasn't right in New York. I just knew it."

His fists clench in his lap and he grinds his teeth.

"Max, I'm not leaving you. You're one of three people in my life who I love and I don't plan on checking out at twenty-five."

"It's not up to you, Knox. If it's your time then that's it," he shrugs.

"Writing me off already?"

"No, I'm just...I don't know," he sighs again, closing his eyes. We sit on the rock until it gets dark. I use the light on my phone to guide us down and we walk back to the house. Dad has dinner ready for us and even though I haven't eaten, I do my best to bite the burger. I send Bailey a quick text telling her where I am. I do not want a repeat of last week.

Bailey: Okay babe, miss you xxx

She replies and my heart hurts all over again. How the fuck am I going to tell her this? As if reading my mind my dad asks.

"When are you telling Bailey?"

"I don't know. I want to marry her, Dad. I don't want anything to stop it."

He opens his mouth, but I hold my hand up, stopping him. "I know Dad, I know. I need to tell her, but I don't want to make her a 'widow' before we even walk down the aisle," I sigh.

"It's a difficult choice, Knox, but it's better that she knows beforehand."

I reach into my pocket and take out two of the pills my doctor gave me. Max and Dad watch me swallow them.

"It's the same medication as before, I can't get anything stronger."

Max blows out a breath and slumps back into his chair. I can see his face clearly now and watch the angry set of his jaw.

"I should get back, Bailey is waiting for me."

Max stands up with me and my dad looks sad that we are leaving. I tell him I will swing by the lake house on Saturday. Climbing onto my bike, Max looks at me frowning.

"Do you want to take the truck?" he asks.

"No way, bro," I laugh at him. Starting up the engine, I smile at the familiar rumble and follow Max out of the driveway. I take my time and stay behind Max on the freeway. I don't feel like tearing home although, I do want to see Bailey. When we pull into the parking lot, I climb off and stretch out my back. Max walks over to me and leans against his bike.

"You okay?" he asks.

"Yeah, for now. I have to wait for more results, but there's not much I can do about it."

"I'm sorry for blowing up at you. I know why you didn't say anything, but it hurts that you didn't tell me after."

"I'm sorry Max. I just got carried away with life, after Lindsey and then Bailey. I didn't have much time to think about myself," I shrug.

"Yeah I suppose, are you coming to work tomorrow?"

"Yeah I am. I don't think Frank will like me taking off more time and I have to do the wedding meeting thing on Saturday morning."

He nods as he stands and hugs me tight, "Love you, bro."

"You too," I answer and walk off to my building. When I get inside the place is quiet. I kick off my boots and jacket. Walking down the hall I hear soft music coming from the bathroom, peeking inside the door, I see Bailey in a bubble bath with her eyes closed. I strip off and walk inside. She smiles without opening her eyes and moves forward so I can slide down behind her.

"Welcome home," she says.

My heart constricts and I wrap my arms around her waist, "Hey darlin'." Tilting her chin up I bend down and kiss her. Opening her eyes, she smiles at me and kisses me back.

"I was home waiting for you at noon," she says, still smiling at me.

"I'm sorry," I sigh. "I was with Dad and Max and time got away."

My answer is crap and I'm sure she can see through my bullshit, but she doesn't call me on it. She nods and settles her back against my chest pushing the bubbles around with her hand. I can't help but kiss her neck making her sigh and lean into me more. Everything in the world I want is here in my arms and everything I can lose.

Chapter 22

Bailey

Over the past few days, Knox has been quiet. I haven't asked him why he is this way because I have a feeling it has something to do his dad or Max. We are in the Edgewater Hotel walking through the main ballroom. It is a beautiful room, with a wide dance floor. Knox has his hand in mine as we follow the wedding coordinator through the room and out onto the balcony/patio area.

"This is where we can have the ceremony. The guests can enter from the main lounge and walk up those steps," she points behind us to a set of stone stairs. "We can do a flower arch if you want or we can do something simple," she finishes and looks at us expectantly.

"Yeah, whatever you want darlin'," Knox says, looking at me.

I know he has stuff on his mind, but he could at least take part. I tell the lady I'll get back to her in a day or two about the arch or whatever. She frowns and nods at the same time looking annoyed. We walk back inside and over to a table with eight place settings with all different, crockery, cutlery and glassware. Looking around, I am slightly overwhelmed and I see plates of all different colors. Some have charger plates and some don't. I squeeze Knox's hand and beg him with my eyes to get in the game and help me out. He smirks at me and kisses my head then walks around the opposite side of the table. I look down at the place setting in front on me and groan, it has loads of flowers on it, and I swear it was dragged up from a sixties wedding storage unit.

"This one," Knox announces. Lifting my head, I look over at him. He is grinning like a maniac so I walk around to see what he picked. When I get to him, he kisses me quickly and I smile. "Just for you darlin'," he points down and I follow his finger.

I smile big when I see the place setting. It is a white plate with three Calla lilies on the side. The champagne flutes are brushed silver in the shape of a Calla Lily, and the cutlery, match the glasses.

"It's perfect," I whisper, looking up at him.

"It's you," he smiles, taking my face in his hands.

"So we've decided on set six," the coordinator interrupts our moment.

We nod in agreement and finally she cracks a smile. We walk to another table and get down to real business, the food. After an hour of tasting meats, sides, and dessert, I am fit to burst. My stomach hurts as we walk back to my car.

"My belly hurts," I moan. Leaning against Knox, he laughs and pulls me closer to him.

"I know what will help you."

"Babe, seriously?" I question him, as he opens the door.

Laughing he bends down to kiss me, "Get your mind out of the gutter darlin'."

Knox drives us to the lake and parks in Dad's driveway. Climbing out he takes my hand and we walk towards the house.

"You know we have our own driveway babe."

He looks down at me and smiles, "Yeah but the walk will help the food go down."

"No, I don't think so. This baby is not going anywhere," I pat my bloated gut and groan. He laughs at me and shakes his head. When we arrive at the house, a big smile spreads across my face. I can't believe in a few months we will be married and living here, it feels like a dream. Richard smiles when he sees us and hugs Knox a little longer than normal.

"How are you doing?" he asks.

"We're good, we just came from the hotel," Knox answers.

I pat my belly and pout, "I tasted too much."

Richard laughs at me and tells me I'll be okay. We walk around the house and mostly all I see is exposed wiring, pipes, and odd markings on the walls, but I love it. He explains the progress so far and answers all my questions. I am happy he agreed to help me. I didn't want to hire just a contractor and have to worry. I know Richard will keep everything on track and in budget. We stay and chat for a while, then decide to walk back over to Dad's.

"So are you happy with the way it's shaping up?" Knox asks.

"Yes, I can't wait to move in. It will be amazing and we can do what we want when we want," I answer.

"We do that now," he laughs.

"Yes, but we have a landlord to answer to and neighbors," I retort.

"True, we do," Knox agrees.

"Are you excited to move in?" I ask him, taking a hold of his hand.

"Of course I am darlin', I can't wait," he says, looking down at me. "How about we spend tomorrow on the beach or up in the mountains?"

"Oh, we haven't been up the mountains for a while."

"Okay then, we will have a picnic and relax up there."

I watch his jaw set and see the muscle jump, he sounds okay, but I know by his body he is definitely holding something inside. I hope he tells me because I really don't want to fight anymore. I don't think I could take it.

I call out to my dad when we walk through the kitchen, he appears at the doorway smiling. He gives me a hug hello.

"What are you doing up here today?" he asks.

"Oh, we went to the hotel and over to see the house," I answer, making myself a drink. My dad and Knox talk about the hotel. Well, when I say talk, I mean a heated discussion.

"Knox, I won't hear of it. I'm paying and that's final, now shut up about it," my dad says.

"Fine, Frank, have it your way," Knox replies, blowing out a breath.

Dad winks at me and I grin at him, poor Knox, he has been beaten by his future father-in-law.

"Don't worry babe, you'll get used to it."

"Yeah, that's the problem," he smiles at my dad. Walking over I plant myself on Knox's lap and kiss him. Dad tells me he will be going back to DC for a few weeks on Monday and I need to keep an eye on the company.

"There are two presentations coming up and a meeting with Hero designs. You need to take that one for me sweetheart."

I groan and bury my face in the crook of Knox's neck. "No Dad, I can't deal with Ken doll."

"You have no choice, they want a new security program for some upcoming design."

Knox rubs my back and kisses my head, "Who's Ken doll?" he whispers.

Lifting my head, I look at him and sigh. "Andreas," I answer. He raises his eyebrows at me and gives me his 'I don't think so' face. Smiling I kiss him, "Yeah I know babe, he is a tool."

"But you have no choice," my dad says, making it clear and final.

"Okay, I get it, Frank," I answer him. He ruffles my hair and laughs at me, telling me I can handle it. "Dad I swear you are trying to give me more responsibility in the company, which I don't want."

"Why would I do that? You're only twenty-three years old," he smirks at me.

Knox chuckles at us and wraps his arms tighter around me. "You're good at it darlin', that's why."

"Don't side with the enemy," I scoff, swatting his arm. Both my dad and Knox laugh at me. We hang out with my dad for a few hours and I hug him hard before I leave. "I love you, Dad, be safe over there in DC."

"Love you too sweetheart," he kisses my head and we say goodbye. Climbing into the car I am a little sad that he is leaving. I have gotten used to seeing him every day for the last six months.

"You okay darlin'?"

"Yeah, I'll just miss him," I sigh.

Knox holds my hand as we drive down the hill, he asks if I want to swing by the bar tonight to hang out with him and Max.

"Where's Chase?" I ask.

"He has some personal time he took," Knox answers, so I agree to hang out with him. When we get home, Max is in the living room staring at the ceiling.

"You okay?" I ask, wondering why he is here and spacing out.

"Yeah just thinking," he answers, in a lifeless tone. Knox frowns as he looks down at Max.

"Okay, I'll go shower while you guys make dinner." Giving myself an out I leave them to talk, I haven't heard from Paige for a few days so I am hoping that she and Max are not fighting again. After my shower, I stroll into the kitchen in my yoga pants and Knox's sweater.

"You look adorable darlin'."

"Really," I frown. "I was going for badass."

They both laugh at me and Max sticks a fork in my leg making me jump. Taking a seat, Knox hands me my dinner of baked salmon and salad. Both of them are smiling now and the moroseness in the air has lifted. After dinner, I say goodbye and kick them out of the apartment. Knox pouts but Max drags him away from me complaining that he will see me in two hours.

Paige and I walk over to the bar she is talking about starting back at BRU next week.

"It's going to be fun."

"Yeah, it will," I agree. "We can chill on the quad again, Abbey and Becky are pretty cool too."

We arrive at the bar seeing Knox and Max with their back to us, from behind most people wouldn't be able to tell the difference between them, especially tonight. They are both wearing all black, only the ring on Knox's finger, which he insists on wearing, is what tells them apart right now.

"Hey, can we get some service down here?" I yell at them. Knox lifts his head and smiles at me.

"Just a sec darlin'."

"You say that to all the girls?" I tease. He laughs while punching buttons on the cash register, then slams the drawer and walks over to me.

"Only the really special ones," he answers. Stretching up I kiss him on the lips, leaving a nice layer of lip-gloss behind. Grabbing a napkin he wipes it off. "Now what can I get you ladies?" he asks.

"You know, I think I want something new," Paige answers, "Can I have a cocktail?"

Knox rolls his eyes at her and I laugh, "I'll get Max on it," he teases her.

"You're gross Knox," she answers.

He walks away and I watch as he shakes the silver shaker above his head. After a few minutes, he comes back with two different drinks. "Cape Cod," he hands Paige her drink. "Sex on the beach," he hands the other to me.

"Yes please," I reply, making him laugh.

"I love you," he says, before turning to get back to work.

Paige and I drink quite a few cocktails throughout the night. We are dancing for so long that my legs are getting tired. The bar is busy and the night goes by fast, we have barely spoken to Knox and Max.

"I'm so hot," Paige shouts, fanning her face.

"Me too," I answer, but keep dancing anyway. I am lost in the music and the lights until a pair of hands slide around my waist and pull me backward. My back molds to his chest and his lips trail soft kisses down my neck. The smell of his cologne wraps around me sending my senses into a riot.

"You having fun?" he asks.

"Yes, it's better now that you're here."

"I can't stay long. I'm on glass collecting duty, but I couldn't resist stopping by."

Turning around in his arms I press my mouth to his, we long ago gave up caring who in the bar saw us. We own it and we can damn well make out if we want. Knox pulls back breaking the kiss and winks at me. "You want another drink?"

"Yes, please," I answer.

He continues to collect glasses and I make my way over to the bar. Max gives me a sad smile before turning away to busy himself with other customers. Taking a seat beside Paige I wait for Knox to come back, he runs his finger down my back on his way past me. After he puts the glasses into the washer, he makes us another drink.

We hear a crash and look over at Max, who has dropped two glasses. Knox claps and shouts at Max, who then bows his head. They are both laughing and the energy between them seems fun like it used to be. Swallowing a mouthful of my cocktail, I turn my eyes to watch the dance floor. Couples are writhing against each other, girls dance in small groups, laughing and checking out the guys. I remember when I first started coming here, the night I saw Knox on the stage.

I'll never forget the way he looked at me like he could see through my façade into the deep sadness that I was barely controlling. His smile then was a little tight around the edges except when he glanced at me. Like now it reaches the very corners of his eyes brightening them and lifting his whole face. Like the night he proposed, that was magical. I can remember every detail, down to the taste of the salt in the air and when he got down on his knee, I knew he was mine forever.

"What's that smile for darlin'?"

Turning my face, I find Knox up close and the green of his eyes blow me away. "I was just remembering something," I answer.

"Oh yeah, was it a hot something?" his eyebrows wiggle as he jokes with me.

"No, not hot. Wonderful and amazing."

He crosses his arms making his biceps bulge and gives me a quizzical look. Smiling I lean over, kissing his lips softly, "I was thinking about you and me."

"Well then think away, because that smile has been hidden for a while now."

Snaking his arm around my waist, he steps closer to me, burying his face in my neck. Just breathing me in like he can't get enough, my focus returns to the bar, which is now almost empty. Knox places a gentle kiss below my ear. "I'll be done soon, would you like another drink?"

"No, thanks, babe." He nods, as he leaves my side to help Max clear out the bar. Stepping outside, I can feel the goose

184

bumps erupt on my skin after being in over stuffy warmth of the bar. My teeth chatter a little and Paige huddles closer to me. "What's with this cold?"

"I have no idea," she answers.

Knox and Max exit the bar and lock the doors. Knox immediately wraps me in his arms, filling me with his warmth.

"Thanks, babe," I chatter, as we begin to walk across the road.

"Anytime Darlin'."

Once home, I wash my face quickly and join Knox in bed. His warm body molds to mine and I instantly relax. "Are you looking forward to our date tomorrow?" he asks.

"Yep, can't wait," lifting my face, I give him a smile and kiss his waiting lips.

Chapter 23

We arrive at the secret mountain spot just after noon.
There is still a little mist clinging to the trees, like soft tendrils
of smoke caressing a lover. Knox spreads out the blanket as I
stand watching him. His movements are jerky and stiff like he
is holding himself tightly. Once the blanket is down he takes
my hand, lowering himself to the ground. I settle myself
between his legs and look all around.

"It's nice up here, even if the trees are missing leaves."

"Yeah, we haven't been here for a while. I like the
peacefulness of this place," Knox says. He sighs deeply and
begins to smooth his hand down my hair.

"You okay Knox?"

"Yeah darlin'," he kisses the top of my head and pulls me
back into him further. "Remember that time when we all came
up here and played football?" he asks, wistfully.

"Yeah, it was fun. Except for the whole back rash I got."

I can feel his chest shake as he laughs, "It was worth it
darlin', every time with you is worth it." His voice grows soft
and quiet. We sit together for a while without talking, just
sharing the comfort of each other. Craning my neck I look back
at Knox, he seems so far away and lost in his own world.
Meanwhile, I am starving.

"You hungry babe?"

His eyes travel from the skyline to my face, slowly. I
watch him inspect every inch of my face before he answers,
"Yeah sure darlin'."

Moving away from him, I watch him take our picnic out of
the basket and lay the food on the blanket.

"You really went to town on the food Knox."

"Yeah I know darlin', just wanted to make sure you are fed. You have your first game soon, right?"

"Yeah, two weeks from now and we have double practice this week too," I answer with a moan. He smiles at me holding out a sandwich to me. "Babe, are you okay?"

"Yeah, why?"

I shrug in answer and take a bite of my food. I can't help but glance up at him. He is just staring at the sandwich in his hand like he doesn't know what to do with it.

"Knox?"

"Yeah," he looks up at me and smiles. "Sorry, I was miles away."

We eat our lunch and lie down side-by-side on the blanket, making shapes out of the clouds. Knox clears his throat and turns to face me. He looks like he is in pain and I feel a knot from in my gut.

"We need to talk darlin'," he whispers.

Nodding my head I sit up, holding my breath, is he getting cold feet? Knox takes my hand in his and moves to enclose me between his legs once again. My back rests against his propped knee and I look at him. His eyes take me in again and his finger traces slowly down the side of my face to my neck.

"I love you, Bailey, you know that, right?"

"Yes," I croak.

He exhales another long sigh and I feel his body tense. I can see the muscle in his jaw bounce and he runs his free hand through his hair.

"Okay," he says, then clears his throat, "I have something to tell you."

My heart leaps in my chest, and I nod back to him. I try to prepare myself, to not freak out when he says he doesn't want to marry me.

"You know these headaches I get…"

I nod.

"Well, I wasn't getting my eyes tested the other day. I was getting a brain scan."

My heart stops.

"I have a lump on my brain darlin', I have had it for years. But now it's getting bigger, and I need surgery to remove it."

187

His words are rushed like he is trying to get this out in one breath. "But the surgery has risks," he whispers.

My throat burns and my eyes sting. My heart is beating too fast, sending blood rushing to my ears and my breathing begins to speed up. Pushing myself away from him I crawl away and stop on the grass with my head between my legs. This panic attack is not like any other I've experienced, this one steals my breath away and won't give it back. I can hear Knox calling out to me, but he sounds far away.

The edges of my vision swim before turning black like I am in a tunnel. Blood pounds away at my eardrums and I feel myself falling, I can't stop it.

"Bailey, darlin' wake up," his voice filters through the haze of blackness. "Baby, come on wake up." The anguish in his voice hurts my heart. Opening my eyes I blink up at the blue sky, my breathing is normal but my mind reels.

"Knox?"

His face appears above mine and his eyes are full of tears. "Baby, don't do that to me again." He cries against my face. Wrapping his arms underneath me he pulls me up off my back and into his arms. His words come rushing back to me and I push him hard.

"Get off me!" I cry, rolling onto my knees.

"Please darlin', hear me out," he begs, gripping my arm tightly.

"Knox, why didn't you tell me before? Why now?" Angry hot tears fall from my eyes. "Why now?"

"I'm sorry darlin', everything was fine up until a few weeks ago."

My head snaps up to look at him. "What happened a few weeks ago?" I ask, trembling.

"I don't know, I'm waiting for more results," he says. Reaching for me again I collapse into his strong arms. How can this be happening? Haven't I lost enough people in my life? Knox holds me so tight it's hard to breathe, but I don't move, I want to say here forever.

"Darlin', I'll be fine, don't worry," he whispers, into my hair.

"When is this surgery taking place?"

188

"I don't know, the sooner, the better," he sighs.

Steeling my resolve, I sit up and wipe my face with the end of my t-shirt. I'm not going to be negative about this I can't allow it, I won't.

"Okay, we can do it soon and then we can get married."

Knox looks into my eyes again, "I'll see what my doctor says; if it's too risky we are waiting darlin'. I'm marrying you no matter what."

"I know, Knox, we are getting married, and living happily ever after, we both deserve it." My words are strong and fierce. I'm not sure who I am trying to convince, but I'm trying no matter what. His lips press against mine, in a soft kiss. Opening my mouth, I allow his tongue access, to taste me and drive me wild with desire.

"Darlin', slow down," he pants.

I grip his hair tight then release it just as fast, remembering his headaches.

"I don't want to Knox, I want you now. I need you."

My words are almost a cry, but I hold my voice as steady as possible. He doesn't wait and crushes his lips to mine, pushing me down and exploring my body with his hands. There's an urgency between us, like never before. Our hands grip and pull at each other as our bodies heat up.

Knox pushes my jeans off my feet and I wrap my legs around his waist, wanting him. No - needing him. Needing him like I need air to breathe, because without him I will surely cease to exist. Knox groans deep from his throat as he pushes inside of me, our hips buck against each other. He grips my hip with one hand while holding his weight on the other and our eyes lock as our bodies move. His emerald eyes bore into mine, filling me with a warmth that penetrates deep within me.

"I love you, Bailey. I've always loved you," he chokes out. His eyes become glassy and he blinks rapidly.

"I love you too, so much."

We tangle our limbs again as he thrusts harder and faster, our bodies come apart together, sending shudders throughout me. Knox collapses on top of me, his sweat-soaked body cooling in the mountain air and his shoulders shake from the weight of his tears.

***

It's been a few days since the mountain trip. Knox has been quiet but attentive, treating me like I am made of fine china. I can't seem to concentrate though, practice is painfully slow, and I am making too many mistakes.

"What's up with you?" Becky asks. She follows me off the field and sits beside me on the bench.

"Nothing why?"

"Your head is not here and I sacked you twice in five minutes."

"Yeah sorry, I just have stuff on my mind," I answer, not meeting her eyes. The sky is blue with big white puffy clouds and I just want to lie on the grass and watch them.

"Yeah, well get your head in the game Bailey because we have an away game in two weeks," Becky comments.

I just nod my head and feel myself deflating, an away game. That's all I need, time away from my fiancé who may be having life threatening surgery any day now. The whistle blows, pulling my attention to the field. Everyone is looking in my direction and I take a quick peek around me, noticing I'm the only one sitting here. Jogging over to the group my coach frowns at me, she gives us another play to run through.

"Mortenson," she says. Stopping beside me she looks at me expectantly, "Well?"

"What?" I ask.

"What is it? I thought the trial was over yet, you look all over the place out there."

"It is over. Sorry, I was just thinking about stuff. I'm okay now."

Pulling on my helmet, I race away from her and onto the field. Becky claps her hands while grinning at me. We run the play and I take off once I get the ball. My legs pound as I race away from Becky, landing a touchdown. It feels good and I smile for the first time today. Once we are done, I grab my bag slinging the strap across my body and head back to the apartment. Pulling my phone out I check the texts from Knox, he says he has pizza waiting for me at home.

My body hurts as I drop my bag by the front door, kicking off my shoes I pad up the hallway to the kitchen.

190

"Hey, Max."

"Hey sis, Knox went for pizza, he should be back in a few." I watch Max take out plates and glasses, laying them on the table.

"Okay, I'll just grab a shower."

"Okay, cool hey, I swapped shifts with Knox tonight," he calls out after me.

"Why?"

"I need tonight off, sorry sis," he peeks his head out of the doorway giving me a cheeky grin. Rolling my eyes I head in for my shower, where I can de-stress and ask the universe to keep the love of my life safe. A few minutes later there is a banging on the door.

"Food's here darlin'."

Emerging from the bathroom I find him waiting for me. A smile lights up his face and he hugs me tight, causing me to wince.

"Careful babe, I'm hurting today."

He frowns as we walk into the kitchen. "Why what happened?" he asks.

Lifting my shirt, I show him the bruise on my hip and ribs. "What the fuck, darlin'?" Kneeling down he inspects my skin and Max lets out a slow whistle.

"How did that happen?" he asks.

"Becky hits like a truck," I smile at Max. Knox stands and shakes his head.

"Why the fuck does she have to hit you so hard? You're on the same damn team," he complains.

"I'm fine Knox, stop worrying about me." I press a kiss to his lips, stretching myself over his crossed arms. He doesn't soften his expression as I grab a slice of pizza joining Max at the table. "Come on babe, sit down," I pat the chair beside me. He runs his hands through his hair and takes a seat.

"I don't like it, she never used to hit you that hard before," his grumbling continues for five minutes until he finally stops to eat. Max pulls a face making me laugh at him, he sticks out his tongue and looks innocent when Knox turns to face him.

"So are we getting new ink?" Max questions Knox while shoving half a slice of pizza into his mouth.

"Yeah I saw a nice one online," Knox answers, pulling out his phone to show Max.

"Oh yeah, that's sweet bro," Max nods his head in approval. Knox puts his phone away without showing me and I kick his leg. He looks up at me then pulls his eyebrows together.

"Don't I get to see it?"

"No sorry darlin', we don't show anyone until it's done," he grins at me.

"You're such a douche," I shake my head at him.

Both of them laugh at me and Knox continues to tell me it's a tradition they have. Each tattoo is done in secret and then they have a drink to celebrate. I remind them they are twenty-five years old and both weirdos. Leaving the kitchen, I start to get ready in my black pencil skirt and white shirt. After I do my makeup and decide on my sky-high black platform pumps, I make my way back to them.

"So how do I look?" I ask while twirling. I smile when I stop.

"Where are you going dressed like that?" Knox scoffs.

"Meeting with Hero, remember?"

"Fuck! I forgot about that asshole," Knox moans and asks Max to swap back his night in the bar.

"No babe, I'll stop by after. Hopefully, he won't go too long," grabbing my purse and my laptop bag, I lean over to kiss him. "See you later." I wave on my way out.

"Hey, hey," he calls chasing me out the door. He catches me on the stairs and walks me to my car. "Be careful darlin'," Leaning down, he kisses my lips.

"Love you."

I arrive in Marion about an hour later and follow the waiter to my seat. Andres and Mr. Hero are already seated. They both stand when I arrive and Andres, makes a point to kiss me on the cheek. Mr. Hero gets straight down to business. He tells me he is working on a project for NASA and needs a top of the line security program. My palms sweat a little and I rub my hands on my thighs.

"So is this something you can provide?" he asks.

192

"Of course, it should be simple enough," I reply, lying through my teeth.

"That settles it then and you can have it ready to run in sixty days?"

I choke on my water and spill some of it down my chin. Andres quickly reaches over with his napkin and dabs my chin.

"Thank you, sixty days is a little soon," I answer. My mind is freaking out at this; it's way too short a time. I was thinking about six months for this type of program.

"Well, Frank assured me that you are the best."

"Of course," I smile. "I can get it done."

We finish dinner listening to Andres talk himself up. I really just want to go. After dessert, I make my excuses and leave the table.

"Well that went well," Andres says, from beside me. He has a smirk on his face.

"Thanks," I reply, walking to the valet. Andres takes my elbow and leans down close to me.

"How about we get a room and have our own dessert?" His eyebrows wiggle a little and I honestly throw up in my mouth. His face is close to mine and I notice his too tanned skin, with his waxed eyebrows. Holding back a laugh, I shake my head no. He pouts at me and tries the wounded look.

"I'm happily engaged, Andres," lifting my ring, I wave it at him. He takes my hand and inspects it.

"Very nice, he must be very well off. What does he do?" his voice is smooth, but there is an edge to it.

Smiling, I thank the valet when he holds open my door. "He's a barman," I reply, climbing into my car, laughing at his face. He looks like he tasted something bad and it makes me laugh harder. When I arrive at the bar, I am weirdly happy. My encounter with Andres allowed me some much-needed stress relief. Walking through the doors I find Knox and Chase run off their feet, it's getting busier every weekend.

Knox smiles when he sees me and sighs in relief. He pulls me through the beaded curtain placing kisses along my jaw line.

"Hey, darlin'."

"I guess you missed me, huh?"

193

"Yes I always miss you, but I don't have time to hang out. I actually need you to me a favor," he begs, gripping my hands in his.

"Okay sure, do I have to get naked?" I tease.

"No, Jesus, I wish," he smiles at me. "I need you to put the order through for me."

I agree and he kisses me, thanking me all the way to the office. He turns on the computer for me and arranges the paperwork. He is buzzing around the office.

"Babe, I've done this before. Go, I'll be out in a few."

"Thanks, darlin', I owe you one." Opening the door, he steps outside.

"A big one," I shout after him, he pokes his head back inside the door.

"It's what you're used to darlin'."

Laughing he runs off and I settle myself down to do his job. I have everything ordered for the next week and I added a few new things for fun. After an hour, I take a seat at the bar. Knox hands me a drink and takes off just as fast. It stays busy until the very end. Knox and Chase take a long time to clear the bar while Amber, and I hang out and laugh at them. Finally the last person leaves and Knox bolts the door, sliding down to the floor.

"Finally," he grumbles, running his hands through his hair. They clean up the bar and we leave after three.

"I have my car babe," I tell him, pulling him around the building. He sighs and holds out his hands. "I'll drive," I punch him on the arm and laugh at him wincing.

"Hey that's spousal abuse," he cries, as we pull out of the parking lot.

"Were not married yet, I still have time to beat you into submission."

"You did that years ago darlin'." Leaning over the seat his kisses my cheek sending a shiver down my spine. "How did dinner go?"

"Okay," I sigh. Pulling into the parking lot, I park beside the bikes. Knox exits the car and opens my door for me. Taking his hand I climb out, the wind is cold, making me shiver.

194

"Are you tired darlin'?" Knox asks, with a hint of amusement in his voice.

"Why, what do you have in mind?"

He smirks at me and tells me I have to change my clothes first. We arrive in the apartment and I throw on jeans and a sweater. Knox hands me my leather jacket and a scarf. "Where are going?" He winks at me, pulling a sweater over his head. He pulls on his own leather jacket and grabs our helmets. I follow him down the stairs to his bike and watch as he starts it, allowing it to warm up.

"I want to take you somewhere if you don't mind." He says, helping me tighten my helmet. When I climb on behind him, I wrap my arms around his waist and snuggle closer. The thrill of the ride fills me with excitement as we travel down the empty freeway and onto the Marion highway. We pass his dad's house and continue along the ocean front road. Pressing closer to him, I rest my chin on his shoulder. He grips my hands in his and brushes his thumb over my knuckles.

We soon travel up a long driveway, lined with trees and wildflowers. I notice the headstones when we turn the next bend and get a little scared. Knox parks the bike under a tree and we climb off. He takes my hand and we walk in silence through the cemetery. I can still hear the distance crash of waves and smell the salt in the air. Knox stops by a headstone and takes a seat on the ground, he pulls me onto his lap, and I read.

Annabelle Porter. Wife. Mother. Beloved.
1955 – 1999.

"I wanted her to see how beautiful you are," he whispers.

"Thank you," I whisper back, unable to stop the lump in my throat.

"I haven't been here in years. The last time Max and I came was before we left dad's." He heaves a sigh and rests his chin on my shoulder. We sit in silence for hours. Knox just holds me and I stare at the rising sun, painting the sky in a gentle pink. "I wish you could have met her, darlin'."

"Me too, babe."

"I have something to give you," reaching into his jacket he produces an envelope. He runs his fingers over the writing on the front before handing it to me. Taking it, I notice it has yellowed from the years. The neat script on the front looks like Knox's writing and I frown.

To the future Mrs. Knox Porter.

"What's this babe?"

"It's from my mom to you," he answers. I'm not sure what to do with it, turning it over in my hands I look up into his eyes. "You don't have to read it now, just before the wedding."

"Okay."

He kisses me softly and we stand to leave, he looks down at the headstone and sadness shrouds him, like a thick woolen cloak. "I'll give you a minute," I whisper and make my way back to the Harley. Sitting on the seat, I watch the sun climb higher in the sky and yawn. Part of me wants to read the letter now and part of me wants to know why he is giving it to me here and now.

I watch him saunter towards me and smile at his beautiful face. I get his megawatt smile back and another kiss when he arrives.

"Ready to get some sleep?" He asks, sliding on his sunglasses.

"Yeah, babe. Let's go to bed."

Chapter 24

Six weeks later.

My fingers are flying across the keyboard trying to meet my deadline. Dad walks into my office and sighs at me.

"Bailey, you have about a month's worth of papers to sign here," he taps the pile of files on my desk.

"Yeah Dad, I know. If you didn't tell Hero how good I was, I wouldn't be trying to fit six months of work into sixty days. And besides, I am almost done and Knox had his doctor appointment today, so right now I really don't care about the files."

"How is he doing?"

"Not good, Dad," I clear my throat and try concentrate on the code in front of me. Dad leaves my office without another word. My eyes blur and I blink rapidly to clear them. I have promised myself I wouldn't call Knox and that I'd wait to get home to find out what is going on. By four, o'clock I am finally done. I feel guilty about not signing the paperwork, but I rush out of my office before I make myself stay any longer. Dad's office is empty so I leave the building and drive home.

Knox and Max are in the kitchen both recovering from a day at the tattoo shop. Knox smiles at me when I rush into them.

"How did it go?" I ask.

"Good darlin', hurt like a mother, but it's all done now."

Frowning I shake my head at him, he stands up and pulls off his shirt. Turning around I see his new ink, spreading across his left shoulder. A dragon, with fierce claws and teeth, breathing out a flame of orange and red, and I'm not sure what to think. Stepping closer, I look at it, it really looks menacing.

In the flame there is writing, Born as one, live as one, fight as one. Brothers born of flame, bear pain, and laughter together.

I look at Max and he smirks, standing he pulls off his t-shirt so I can see his one beside the other. They face each other when standing side by side. Knox's is colored reds with purples. Max has reds and greens.

"They are different."

Knox turns to me, "Don't you like it?"

"Yeah I do, it's just completely different than all the others."

He frowns and pulls back on his t-shirt. Max does the same, giving me a weird look. Both look at each other, and shrug then laugh, like they don't give a shit either way.

"I meant the appointment," I say, biting my lip nervously.

Knox turns his back to me and fiddles with the coffee machine. Max stands up and stretches, saying he is going for a nap and leaves the room. "Babe?"

"Yeah darlin', I know what you're talking about," he keeps his back to me and his shoulders are tense. I can see the veins in his forearms standing out as he clenches the counter. I watch his shoulders rise and fall with each breath he takes. I want him to face me, to tell me what is going on. But I know he needs time to figure out how to say it. My hands shake nervously on my lap as I wait. And wait, and wait. Finally, giving up, I leave him in the kitchen and walk down to the bedroom to change and get some homework done.

After some research and a half written paper, I surface for some snacks. Grabbing a can of soda and chocolate, I plant myself on the sofa. The whole apartment is quiet and I didn't hear anyone leave, so I get up to investigate. Chewing my candy bar, I stroll into the music room where Knox has his headphones on again while he plays the piano. I take a seat beside him on the bench and unplug the jack so I can listen too.

His fingers glide over the keys as he plays. I don't know what he is playing at the moment, but it sounds nice. I sway as he plays and close my eyes. I lose myself in the sounds. I love it like this. Just him and me, together. Knox clears his throat and begins to sing, changing the melody as he does.

You have my heart and you own my soul.
A fire burns between us - hot enough to melt gold.
When I catch you smile, thinking you're alone.
I know I'm forever yours, darlin', and I want you home.

I want you home
Back in my arms.
I want you home,
Protecting your heart.
I want to take all your sadness away,
Come home to me,
I want you to stay.

The light in your eyes has dimmed its glow,
The pain on your face,
Trying not to show.
I want to take you in my arms,
To keep you close,
I know you're my forever, darlin', and I want you home.

I want you home
Back in my arms.
I want you home,
Protecting your heart.
I want to take all your sadness away,
Come home to me,
I want you to stay.

Finding peace, it's hard to say
If love alone, will make you stay.
Keep my heart, it will keep you safe.
My soul is yours
Forever and always.

I want you home,
Come back to me.
I want you home, darlin'.
At home with me.

My eyes drip big fat tears as he sings, each word pulling at my heartstrings. I recognize the melody now; it's the song he was playing on the guitar a while back. The music stops and I feel him shift on the small bench. His thumb brushes away my tears and I refuse to open my eyes.

"Hey don't cry darlin'." He wraps me in his strong arms and holds onto me.

"I'm not losing you too," I whisper.

He doesn't answer only holds me tighter to his chest. His heart is beating fast and I can feel each racing thump against my cheek. "W-when is it?" I manage to choke out. His body sags in defeat.

"Soon," he whispers into my hair. "I love you darlin' and I'm not going anywhere."

Lifting my face I take in the sadness in his eyes, they no longer shine like emeralds in the sun. Now, they hold a dark sadness, and a heartbreak so real, it scares me.

"What did the doctor say?"

"She wants to do it at the end of May, the sooner, the better, apparently," he shrugs his shoulders.

"How risky is it? Don't lie to me," I beg.

"Very."

I nod, understanding sinking into my heart. I always knew, but I refused to believe it. However, sitting here now and seeing the pain in his eyes and the fear on his face makes me want to roll into a ball and cry for days. His lips brush off my temple and he gives me a cheeky grin. "I'm not leaving you though, so don't get any crazy ideas darlin'."

"I know you're not because I'm not letting you go."

He winks at me and chuckles. "See, I always knew you were a control freak." He teases, bending down to meet my lips. We kiss softly for a while. No rushing, no pulling at each other, just soft tender kisses. Knox holds me close as I straddle him, his eyes take in every inch of my face and body.

"I can't wait to marry you darlin'."

"Same here," my fingers trace along his chest, resting against his beating heart. A heart that is so amazing and full of love, all for me. We eventually leave the room and I try to finish my assignment while Knox makes dinner. My phone beeps from the dresser with a text.

Mom: When are we going dress shopping? It's getting close.
Me: Soon Mom, I promise I'll call you.
Mom: Are you ok? Not getting cold feet?
Me: No way!!
Mom: Good, I like seeing you happy baby. Call me soon.

Her text has me in tears again. I feel so desolate. Empty. Dragging myself off the bed I manage to wash my tear soaked face before Knox comes looking for me. We eat dinner in silence. Knox suggests we watch a movie and I agree, climbing onto the sofa with him. I settle between his legs and pull the blanket over us, his arms are wrapped around me. This is what I love, the simplest things we do are usually the most forgotten, but I intend to savor every minute together for the next four weeks.

I wake up to the early morning light shining through the window. It takes me a minute to orientate myself as I look around the sitting room. Knox shifts behind me, and kisses behind my ear.

"Looks like we fell asleep darlin'."

Turning around I attack his lips, not allowing him any time to talk. He starts to laugh and I pull away. "What are you? A sixteen-year-old boy?" he teases. I run my fingers through his hair, and mess it all up. He laughs at me and picks me up into his arms. "I think you need a cold shower there mister," he grins at me.

"No Knox, don't."

But the gleam in his eye tells me I am getting wet and I won't like it. As soon as the water is on, he deposits me into the shower. The water is like ice and I screech. He laughs at me while stripping off his clothes and I quickly turn the knob to hot. Climbing into the shower he helps me pull off his sweater I am wearing and my shorts. He 'accidently on purpose' drops my shower puff and smirks when I have to bend down to get it.

He pushes his hips forward on my way back up and I get smacked in the face with his manhood.

"Hey, that was assault!" I cry, rubbing my face clean while making faces at him.

"You love it and you know it!" his cheeky grin is back and I can't help but smile at him. Knox climbs out first and fills the sink to shave. Climbing out, I wrap myself in a towel and watch him. He never complains when I watch him shave. I secretly think he likes it when I do. Once he is done, I get to kiss his smooth face and that is my favorite part. He smirks again as I leave the room to get dressed.

"I'll see you tonight babe," I call, on my way out the door.

"Wait!" he shouts. Turning around I see him exit the kitchen in jeans and a t-shirt, "You can't leave without me."

"Aren't you going to work?" I ask, taking in his clothes and boots.

"No, I'm taking a few days off," he smirks, linking his fingers through mine. He walks me to class, all the way to the door.

"Love you," I kiss him softly and make my way into the room. I slide into the seat beside Ryan and nudge him hello.

"Hey, you all set for finals?" he smirks at me.

"No," I snort and shake my head. I am in no way ready for finals, especially since Knox's operation will be around the same time. Most of my time is spent staring at a blank page or out the window. I have no idea what my professor is talking about. After class, Ryan is laughing at me.

"What?"

"Did you hear any of that?" He asks, nodding back towards the room.

"Nope."

"I'll email you later, he gave us some pointers for finals."

I smile as we part and make my way across the quad to the café. I get my coffee to go and find my favorite table empty. Taking a seat, I look around, remembering when we were all here together. I miss seeing Knox walk around, that easy swagger he has and his handsome face.

"What you smiling about?" Paige asks, plopping down across from me.

"Nothing, just remembering when we were all here."

"Yeah seems like forever ago. It's weird not seeing Knox and Max," she says.

Sipping my coffee, I nod. "Hey so how are you holding up?" she asks.

"With?"

"Max told me," she gives me an apologetic smile.

"Yeah, I guess he would. So are you back together?" I ask, changing the subject.

"No, I told you we are just friends."

"You don't sound happy about that," I say, watching her look everywhere except at me. "What did Max say?"

Her shoulders slump a little and turns back to face me. "He says he wants to wait. He thinks you will need him when Knox goes for surgery."

"Yeah, I probably will." My words are low, but I know she hears me. "Listen, Paige, you're my friend and I love you, but you need to get over the fact that Max and I are close. He is like a brother to me and he leaned on me after you left; he was in a bad way. Knox even disowned him for a while, which hurt him more. I got him through it, helped him to stop drinking and Knox finally came around and we got Max back on track. I love him, Paige, as a brother though, so if you can't accept that then maybe you're better off being just friends."

I watch her for a few minutes, I feel like shit for saying all that, but it's the truth. Max is a great friend to me and I'm not giving him up for someone else's insecurities. Paige looks at me and smiles.

"I know you guys are close and I do accept that, but I have to prove it to him. I think he still thinks I have a problem with it."

"Are you sure you don't?"

Shaking her head, her hair bounces around. "I don't, I swear." She grins at me. I nod and sip my coffee. I feel like I am becoming a bitch again.

"Sorry, I didn't mean to be harsh."

"No, you weren't, I'm glad you said it. I know you love Knox and I have always known it. I guess I was actually jealous of it, you know. I had Max, but I fucked it all up with the baby thing and then I left..." she shrugs.

"Well that's in the past, so we can move on and enjoy the days we have left."

We sit on the bench for a long time, both of us skipping our class without really meaning to. Paige stands and heads off to the library to finish an assignment, so I just leave campus. My feet take me home automatically because as soon as I put my key in the lock I am wondering how the hell I even got here. Dropping my bag in the bedroom I change into shorts and a tank top. I grab my iPod and sound dock, bringing them into the kitchen, where the acoustics are better.

Turning on Nickelback, I blast it so loud I can feel the vibrations hit me in the chest. It makes me smile, grabbing the vacuum, I get to work cleaning the apartment. I scrub and sing my way through the whole apartment. My mood is better and I dance around singing along with a can of furniture polish. A few minutes later I catch a shadow from the doorway, spinning around my eyes fall on a laughing Knox. His shoulder is leaning easily against the doorframe and his arms are crossed.

Grabbing the TV remote, I throw it to him and sing into my spray can again. Knox winks at me, then joins me on the sofa for our version of S.E.X and Trying Not To Love you. Once the songs are over, I turn down the volume and kiss him hard.

"Hi babe," I whisper.

"Hi," he replies against my mouth. His hands are on my hips and we sway to the music. "You looked like you were having fun darlin'."

"I was," I smile at him.

"You're so damn cute," he smirks at me.

"Where have you been all day? You smell like wood," I ask, taking a deep inhale of his neck; sweat and wood for sure.

"I was busy darlin' and I can't tell you," his lips trail along my jaw, but then he steps back away from me. I follow him into the kitchen and watch him open a paper bag from the chemist.

"What's that?" I watch him line up three bottles on the counter.

204

"Pre-op meds," he sighs, clenching his fists. Reaching out, I wrap my arms around his middle and rest my cheek on his back. He rubs his hand over mine and leans his head back. "Sorry darlin', I wish this wasn't happening to us," he whispers. I squeeze him tighter and kiss his cheek.

"We'll get through this babe, we love each other too much."

Chapter 25

Knox

"Hey Dad," I call out as I walk into the house. The noise of the hammers and table saws jar my head.

"In here."

I can just about hear him shouting and make my way through the hallway to the kitchen. "Morning."

"Morning son," he looks up and smiles at me, taking the coffee I hand over to him. "How are you feeling?"

"Fine," I shrug. I'm hardly going to tell him that I feel like I got smashed in the head with a hammer, because I know for sure he'd make me leave. My eyes survey the room and I take in all the progress we have made. I know I asked Dad to do the kitchen out of his sequence, but I am happy he agreed. I wanted Bailey to have a beautiful place to sit and feel loved, in the event my surgery goes wrong. My dad moves around the room, and checks out fittings and makes sure they are all where they are supposed to be.

I have been wondering why he is doing this, why he is helping with a house, when his normal clients are multi-billion dollar corporations or governments. I get a feeling Bailey has him wrapped around her finger, which I can't complain. I pretty much think she has all three of us Porter men that way.

"You going to stand there all day?" Dad says.

"No sir," I laugh and take off my sunglasses. Draining my coffee, I throw the cup in the trash and go stand beside my dad. Throwing my arm around him I give him a squeeze. "I love you old man."

His eyes snap to me, "I love you too son. What's going on?" His face is creased with concern and he claps me on the shoulder. I tell him about the surgery. I actually for once tell him the truth about how dangerous it really is and that I only have a sixty to seventy percent chance of survival. His face pales and his knees give out, I grab him quickly.

"Sorry, maybe you should have been sitting down."

"Knox Andrew Porter," he glares at me, he looks so pissed off, but I know it's because he is hurting.

"I'm sorry Dad, but don't tell Max or Bailey," I beg him. "Besides, I'll be fine, I'm not checking out yet."

He shakes his head and walks out to the lake. I give him a minute before I follow him. "You okay?"

"Not really son, this is harder than I thought it would be. Losing my wife was tough. But she was sick, so we knew, we could see it. But you're my child and you're young, this shouldn't be happening," he shakes his head and rests his hands on his hips. Picking up a rock, I toss it into the lake.

"Bet you can't beat that."

He looks at me from the corner of his eye and smirks. I bend down and pick up two more rocks and hand one over. "Come on mister, you played baseball, show me your arm," I tease. He reaches back and throws the rock and we watch as it sails out over the water and splashes a fair bit out. "I think you beat me." I throw the next rock but I can't get it out as far as his.

"Looks like you're buying lunch," he says, patting my shoulder and telling me to stop playing around and get back to work. We work on the house for a few hours. I am actually physically putting in the window seat for Bailey. I want her to know that every time she sits here, that I built for her.

"Looks good," Dad announces from behind me. I am being a little childish and scratching on the top of the wood. "What

206

are you doing?" bending over my shoulder, he chuckles. "Knox loves Bailey," he reads aloud.

"Yeah, she'll find it funny and the cushion will be on top," I answer, admiring my act of vandalism. Dad tells me he feels like pizza for lunch, so I drive him down to Pizza Mia. We take a seat by the window and order. "You want a beer?" I ask, lifting my eyes over the menu.

"No, maybe later. I'll need more than one," he sighs.

"Don't Dad, I need you to be the strong one," I reply. He nods at me and gives me a small smile. We talk about the wedding over lunch. I tell him about Frank paying, and he tells me to leave it alone and not to get in between a man and his daughter. I can't help but laugh at him.

"Did you ever regret having two boys?" I ask.

"No, it was a blessing and twins was even better. We tried to have a girl, but I guess we weren't meant to. But I have one now," he smiles.

"Yeah, I know you do. She loves you like a second father too."

He smiles big and proud at me "I like Bailey, she's a wonderful young woman and I'm happy you have each other."

"Me too, she's amazing all right."

My heart is ready to burst with how much I love that girl of mine. She is everything to me and I just hope I get to see it for myself, not from afar. Dad and I go back up to the lake and finish up some more little things. Dad tells me that we should have the flooring for the whole house next week and the painters will be here on Friday and work through the weekend.

"Sounds good. So can I see upstairs?" I ask, heading that way.

"No!" he shouts at me, grabbing my arm. "I was told not to let you up there."

"Why?"

"Because that's what I was told, now go home. Will you be here next week?"

"No, sorry I have to get back to real life," I sigh.

"Okay then, how about you kids come over on Sunday?" he asks.

"Yeah I'll bring steaks."

I give him a hug and leave the house. On my way out I notice all the grass has been delivered and a few trees are placed beside it. I didn't know we were getting a new garden. When I get home Bailey, is already here and studying.

"Hey darlin'," I bend down and kiss her, tasting chocolate.

"Hi, how was your day?" she asks.

"Good but way better now. I'm grabbing a shower."

She smiles at me and goes back to her homework. Making my way down to the bedroom, I text Max telling him about Sunday. My whole body aches and my head is pounding. After a quick shower, I chill on the sofa. It's hard feeling like this, so drained and fucking useless. There are so many things I want to do, but I have to relax for these few weeks. Bailey strolls into me carrying a glass of water and my medication. Taking them I swallow quickly and drain the glass.

"Thanks."

"You're welcome babe," she climbs up beside me and asks if I am going to attend her last game next week.

"Shit darlin', I'm sorry I missed your games. I'll be there. How can I not? It's the sexy Super Bowl," I tease.

"Yeah and it's a home game so that's easier," she says, wrapping herself around me.

"I'll be there, I promise," I assure her. We hang out on the sofa until my stomach grumbles. We make dinner together and eat watching a movie. Bailey tells me that her finals start soon and she has all early exams, then a four-day break, and her last exam is the day of my surgery.

"Oh, that's okay darlin', it's probably better like that," I tell her, but I feel crap.

"I'm not taking it," she says.

"What? You won't graduate without it darlin'."

"I don't care. I have a job and I have money," she shrugs. I look at her for a few minutes. She is pretending not to care but I can see it, by the way she is staring straight ahead.

"You know they have an emergency program thing that you can do your exams after the date; but only if there is an emergency. Maybe they will let you do that."

"Maybe," she answers.

After dinner I flake out while she studies. I am watching her. The way her lips move as reads silently and the way she taps the pen on her knuckles when she is looking for answers. My eyes follow the curve of her neck down her shoulder, and back, she looks so small.

"Stop staring at me," she says.

I laugh at myself and at her. "I like staring at you darlin', it's my favorite pastime."

She lifts her head a little and watches me back. Her lips tilt at the corners, like she is trying to hold back a smile.

"You're my favorite pastime," she answers and looks back down to her book. I jump off the sofa and grab her around the waist, knocking her to the floor. I straddle her hips and begin a slow torturous tickle war. My fingers work up and down her ribs, while she squirms and screams. Her knees are hitting my back and I think I already have a bruise from it.

"Stop! Mercy! Mercy!" her voice is a mixture of laughing and crying.

"Never darlin'," I keep tickling her until she is barely able to breathe. I rub her ribs while she gets her breathing under control, she wipes at the tears rolling down to her hair.

"You're mean," she smiles at me.

"Only because I got mad love you for you darlin'," I grin at her.

"Mad love?" she giggles again.

"Yep, all for you baby," leaning down I kiss her gently. I feel her hands in my hair and I love it. I love the way she can make my scalp tingle with just a slight touch or the way my body responds the minute she walks into the room.

"I love you darlin'."

"I love you too, you know I think we should go for a drink." She bites her bottom lip and I pounce.

"Okay let's go," I announce, pulling her off the floor. On the way through campus, she jumps onto my back. I spin us around, and walk to bar with her on my back. I let her down, so we can fit in the door, gripping her hand as she walks past me, our fingers twine together.

"Hey what's up douchebag?" Max says, to me when I sit down.

"Nothing why?"

"Where have you been all week?" he asks, putting a beer down for me.

"Helping Dad," I reply. Bailey looks at me, and pouts.

"You never said."

"I know darlin', it's a surprise."

Max laughs at us and grabs a beer for himself, we chill in the bar for an hour or so, and I take Bailey home. We walk through campus slowly, taking our time. I watch her smiling as the wind blows into our faces.

"What are you thinking about darlin'?"

"You," she sighs. "I'm always thinking about you Knox. I love every day with you and I kind of get annoyed with myself."

"Annoyed for what?"

"For all that drama with Ben. We wasted too many days being stupid and careless with each other's hearts."

I pull her to stop in front of me and cup her face. She smiles up at me and leans her face into my palm. "Don't think like that darlin'. We have always loved each other and just like every other couple, we had a rough patch."

I really want to make her understand that I never fell out of love with her. Just that thought alone makes me feel sick. "You know that song I sang to you?" she nods her head. "I wrote it about how I felt at that time. How I felt like I pushed you away and all I wanted was for you to come back to me. I missed you like I'd miss my shadow. I'm not giving you up so easy darlin'."

"Because you got mad love for me?" she smirks.

Nodding my head I chuckle at her, "Yeah, darlin', mad fucking love." I lean down and kiss her, closing my eyes I fight to stay upright. A blinding pain rips through my head and I can feel my hands shake from it. Pulling back I hold her close and breathe through it, "I think we need bed."

210

Chapter 26

Bailey

Leaving my advisors office I am pissed off; she refused me the emergency test thing. She said a fiancé having brain surgery didn't constitute as one. My mouth ran away with itself and unfortunately she got the sailor version of myself.

Her face turned red and she pretty much 'asked' me to leave her office. I stomp all the way to my computer class and slide into the seat beside Paige, dropping my bag on the desk with a thump.

"So I guess that didn't go well."

"No," I sigh, "she said it didn't count." I clench my fists on top of the table allowing my nails to pierce the skin. "I can't believe this," shaking my head, I close my eyes to keep my tears inside.

"Go talk to the Dean, maybe he can help," Paige suggests.

"Yeah." Grabbing my bag I take off. My feet stomp all the way to the admissions building again and up to the Dean's office. I am met with yet another assistant who is uncooperative.

"You need an appointment Miss Mortenson."

"It's an emergency," I grind, through my teeth. She won't budge, so neither do I. Taking a seat on the leather chair, I wait. It's not long when the Dean's door opens and he walks out followed by Agent Daniels. I shoot to my feet and square my shoulders, Agent Daniels notices me first.

"Hey shouldn't you be in class?" he says, smiling.

"Yeah, but I need to speak with the Dean," I answer.

Agent Daniels looks concerned and asks if everything is okay. Shaking my head, I am barely able to hold on. My resolve is cracking and I'm losing it. Dean Chambers stretches his hand out to usher me into his office, when his assistant reminds me I don't have an appointment.

"I told you it's an emergency," I snap at her. My hands are shaking from anger now. I need to run, I need to calm down before I get kicked out with two weeks to go. Agent Daniels puts his hand on my back and moves me into the room. We all sit down and I get my story out, and pretty much beg the Dean to let me take my last exam on a different day.

After a few sighs and repeating my dilemma, he tells me he can't change the date because he won't have an available proctor. My hearts sinks and I just nod, not trusting my voice. Standing, I leave the room and walk to the gym where I change into my football training gear and head out to run. I don't know how long I run for, but all I know is my life is fucked up right now. Of all the days that test could be on, why did it have to be on that day?

My eyes see the remaining students leaving campus, but I am not really registering it. My legs just keep going and going - it feels good to run like this. It's been way too long, that's one good thing about moving back up to the lake. I can run again. My feet pound the track in time with my raging heart. All the pain I have been holding onto is finally being released and although it feels good, I know the minute I stop it all come crashing back down on top of me. Rounding the bend in the track, I notice a figure strolling out into my path. Honestly I am about to run them over when Knox smiles at me. I pretty much fall into his arms and hold on tight.

"Hey what is it?" concern and worry lace his voice, as his eyes scan my whole body looking for something amiss.

"Nothing babe."

He stretches his arms out moving me backward. "I don't buy that darlin'. You've been running for an hour solid and I know that means something is going on in that pretty blonde head of yours."

"I'm okay, just a bad day."

He nods but still looks worried.

"How do you know it's been an hour?"

"I've been watching. I came to walk you home, but Paige told me you left class and she didn't see you again. So after my heart calmed down," he smiles, "I walked over here and saw you."

"Sorry," my body deflates against him again. Knox walks me back to the locker room so I can grab my stuff and we walk home. He runs a bath and pours some bubbles into it. I watch him smell all my essential oils and he pours nearly half a bottle inside before I stop him. "You only need a tiny bit babe," I laugh.

"Oh," he shrugs, "smells good though."

Peeling off my sweat soaked clothes, I climb in and sink down into the too hot water. Knox appears back with the lighter and a few candles. He is doing all this for me and he is the one facing something horrible. Reaching out I take his hand and tug it.

"Come in with me?"

I don't have to ask again, he pulls off his suit and climbs in behind me. "Holy fuck! It's hot," he shouts. Laughing, I turn around to see his eyes huge and his mouth open, trying to breathe through the scalding water.

"Sorry, I added more hot," I wince and kiss his cheek. We relax together in the bath and I watch the shadows from the candles dance on the wall.

"So what happened today darlin'?"

Sighing, I tell Knox about my day from college hell. He holds me closer and kisses my shoulder, telling me it will be okay and I have to do my exam. "No Knox, I'm not leaving you to face that alone."

"I won't be alone darlin', Max and my dad will be there."

"It's not the same, I'm supposed to be there with you," my eyes prick with tears again and I swallow the lump in my throat. Knox tilts my face to his and kisses me tenderly.

"I'll be okay, baby, I promise."

His words penetrate my heart and try to comfort me, but I know deep down that he can't make such promises. Deep down, fear consumes me. It reminds me every day that no one can make such promises and it makes me remember the last few days before Summer died, and before Nan died. She

213

seemed so full of life and energy, then bam, she was gone just like that.

Knox rubs my shoulders and sings to me, his voice echoes in the bathroom and surrounds me, just like his body. We stay together until the water gets cold, then climb out, wrapping towels around ourselves. In the kitchen I make us some hot chocolate and bring it back to the bedroom. Knox is in bed already rubbing his eyes.

"You okay babe?"

"Yeah, the usual." He frowns and points to his head. My heart breaks all over again as I climb in beside him. We watch some tv and fall asleep together - everything feels good right now.

It feels normal.

***

"Come on Abbey!" I shout across the field. I know she can't hear me with the crowd here, but I try anyway. I watch her move through the other players only to be brought down, shit. Georgia groans beside me and we exchange glances.

"Ready girl?" she asks.

"Yeah let's do this," I reply.

We stand off the bench and pull on our helmets. The crowd is yelling and shouting and the cheerleaders are causing some excitement. Our cheerleaders from the men's team offered to cheer for our last game and coach thought it was very nice of the girls. I am actually happy to see Chase's sister get in on school spirit. Glancing over my shoulder, I find my number one cheerleader, a huge smile splits my face when I see him. He waves at me and I wave back, earning one of his megawatt smiles. Max, Paige, Richard, Ryan, and Dad are all there shouting along with the rest of the people. But my eyes stay on Knox. He winks and clenches his hand into a fist, giving me a sign to go 'get em.'

We all huddle around Georgia, who calls the play. Once we get in position, things happen fast. Before I know it I am off running like a wild hare, glancing over my shoulder, I see the ball sailing my way so I take a chance and jump. Reaching out my fingers grip it and I clutch it close to my chest. My legs keep moving and my eyes are scanning, but out of nowhere I am on my ass with about a hundred girls on top of me.

After I am finally free, the referee checks to see where the ball is. Rolling over I clutch it to my chest like a newborn baby, the home crowd gets louder as I stand up. My eyes find Georgia and she makes what one would call a 'gang sign' but we know what play she is calling. One we call 'holy fuck' because every time we practice it, it goes wrong. It's first down on the five-yard line with six seconds on the clock. My heart pounds and my mind blanks. All I can see is the play in practice, the whistle blows, and I'm gone.

Jumping away from some menacing looking chick. I turn my head and the ball is there. "Fuck!" reaching out I plead with myself to catch it. The laces bounce off my fingertips and it rolls in the air. Fear grips me and I grab at it again, the corner of my eye registers a white and gold blur heading straight for me. With the ball firmly in my hands I run like hell, like the devil himself is chasing me. My foot just crosses the touchdown line and whistle blows.

Falling to my knees I clutch the ball to my stomach and cry. I get slammed from all directions when the girls jump me. They are screaming and cheering, but I lay on the ground still.

"Come on girl we did it." Georgia's voice sounds from beside me. Opening my eyes I turn to look at her. She grins at me and slaps my back, reaching out a hand to me. Gripping it she pulls me into a hug. Abbey and Becky jump on us, jostling our bodies together.

"We did it!" Abbey shouts, hugging me close.

"I'm keeping the ball," I shout at Georgia. She smiles and shrugs like it's no big deal. Finally I remove my helmet and run over to our bench. My family is going crazy behind our bench. Pointing to Knox, I throw the ball to him. He catches it and then runs down to me. Excitement rips through me at the sight of him pushing through the crowd, once he is on the field, I run into his arms.

"Holy shit darlin', you were amazing!"

He twirls me around in his arms squeezing me hard. Our lips crash together and I wrap my legs around him. Our kiss is hungry and passionate, as we devour each other.

"Get a room!" Someone shouts before a very cold dose of water sloshes over us. Knox drops me with shock but I hold onto his neck, everyone is laughing at us and join in.

"Well I guess that's that," Knox says.

"Hell no," I chatter and kiss him again. Knox and my family leave after the trophy is awarded. We have opened the bar to the team tonight in celebration. Max had some food catered and heads off to get it all ready. The whole team is on a high in the locker room, grabbing my stuff I remind them to come over to the bar and head home to get ready. Paige is in the apartment waiting for me.

"Hey what you doing here?" I ask, smiling at her.

"I'm your official escort to the after party," she laughs and twirls around.

"Thanks, I'll be about thirty minutes." After another shower and hair wash, I get ready in a new short cream mini dress. I slip on my platforms and grab a small black clutch for my phone and keys. I know I don't need money, so I leave my purse and head out to Paige. We walk through campus and the blood in my veins is still coursing with adrenaline and joy.

"You played really well Bailey, congrats."

"Thanks Paige," I can't help the huge smile on my face as we walk across the street. The bar is jammed so we use the side door. I slide through the beads and find Knox waiting at my seat with our dads. He smiles at me, as I walk around the bar and Dad hugs me tight congratulating me. Richard grabs me after my dad and hugs me too.

"Congrats darlin'," Knox takes me into his arms and shelters me from the world. We have a few drinks and eat some food. Knox and I hit the dance floor with Max and Paige. Knox's hands grip my hips as we move together and I can feel his body heat wrap around me. He kisses down my neck and pulls me closer, while his thumbs graze my ribs.

"Are you sure you were never a stripper?" I ask, teasing him.

"Nope, never, but I can be if you're short a few dollars for your student loans," he smirks at me. Laughing, I kiss his lips and wrap my arms around his neck.

"Thanks," I whisper.

"What for darlin'?"

"For everything you do for me."

His lips brush off mine, "You don't have to ever thank me darlin'. I love you, that's why I do things for you."

"Love you too but I'm still grateful for it all." My lips brush off his as we talk, our bodies slow down with the rhythm of the music. Resting my head on his shoulder I close my eyes and enjoy every second of being in his arms.

Chapter 27

"Mornin," Max groans and crawls onto our bed. Opening my eyes, I find his face right at mine and laugh.

"Hey, why are you here so early?" I ask. Knox groans and pulls me closer into him.

"We have some stuff to do and so do you," Knox answers. Max leans forward and presses his nose to mine, then pulls a face. Knox pushes him away from me and laughs.

"Get away from my woman, asshole."

"Why, you know the three of us would make a hot ass team," Max winks at me, because he knows Knox will get pissed off. I mouth 'stop,' at him, as Knox lifts up on his elbow, to look at Max.

"Seriously Max, if you weren't my brother I'd fuck you up."

Max leans forward and plants a kiss on my forehead before rolling off the bed and dodging a slap from his brother. "C'mon douche get up we have shit to do," he says, on his way out the door.

Knox bends down to kiss me hello and smirks at me. "You need to shower darlin', your mom will be here in an hour."

My head whips around to watch him hop out of bed. "My mom? Why?"

"Wedding dress shopping darlin', unless you want to walk down the aisle naked. Which is totally cool with me, but there will be family and friends there."

"Knox," I moan, burying my face into his pillow. His arms circle my waist, and he kisses my cheek then, pulls me up from the warmth of the bed. "Okay, I'm up."

"Good now go have fun and I'll see you later. If you want we can take your mom to dinner, just let me know."

218

"Okay, but where are you going?" I ask, watching him smirk.

"Never mind," he kisses me gently, then a little rougher while sliding his hands over my naked butt. "Ugh, I need to go before I can't." I watch him leave the room and shout for Max. I hear him brush his teeth and then he turns on the shower. "Shower's on darlin'," he calls then leaves the apartment.

After my shower, I pull on a dress and sandals. I hear a knock on the door, opening it my mom smiles at me.

"Surprise!" I give her a hug and laugh at her. "I'm sorry I couldn't make the game last night," she says.

"That's okay Mom, I didn't expect you to come all the way here for a game." This is the first time she has been to the apartment and I give her a quick tour. On our way out I call Paige and ask if wants to come along. We meet her at my car and take off to the mall.

"So what's first on the agenda?" Paige asks.

"A wedding dress," Mom laughs at her. Rolling my eyes, I park the car and climb out. We walk through the mall into the only store here. I flick through the racks, but nothing jumps out at me. Paige and Mom are pulling out dress after dress and my eyes hurt, from all the tulle and bows.

"No, let's just go," I moan, planting myself against the door. Mom says five more minutes and Paige takes off with her. My phone beeps with a text from Knox, asking how it's going.

Me: Horrible, I want to go home.
Knox: don't give up darlin'.
Me: I'm not, just annoyed. You know there is only one dress shop in this place.
Knox: go to Marion, the high street has a couple xx
Me: How do you even know that?
Knox: Ha ha not telling now go, love you.
Me: love you too. I want a date night tonight.
Knox: done!!

"Hey Mom, come on I have more shops to annoy myself in."

219

I shout from the door of the store. The sales clerk scowls at me and I push open the door to leave. When we leave the store, I drive to Marion and Google the High Street shops. I find five bridal stores and we make a plan.

"Okay, we'll do two then get lunch and then the other three," I announce.

Mom and Paige agree only because they have no choice and I'm not in the mood. I always thought I'd have a great time buying a wedding dress. Summer and I used to dream about it when we were kids. We'd often walk into a bridal boutique in Grove just to play out our fantasy.

"What about this one?" Paige asks. She holds out the most god awful looking thing. She is snickering behind the dress and I can see her shoulders shake.

"Yeah I like that," I answer. Her head pops up and she looks at me.

"You freakin' liar!" She puts the dress back and moves on. We spend about an hour in this store and leave. My stomach is rumbling already and I'm getting more annoyed.

"Who wants food?" I sing out. I think my mom is getting annoyed with me because I catch the scowl on her face.

"Sorry Mom, I know I'm being a pain," I sigh and link my arm through hers.

"It's okay baby, I get it."

She pats my hand and agrees that food is in order. We find a little café and stop in. Our lunch consists of coffee, cakes, and more coffee. In the next shop, I make an effort to look for a dress and go so far as to try two on. Mom shakes her head at both so we leave that place. Walking into the next place we are accosted by a sales clerk. He greets us with air kisses and a glass of champagne each.

"Oh I'm driving," I smile, putting the glass back down on the tray. He clicks his fingers and a woman brings over a glass of orange juice for me. I thank him and turn away not knowing what the heck is going on. The store is bright and airy with a huge crystal chandelier hanging from the ceiling.

"So which of you young ladies is the lucky bride?" he asks, smiling at us.

Raising my hand, I give him a slight wave. His smile never leaves his face as his eyes zoom from my head to my toes then, back to my face.

"I'm guessing, 36, 26, 30," he says, nodding to himself. With that, he is off, and pulling dresses from the racks. He puts them on one of those roll away rails; the ones you see on movie sets and brings it over to me. Taking the glass away from my lips and removing my handbag from my shoulder, he puts them on the table. I just stand stiff as a board at his boldness.

"Now tell me is there anything you don't like?" His eyes are open wide and he is staring.

"I...I...eh...flowers, I'm not into floral," I answer. His eyebrows shoot up to his hairline and laughs at me.

"Oh dear," he says, then leans closer, placing his hand by his mouth he whispers, "I thought you said oral," he giggles.

"Oh...oh god no!" I answer and feel the heat bloom on my cheeks. He claps his hands and howls with laughter at me.

"I'm Gordon ladies, and I'm here to make all you fantasies come true. Well wedding ones at least," he says, waving his hand.

Mom and Paige crack up at him and I just look at him like he is from Mars. He puts a dress in my arms and pushes me toward a huge room with no mirrors. Slipping off my clothes, I pull on the puff-ball he handed me.

"You doing okay Bailey?" his voice calls out.

"Eh yeah, I think so."

The next thing I know the door is open and he is in the room with me. I scream at him, but he waves me off, telling me he is not interested and helps me button up the dress. We walk out to the waiting area to Mom and Paige, who are both in hysterics.

"What's so funny?" I ask, stepping up onto the little stage thing in front of three mirrors. They stop to look at me, and Mom gets all 'emotional' now.

"No don't like it," Paige shakes her head. I have to agree with her though. It's just too much for me.

"I want simple and elegant," The words tumble from my lips before I know I've spoken. Gordon smiles and claps his hands.

"I know the perfect one," he sighs.

I trudge back to the changing room and wait for him. "Okay, this one has just come from the runway and I was saving it for someone special and look, you just happened into my store."

His brown eyes are soft when he smiles at me. He helps me out of this dress and thank God I wore nice undies. Stepping into the second dress, he slides the cool fabric up my legs and torso. Holding it against my chest, he closes all the buttons at the back.

"Ready?" he asks, reaching for my hand, like Prince Charming in a Disney story. We walk out to the mirrors. Mom and Paige both gasp, and jump to their feet.

"Oh Bailey," Mom has tears in her eyes again and she nods.

Turning, I look into the mirrors and I can't believe it. I look like a princess. The dress is the most beautiful gown I have ever seen.

"This ivory dress is strapless corded lace appliqué, tulle, and organza, over a satin ball gown wedding dress with scalloped sweetheart neckline. Corded lace appliquéd bodice with dropped waistline and back bodice features covered buttons, softly gathered tulle and organza layered full skirt with matching lace appliqués cascading down to scalloped hemline and chapel length train," Gordon gushes.

"It's amazing," my voice cracks a little.

"How do you feel?" Paige asks. Her smile is contagious.

"Like a princess," I confess and she nods.

"Good because you look like one and Knox will die when he sees you."

Once the words leave her lips, she gasps and covers her mouth. "I'm sorry, oh shit. Bailey, I didn't mean it like that."

"I know Paige, calm down. He will though," I smile.

Paige walks away from us with her head down and Gordon looks really interested in the little tidbit.

"My fiancé is having brain surgery in a few days," I explain.

"Oh I'm so sorry," he says and hugs me.

"It's okay, he'll be fine. We will get through it," nodding to myself I take another look in the mirror. My own eyes tear up and for once in the last few weeks I feel a little ray of hope bloom in my heart.

"I'll take it," I whisper.

"Of course you will," Gordon scoffs at me. "It was practically made for you and no alterations needed, so perfect," he says, resting his chin on his fist.

Looking in the mirror again, I check the store for Paige, but I don't see her.

"Mom can you check on Paige, please? We need to pick her dress."

She leaves to find Paige and I go back to the room to change. Gordon asks about Knox and I find myself telling him my life story from when we met up until now. His mouth is gaping open at me.

"How old are you?" he whispers, shaking his head.

"Twenty- three, but my birthday is in August."

"So much pain for someone so young."

Shaking his head, he leaves me to get fixed up. When I walk back outside, Mom and Paige are ready. Gordon takes us up to the second level and it is filled with every color dress you can imagine. We browse for a while and I find a nice asymmetrical cut dress.

"Hey Paige, what about this?" I call out and walk towards her. She pokes out from behind a rack and smiles.

"Ooh I like," she takes it from me and walks to the changing room. She waltzes back out a few minutes later, with a smile on her face.

"Wow you look hot," I nod to her.

"I know," she smiles and twirls for us.

The dress is a crinkle chiffon, with a halter neckline and asymmetrical hemline. She looks really pretty.

"What do you think of the color?"

"I'm down, I mean it's your day so I'll wear whatever color you like."

"I like that color on you, rose pink," I nod in appreciation.

"Rose pink it is then unless you want purple," she asks.

"No, you look pretty."

We agree on the dress and then we try find Mom something, but she declines, telling us she all kinds of dresses at home. We find Gordon at the checkout area, but there's no register. I take out my credit card and phone, snapping a picture of it, I text it to Knox with a smiley face. Mom snatches it from my hand and hands over her own.

"Mom, no way!"

"Yes way," she answers. Gordon doesn't argue with Mom and runs her card through this odd looking thing attached to an iPad. Once we leave the store and agree to have my dress delivered to the hotel the day before the wedding, I am feeling a little lighter.

"Mom, do you want to have dinner with Knox and I tonight?"

"No baby, I have to get back. My flight is at six," she gives me a hug. "I'll be back a few days before the wedding to help you out."

"Okay," I nod to her. I drop her off at her hotel just after four and say goodbye. When Paige and I get back to the apartment, we just sit in the car for a minute.

"You doing okay?"

"I think so, part of me didn't want to buy a dress. Just in case the worst happened then I'd have a reminder of what never would have happened."

"I get that, but now you have something to hold on to. You know Knox will shit a brick when he catches a glimpse of you in that dress."

."I know," I sigh and open the door, climbing out "I just hope he gets to see it." Paige hugs me and I walk up to the apartment. Opening the door, I can smell Knox, taking a deep inhale I smile and walk toward the sitting room.

"Hi," I smile, when I see him all dressed up.

"Hey darlin'," he gets up to give me a hug and kiss.

"You look nice," taking another deep inhale and I bury my face into his neck.

"Got a hot date tonight," he answers, running his hand up and down my back.

"Really, well she better have you home by midnight, or else you'll turn into a monster."

"Oh I'll be a monster alright," he growls in my ear and tickles my ribs. "Go get ready darlin', dinner is at six." He kisses me quickly. I run down to the bedroom, pulling off my clothes along the way. I have another quick shower and redo my makeup. Knox strolls into the bedroom and sits on the bed watching me.

"You okay babe?"

"Yeah, just bored sitting on my own," he answers. I walk into the closet and pull around my clothes. He is dressed in a white shirt and jeans so I'm guessing casual is okay.

"Will I wear a dress or pants babe?" I shout out to him.

"A dress, the shorter the easier the access," he shouts back, laughing at himself.

Rolling my eyes, I grab my black swing dress and my purple suede platforms and purple purse. Slipping them on, I walk out and twirl for him.

"So does this look okay?"

He has me in his arms in two seconds, "More than okay darlin', you're beautiful."

We drive out to a beachfront restaurant and enjoy our dinner, we talk about everything, and it feels like when we first met. After dinner Knox takes me dancing in Black's, it's been so long since we were here last but I still have fun. After our date, he drives us home and helps remove my shoes and dress. He stands staring at my body while holding my hand.

"Knox?"

"Yeah, darlin'?"

"You're staring."

He smirks at me and pulls me close to him. His hand moves up my arm to the back of my neck and his fingers tangle in my hair. "I love you darlin'," he whispers, before kissing me passionately and taking me to bed.

Chapter 28

Walking to campus I take a look around, admiring the buildings and the grounds. The years have gone by so fast, yet sometimes it feels like I only just arrived here. I'm torn between doing my exams and running home to be with Knox. He forced me out the door this morning, telling me if I didn't graduate then he is not marrying me. We both knew he was bluffing, but I let him have his little lie.

Pushing open the door to the room, I take my usual seat and wait. There are a few people here already but no one I know. By eight, thirty the room is full and our Proctor arrives holding two big envelopes. Just before nine we are handed a test sheet and an answer sheet. He stands with his left arm out in front of him and his eyes are glued to his watch.

"You have three hours you may begin," he announces the minute the clock strikes nine. By eleven, thirty I am done and leaving the room. I grab a quick sandwich and soda from the café and make my way to another room in the computer building.

"Hey, you all set?" Paige asks.

"Yeah, this should be easy. You?"

"Yeah, same. Are you done after this?" she asks.

Shaking my head, I down the last of my soda. "No, I have one more today then I'm done until Friday," I frown. After a quick bathroom trip, I find a seat beside Paige and wish her luck. This test is easy enough for me and I finish with an hour to spare. Leaving the room, I walk out to the quad and sit in the shade of a tree. Putting my earphones in I play my all-time favorite Nickelback and close my eyes. Friday is the day my life will change. Knox has his surgery at nine in the morning, and my last test starts at the same time. I am torn between being at the hospital and taking my final exam. Grabbing my phone, I scroll through the pictures of us, every memory we have made together floods my heart.

A shadow falls across me and I look up. Agent Daniels smiles at me and I pull out my earphones. I realize I am crying and quickly wipe my face.

"Everything okay?" he asks.

"Oh yeah, just being silly," I answer and wipe my face again. He sits on the grass beside me and holds out his hand. I'm not too sure what he wants, but I put my phone in his hand. He smiles at the picture and hands it back.

"Why are you crying?"

"His surgery is Friday and I have a choice to make."

"What's the choice?" he asks, sounding concerned.

"Like I told the Dean, I want to be there for him, but I have my last test. What if he doesn't make it and I'm here taking a stupid test? I'll never forgive myself."

We sit in silence for a few minutes before he tells me to leave it with him. He helps me up and I walk towards the room of my last test. After the exam, I make my way home finding Knox making dinner.

"Hey beautiful," I call out and smile when he turns.

"That's my line darlin'."

I kiss him hello and shrug, snaking my arms around his waist.

"How did it go?"

"Okay, I'm done," I answer, resting my head on his shoulder.

"No, you have one more on Friday, Bailey," he kisses my head and moves me back. He gives me his stern face and I roll my eyes at him.

"I'm not arguing babe, it's you over a test any day."

Taking a seat, I kick my feet up onto the chair and rest my head against the wall. "It will be weird packing up this place."

"Yeah, it will. Remember when I got it?" he asks.

"Yes I do," I smile at him. Do I ever. "We had so much crap going on, how did we ever get through it all?"

"Love darlin', that's all it takes."

Moving my feet, he sits down to eat with me and we don't mention Friday again. I don't want to argue with him, especially now. "What are you doing tomorrow?" he asks.

"I'm going to work with my fiancé."

"Yeah? Cool, I like it when we can spend our lunch break together," he teases.

"I think I have a lunch meeting with Dad actually."

He groans at me and I laugh, "You're a big baby Knox Porter."

"I know," he says leaning over for a kiss.

***

I have spent the last two days here at work with Dad. I am trying to keep busy and not have to think about tomorrow, but it's all I can think about.

"How are you holding up sweetheart?"

"Dad, honestly I don't know," I sigh.

"I know you want to be there for Knox…"

"Dad stop…you sound like him right now and I really can't hear it. I know what's at stake, but his life is more important than some stupid exam. I have money Dad, lots of money, and a job, so a degree is not really needed."

Leaning my head back on the chair, I let out a breath and close my eyes.

"I understand that you have money sweetheart, but isn't getting a degree a big achievement for you? Considering you weren't even planning on attending college after Summer died."

"Yeah it is Dad, but Knox is more important."

Climbing to my feet, I give him a hug, he holds me just a little bit longer and kisses my head. Leaving his office, I stroll back into my own and take a seat at my desk. Picking up the phone I dial Knox's extension.

"Hello."

"Hi handsome."

He laughs down the line at me. "I knew it was you, I have caller ID."

"No, you don't, my extension doesn't come up."

228

"I got a tech friend to make it display. It says, watch out the boss is calling."

"You're such a liar," I laugh at him.

"Okay then bye darlin'," he hangs up on me but I don't care, I have a smile on my face. A few minutes later he walks into my office with a coffee. "Beautiful."

"Hi babe, nice surprise."

He bends down to kiss me, but I don't let him go, deepening our kiss. Finally, we break apart and he looks at me. "What's up?"

"Nothing why."

"You don't usually kiss me like that," he says.

"Like what? I do so kiss you like that, all the time," I argue.

"No, you don't darlin'. That was a feisty, I wanna fuck you in the bathroom kiss," he says.

"Oh really and how would you know what that kind of kiss is like?"

He smirks at me then laughs. "I have given a few out."

"Oh well, pray tell my love," I watch him duck his head a little and allow his hair to fall forward. His cheeks turn a little pink, and I move so I can look at him.

"Are you blushing? You little slut!"

He bursts out laughing at me and twirls my chair around with me in it. "No, men don't blush. Let's just say before you, I had a few lady frogs to deal with."

"Oh bullshit, you're a man whore, I was right! All those nights spent working in Black's. I knew you were trouble, Knox Porter."

"Yeah, well why did you chase me?"

"What! I never did any sort of chasing babe. Your memories are a little fuzzy." Shaking my head, I smile at him - perched on the edge of my desk. He is grinning back at me and chuckling.

"I distinctly remember you chasing me down and accosting me in the street."

"I think you're full of shit babe."

"I think you see something you like," he smirks and leans closer.

"I think I wanna fuck you in the bathroom."

I answer, grabbing his face between my hands and pulling him closer. We kiss hard and fast, Knox grips my hair and pulls me into his groin. We stumble over to my door, pulling away from him I quickly close it and lock it. His lips are on mine again and his hands are pushing up my skirt.

"Damn darlin'," he says, against my neck as he leaves a trail of hot wet kisses. His fingers are already slipping inside of me, making me moan with pleasure. My cell phone rings and we ignore it.

"I want you now, Knox," I whisper, in his ear.

Lifting his head, he looks into my eyes. His lips are swollen and I want to bite them, his eyes are darker than normal as he looks into mine.

"I love you," he tells me.

"I know, I love you too."

My phone rings again and I ignore it again. Slipping my hands down, I open his pants and push them off his hips. Knox spins me around and pushes me over the edge of the sofa. He enters me from behind and we move together, hard. The only sound in the room is our skin slapping off the other and my phone ringing. We reach climax together and Knox holds my hips tightly as he pushes into me one last time.

After we get dressed, he asks who keeps calling me. Grabbing my phone I shrug and he wraps his arms around me as I listen to the voicemail.

"Afternoon Bailey, this is Agent Daniels. I hope you get this message on time. I can proctor your last exam today at two o'clock. Call me back to confirm if I don't hear from you then I will take that as a no."

Checking my clock, I notice it is one twenty already. "Fuck!" pressing the callback button I kiss Knox one more time and grab my purse running out of my office. I leave a voicemail back and race through the town of Blackrock towards the college. Traffic is shit and I am freaking out. "Come on!" I shout at the cars in front of me. Banging my hands on the steering wheel I bounce in my seat. When my phone rings, I almost scream from fright.

"Yes, hello?"

"Hi, Bailey I got your message. I will be in the Science Building room SC201, see you in ten."

"Okay," I answer. The traffic moves a little bit and I am able to pull into the parking lot at the apartment. Climbing out I race all the way to the science building in my heels and suit, barging into the room at one fifty-seven, panting like a mad dog.

"You okay?" Agent Daniels asks.

"Yeah," I pant. "I was at work."

He frowns at me and points to a seat. Taking it, I notice about fifteen other students here and try to calm myself.

"Did you run from work?" he asks, handing me my test.

"No, I drove to the apartment. The traffic was bad so I ran from there."

Shaking his head, he pats my shoulder and wishes me luck. Before I know it, I am on the last question. I just finish writing and he calls time, my head snaps up and I sigh. No time to revise. Walking up to him, I hand over my answer sheet and say goodbye. I'll miss him.

"Thank you for helping me."

"You're welcome and I hope everything goes well tomorrow," he answers.

Nodding I leave the room and exit the building; wow college is over. How did that happen? I take my time to walk through campus and arrive home to find Knox pacing the floor.

"Darlin'," he grabs me in a hug the minute I step into the apartment.

"You okay?" I ask, a little concerned.

"Yeah, when I saw the car I thought you didn't make it on time," he sighs, running a hand through his hair.

"I'm done babe, all done." Tears prick my eyes as I digest that fact. Tomorrow seemed so far away and now here it is.

"Don't cry baby," he whispers, "It will be okay."

After a shower, I smell pizza and walk into the sitting room. Max and Knox are playing video games while Paige munches away.

"Hey guys," I grab a slice of pizza and sit next to Paige. She squeezes my hand and smiles at me. Knox and Max are acting the way they always do, trying to grab the others controller and pushing each other. My heart hurts looking at them, knowing tomorrow everything may change.

Chapter 29

We all get up at six in the morning. Knox has a shower and complains about being hungry.

"Aren't you eating?" he asks, walking into the kitchen.

"Na bro, we're starving in solidarity," Max grins.

"Lying fucker, you're just waiting until I'm knocked out."

"See you know me so well, we should be twins," Max answers.

Knox rolls his eyes and kisses me hello. After a while, we leave the apartment and climb into the truck. Knox and I take the back seat and he holds my hand in silence all the way. I can't help but stare at him while he looks out the window. I catch Max's eyes in the rear view mirror a few times, and we both have worry on our faces. When we reach the hospital, Knox checks in and is shown to his room. He gets changed into the gown, moaning about it the whole time and climbs into the bed.

"Darlin'."

"Yeah?" I smile, taking a seat on the bed beside him.

"I love you so much. Don't ever forget that. I am happy I got to spend the last four years with you. I could never love anyone the way I love you..."

I press my finger to his lips. "No babe, you can tell me all this on July 29th."

He smiles at me and pulls me close whispering in my ear.

"Just in case darlin', know that you mean the whole world to me, okay?"

Nodding, I pull back when Max and Richard enter the room. I leave them alone to have some family time and wait in the hall. I watch a doctor walk into Knox's room and Max calls me in. Knox takes off his ring, placing it in my hand.

"Love you darlin'."

Bending down, I kiss him and wrap my arms around him so tightly. After a few minutes, he is getting wheeled out of the room. "Max, take care of her," he shouts, over his shoulder.

"I know," Max chokes out and grabs me closer to him. We follow the bed down the hall. I watch Knox run his hands through his hair, and then he smirks at me as the doors close to the elevator. As soon as he is out of sight I allow my tears to fall and cling on to Max.

"It's okay sis, he'll be okay," he whispers, holding onto me as much as I am holding onto him. We take a seat in the waiting area. The doctor said it was going to be at least four to six hours for the surgery. I stare at the blank wall for a while, I'm not sure how long. When I look around, I notice Max and Richard are sitting together in silence.

"I'll be outside for a minute," I tell them.

Richard smiles and nods at me, so I walk outside and find a small tree with a bit of sunshine, and I sit down. I take the worn envelope from my purse and turn it over in my hands. I'm not exactly sure why I brought it with me, but I did. Brushing my finger over the writing on the front I smile. I don't know if I am supposed to wait for my wedding day or not, but right now I think I need to be close to Knox's mom. Sliding my finger along the top, I rip the paper open and take out the blue writing paper inside. Lifting my eyes to the sun I close them for a minute and ask Nan and Summer to keep Knox safe for me, I can't lose him.

Opening the pages, I begin to read the script writing that looks so much like Knox's.

Dear Mrs. Knox Porter,

I am not too sure what to call you, so I hope you don't mind. If you are reading this letter, then I know my son has found a truly special person to love. I am only sorry that I can't be there to see your wedding. I wanted to introduce myself to you. I am Annabelle Porter, wife, mother, and friend.

I am writing this letter as a way for you to get to know me a little better, but also as a way to tell you about my son. He is a wonderful boy and I know he has grown into a wonderful man. I am sure Knox has told you that I am a music teacher and both he and Max have learned everything they know from me, well, they are right. Some days not by choice, but I hope music plays an important role in their lives today. I love my children so much and it hurts to know that I will miss out on many special occasions in their lives. But I also know that my husband will be there for them and see them through it for me.

So, on to Knox, my handsome young man. You may already know this about him, but I will tell you anyway. Knox is my sweet, sensitive son, he is caring and loving and has a kindness that he tries to hide, but he can't. It is him, and it will always, be him. He loves, not only with his heart, but with his whole being, and that is a very special love to have.

He will treat you like a princess and give you all of him. I just hope you give all of you in return because he deserves a woman like that. When he hurts it will be deep and he will not forgive easily, but eventually he will come around. I am not trying to scare you away. I know he must love you very much.

I hope you have a beautiful wedding day and spend the rest of your lives together, living in pure happiness and joy. Love each other passionately, and live each day to the fullest. Life is short but with the love of Knox, you will have a happy heart. I am blessed to have had sixteen years with my sons and I hope you have much more than that together.

Please give my son a hug and kiss from me, and tell him I love him more than anything. I miss them both and to you, I love you for loving my son, treat each other with respect and love will always bloom.

All my love,
Annabelle.

I read the letter twice and close my eyes, hoping that Knox will be okay and I can show him how much I love him for the rest of my life.

"Hey, sis, what you doin'?"

I allow a small smile to grace my lips as I look up at Max. "Nothing. Just reading," I answer, holding the letter in my hand. He takes a seat beside me wrapping his arm around my shoulders.

"Anything interesting?"

"Yeah, a letter from your Mom," I reply. Max stiffens beside me and I look over at him. He looks a little worried and confused so I pass it to him.

"Here, don't tell Knox."

Taking the letter, he looks at it then at me. "You sure?"

"Yeah," I reply and close my eyes again. I hear a snort and grunt a few times, and then the sound of the paper, as he puts it back inside the envelope. Opening my eyes, I look at him. He blows out a long slow breath and pulls me into a hug. Neither of us speaks for a long time and I finally pull back.

"You okay?" I ask, watching as wipes his eyes.

"Yeah," he clears his throat. "I wonder what she wrote in mine. Max is a cheeky fucker and doesn't take life too seriously."

"Well it's true," I smile over at him. He nods and wipes his face again.

"I doubt I'll get to hand mine over anytime soon, though."

"Why's that? I thought you and Paige are doing good."

"Yeah, we are…I mean, we're friends and it's good, but…I dunno Bailey, she wrecked me the first time around…I'm not sure if I can chance it again," he sighs.

Taking his hand in mine I link my fingers with his, "I know how you feel. I was like that when I first came here. I was closed off and stayed up at Dad's for nearly two months before I ventured into town. I wasn't sure I'd ever be able to open my heart to anyone again," I tell him.

"But you met Knox," he says.

"Yep and he wrecked me too, but I took a chance again and now look at us."

Max smiles at me and leans over to kiss my forehead, "I'm happy you two got together. I think you're perfect for him sis."

"Thanks, Max."

Standing, we walk back into the waiting room with our arms around each other. Apart from Knox, Max is by best

236

friend and I'd be lost without him here. I watch the hours tick by, one after another. Four hours turns to six, which turns to eight and I am beginning to get a little nervous. The operation was supposed to be four to six hours; not an eight going on nine. We are all feeling a little restless. Max is bouncing his knee. Richard is scrolling through his phone and I'm pacing a hole in the floor.

As the clock moves on to the tenth hour, I get agitated. Max keeps watching me and I run my hands through my hair. Tying it up, then taking it down, and repeating it over again. I am about to lose it when the doctor finally walks into the room.

"Hello," she greets us. I can see the tiredness around her eyes and weariness about her too. My heart bangs against my chest as I wait for her to speak to us.

"Knox is out of surgery. He is in recovery, but I'm going to keep him in for a few days longer than normal."

Richard jumps to his feet, startling all of us. "What happened?"

"There was more bleeding than there should have been, but we got it under control. Right now, he is still sedated while the swelling goes down. I can only allow one person to see him for now," she nods at us.

"You go," I say to Richard. He looks at me, lost, but I nod and motion for him to go. He follows the doctor and I drop into the chair, closing my eyes.

"He's okay sis. He'll be awake soon," Max says. I'm not sure if it's meant to ease my mind or his.

"Yeah, I know," I whisper.

Chapter 30

Finally after two days of waiting, I can go in and see Knox. Once I'm in the room, I almost break down and sob. He has a bandage wrapped around his head and his eyes look like he got punched, repeatedly. Slipping my hand into his, I lift it up and kiss his knuckles.

"Lips darlin'," he whispers. His eyes are still closed and his hand tries to pull me down.

"I missed you, babe," I tell him and place my lips on his.

"I missed you too," he whispers back, turning his face away from the window.

"How's the head?" I ask.

"Sore, feels worse than before, but I guess I did just have brain surgery."

"You're not funny," I answer.

He gives me small laugh. "Am too," he sighs. "Tired," he says and then his breathing settles into a soft rhythm.

Letting his hand go, I close over the blinds on the window then resume my position beside him. I read two books and listen to my iPod before he even moves. Once he does he mumbles but remains asleep. Max strolls in after work and sits down opposite me.

"How is he?"

"Okay, made a joke about five hours ago," I shrug.

"Doc says he will be in and out for a few days. Do you want to go eat? I can sit for a while," he asks.

I know Max misses his brother and I really don't want to go, but I do. Nodding, I stand up and tell him I'm going to the café across the street. It kills me to walk out of the room, but I need to. Entering the café, I smell the food and instantly my stomach grumbles. Taking a seat, I order a burger and fries.

Sipping my milkshake, I text my mom back and let her Knox is doing okay, but he still has a ways to go. When my food arrives, I force myself to eat it and slowly too, giving Max some time.

Life right now is on hold, although Knox is out of surgery, his brain still has swelling and the lump they removed is being tested for cancer. I have numbed myself to the whole thing. Part of me feels bad, but the survival part is keeping me numb just so I can function. I need to be strong for him, not to break down and lose it while Knox depends on me. Walking back to the hospital, I school my features and put on my brave face, the face I have adopted since the other day.

Walking into the room I can hear Max talking. As I round the corner, I see Knox sitting up and awake. I almost drop the remainder of my shake with my sudden shock.

"Hey babe," my voice is barely a whisper.

Looking over he tilts his head a little, "Hi."

I'm confused. Walking closer, I look at him, trying, to gauge what is going on here. Max stands and reaches for me, but I shrug him off. "Hi babe, you feeling okay?" I ask. Knox looks at me for a minute, then over to Max.

"Hey sis, maybe we should step outside for a sec," he says.

Following Max out into the hallway, I cross my arms and glare at him. He holds his hand up in surrender and takes a step back from me.

"He kind of doesn't know you," he says.

"What?" my eyes grow huge and I breathe hard. "What do you mean he kind of doesn't know me?"

"He doesn't remember much of the last two years," Max shoves his hands deep into his pockets.

"Are you fucking kidding!" I whisper shout. He shakes his head no and I crumble. My body slides down the wall and I sit on the floor. My eyes just stare at nothing. Max walks back into the room leaving me on the floor. After a while, I pull myself up and enter the room. Both of them watch me pull up a chair and sit myself down. Knox gives me his trademark smirk but says nothing.

"Do you really not remember me?" I ask.

"Sorry," he answers and I can see the sadness in his eyes. Letting out a sigh I nod and decide to make him remember.

"Well that's not good enough," I tell him and pull my phone out of my purse.

"What do you mean?" Knox asks. He looks scared as he searches my face.

"Knox, we have been through so much in the last few years. I am not letting you forget anything about us. We are getting married in two months."

He laughs at me, I'm not sure if it's a nervous laugh or a 'fuck you' laugh.

"I'm sorry, but I don't know you and I am not getting married to you."

Max stands up and opens his mouth, but I hold up my hand. "Don't Max." He nods and takes a seat. I pull up the photos on my phone and sit myself beside Knox, who moves away.

"Max I think…" he starts but stops as soon as I hold the phone out to him. Taking it he stares at the picture of us, his favorite one.

"Wow," he says. I watch him slide his finger across the screen and take in all the photos. I have a year's worth of pictures on my phone and I am glad I didn't remove them. After about an hour, he hands my phone back to me and smiles. I'm not sure what to make of it and I pray my Knox is in there.

"It seems like we have a good life together," he says. I nod back to him, swallowing hard. Max shakes his head and leaves the room. I watch after him trying to figure out what is wrong with him. Knox slips his hand into mine and links our fingers.

"I could never forget you darlin'," he grins at me.

"You fucking asshole," I breathe. Tears spill from my eyes and rip my hand away from his. "That was mean Knox." Climbing off the bed I shove my phone back into my purse.

"Baby, I'm sorry. It wasn't a joke when I woke up I didn't recognize Max for a while but after a few minutes I did."

"So you think it was funny to do that to me?" I hiccup.

"Darlin', come over to me, now," he holds out his arms and I shake my head. He grunts in frustration at me, "Now Bailey."

"That wasn't nice," I cry, as I climb back up on the bed. He wraps me in his arms and kisses my head.

"I'm sorry darlin', but I did like all the pictures. I love you, even if I forgot you, those pictures would have made me a believer."

Shaking my head, I refuse to let him away with what he has just done on me. I can't believe he thought now was good time for a practical joke. And Max, just wait until I see him again.

"Do you still love me?" He whispers.

"No."

"I thought so," he says. Lifting my face up to his he kisses me softly.

***

Three weeks later

"I can't believe we are moving," I sigh.

"Yeah I know," Knox replies. We have the truck loaded with boxes for our first trip up to the new house. Knox has a bald patch on the side of his head where he got cut open, but the hair is starting to grow back, finally. We climb into the truck and take off up the hill to our new home.

"Are you excited darlin'?"

"Yes, you?"

"Hell yeah, I can't wait to make love in every room," he grins at me.

"Is that all you think about Knox Porter?"

"Pretty much when I think of you, yeah."

Rolling my eyes, I press on the gas and take us up the hill. Knox links his fingers through mine and shakes my hand. "You know you love me darlin'."

"Yes, I do."

When I pull into the driveway, I can't help but smile. The front garden is beautiful. I had the water fountain removed and replaced it with a flower garden. Knox gives me his megawatt smile and we climb out of the truck.

"I can't believe we are finally moving in," he sighs, wrapping his arms around my waist.

"I know, I can't wait to see it all together."

We have only seen rooms, but not the whole house. "Ready?" I ask.

"Hell yeah!"

Knox pulls me to the house laughing. We both pull out our keys and laugh with excitement.

"Ladies first," he says, holding out his arm. Grinning, I run into the house and stop to look around. Knox has his arms around my waist again as we make our way through each room. The sitting room is amazing with the full-length windows and the stone fireplace for the winter. The hardwood floors run throughout the house, but in this room they look so good.

"It's beautiful," I whisper.

"Yeah, it is. Wanna check out the kitchen?" he asks.

"Sure, I'm dying to see it." He grips my hand taking me through the hall to the kitchen door.

"Close your eyes," he teases, kissing me first. I follow his instructions and close my eyes. Knox takes my hand leading me into the room. "Open baby," he whispers in my ear. Once I do, I have to blink a few times against the sun shining through the massive windows. The room has been completely transformed from the last time I saw it. The walls are a rich tan color, making them warm. The floor is tiled with terracotta and the counter tops match the rich bronze color.

"Holy crap babe," I breathe. "This is amazing."

"Yeah I know," he answers. He brings me over to the window seat, which I completely missed and he lifts the cushioned seat. Bending down, I read the writing and laugh.

"Yes I do, I love you, Knox Porter."

I take his hand now and bring him up the stairs. We check out the spare empty bedrooms, then move on to his surprise. "Now, close your eyes babe." He complies with a big grin on his face. Opening the door, I walk him inside and stop.

"Can I open now?"

"Sure."

242

When he does, his eyes grow huge and his mouth opens. "Darlin'…" turning slowly, he takes in the room. His guitars are lined up against one wall in a custom made stand. I got him a real piano, which I was told was a bitch to get up here, but it looks great in the middle of the room. "I don't know what to say…I," he tries to speak but can't. I'm giddy with happiness, just watching his reaction.

"You like?" I ask.

"I love it darlin'…Jesus…I mean… I love you." Stepping closer to him, I wrap my arms around his waist and hug him. He kisses my head and squeezes me tightly.

"Let's go check out our room," I mumble into his chest. We make our way into the master bedroom. The bed is huge and centered in the middle of the room. We picked a soft gray carpet and curtains with a cream wall. Knox sighs as he stops beside me.

"I can't believe we have our own house," he says.

"I know." Turning, I smile at him and we run out onto the balcony. "Wow." I look at the job Richard has done on the balcony, it looks completely different.

"Dad did a great job," Knox says, wrapping me up in his arms again.

"Yeah he did," I agree. Knox bends down brushing his lips off mine. We stand together just staring into each other's eyes, for a long time.

"I really love you darlin'," he says.

"I love you too." My eyes glance at the side of his head and he sighs. Turning me in his arms, he pulls me back into his chest.

"Everything will be okay darlin'. I'm okay," he assures me.

"I know babe. I just…I don't know…you're different now, since the surgery."

"Different, how darlin'?"

Tilting my head back, I smile up at him. "You're actually more like Max. Kind of carefree, I guess." I shrug because I don't know how to describe him really.

"No darlin', this is me. We have been through a lot in the last four years and now it's our chance to be really happy. I'm

243

just me again, without headaches, without the possibility of some crazy fucking stalker coming after the woman I love, and without a terminal illness. This is our chance darlin' and we both deserve it."

"I know babe…I just mean you seem giddier. It's not bad, I like it."

"Good, because life is too short to be moody and not have fun," he chuckles.

"Yeah, because we both know who is the moody one," I tease him.

"Hey now," he warns. We walk back into the house only stopping at the bed. Knox presses his lips against mine and walks backward until my legs bump off the bed. "I think we need to take a rest."

"We haven't started," I answer.

"Oh we're starting darlin', can't you tell?"

He grins at me while sliding his hand up into my hair and gently laying me back on the bed. I watch as he pulls off his t-shirt and kicks off his boots, then he slowly opens his jeans and pushes them down his legs all while keeping his eyes on mine.

Reaching out I grip his hand and pull him down to me. Our lips collide in a hot wet kiss, as my hands roam over his back. Knox pulls my dress up over my head, discarding it on the floor. His eyes drink me in while he traces a line from my neck all the way down to my stomach.

"You're so damn beautiful," he whispers.

"Are you going to stare all day?"

Lifting his head, he smiles at me and chuckles. "So impatient my love." He teases. Arching my hips, his hand moves lower between my legs eliciting a moan from me.

"I want you now," I pant. He works his fingers slowly while his mouth explores my body. My body tightens as he pushes his fingers deeper inside bringing me to climax.

"That was fast darlin'," He smirks.

"It's been too long," I answer, gripping the back of his neck and pulling down to me, to finish what he started.

Chapter 31

"Where are you going?" Mom asks, looking shocked.

"For a run, I'll only be thirty minutes."

I slip my iPod into my armband and wave to her as I step out the back door. I blast my music as I start my run around the lake. The sun is already blazing in the blue sky and it beats down on me. As I pass dad's house, I catch him waving from the kitchen. Waving back I keep going around, sometimes it's weird to run by his house. I am so used to stopping there on my runs but today I can't, today I need to expel all this nervous excitement building inside of me.

Today I'm finally doing it, tying the knot, getting hitched, taking the plunge. As I round the corner on my last lap, I find my dad patiently waiting for me.

"Hi Dad," I smile, pulling my ear buds out.

"Morning sweetheart," he gives me a quick hug. "Are you coming in for breakfast?"

"No sorry, Mom is cooking up a storm over there." I nod in the direction of my house, "Why don't you come over and eat with us?"

I watch him hesitate, but I grab his arm and pull him with me anyway. "I guess I don't have a choice," he mutters.

"Stop being a brat, Dad."

He laughs at me and holds tight to my hand. "I'm going to miss having another Mortenson around."

"I'll always be here Dad, no matter what my last name is."

I know he has been feeling sad about me giving up my name because there is no one else after him to carry it on, but I'm ready to be Mrs. Porter, so ready. When we enter my house, the kitchen is full of food. Mom and Paige are eating already so Dad and I join them.

"Morning," Dad says as he sits. Paige waves and my mom smiles at him. I thought it would be awkward with them, but they have actually really been okay together. Grabbing a fork I pile my plate with pancakes, strawberries and drown it all in maple syrup. Licking my lips, I look up to find all three staring at me.

"What?"

"You won't fit into your dress after all that," Mom says, shaking her head.

"Yeah I will, don't worry Mom, I'll work it off later," I wink.

Paige bursts out laughing while my parents hang their heads in embarrassment, but I catch Dad smiling. We eat in silence and I savor every bite because I know later, I'll be too caught up in everything to eat. My phone beeps and I grab it off the counter.

Knox: mornin' darlin' xx

Me: Hi babe, you're up early.

Knox: Yeah Dad insisted we head out for breakfast. I'll have a nap later.

Me: lazy ass

Knox: saving my strength for tonight.

Me: you better because I plan to give you a workout.

Knox: Can't wait xxx

Me: see you in a few hours, love you

Knox: love you too

"Well, no need to ask who that was. The smile on your face is a dead giveaway," Paige says.

"Yes, it was my future husband," I smile.

After I eat, I head up for a long soak in the tub. I warned my mom to leave me alone for an hour, just to chill out. We originally planned to stay in the hotel last night, but Dad organized a car for us, so we stayed here instead. Lowering myself into the bubbles, I close my eyes, memories of Knox and I run through my head like a movie reel.

He is the most handsome guy I have ever seen and that thought alone makes me giddy. Before long my mom is knocking on my door telling me my hour of solitude is over. Climbing out of the bath, I wrap a fluffy robe around myself, which Knox bought me for today. He said it will remind me of him when he is not with me.

"Are you out?" Mom asks.

"Yes Mom, I'm out," opening the door I smile at her. "See all done."

"Okay good, the hair and makeup ladies will be here soon and your dress is hanging in the spare room."

"Thanks," I smile. Once she leaves me again, I slather body lotion all over my skin. Throwing on a tank top and shorts I head down to the kitchen.

"Finally," Paige says. Grabbing my hand she pulls me down into a chair and begins to attack my feet with nail polish. I'm doing my best to remain calm and relaxed, and not get worked up. I watch Paige as she gets to work and accept a coffee from my mom.

"Where's Dad?"

"Oh, he went home for a shower. He said he will be back with the car," Mom answers. Once Paige is done with my toes, she starts on my fingers. By two, o'clock the hair and makeup ladies arrive, along with the photographer. I really didn't want him here while I am getting ready, but apparently that's what you do. After some serious struggling, my hair is finally pinned up with weird diamond things twisted into it. Paige has her makeup done and now it's mom's turn. I make an excuse to leave and race up to my room for a five-minute break.

Me: Hi babe, cold feet?
Knox: Hell no! Just woke up, what are you doing?
Me: Hiding from the evil twins downstairs lol
Knox: ???
Me: Hair and makeup. I have a headache already
Knox: Sorry darlin', are you okay though?
Me: yes I can't wait to see you.

"Bailey are you ready?" Mom shouts up the stairs at me.

Me: have to go Mom is stalking me.

247

Knox: ok darlin', see you soon xx
Me: xxxx

Leaving my room, I walk back down to the kitchen slash salon. It's already four o'clock and I could use a nap myself. Sitting on a stool, I close my eyes and let the makeup artist do her thing. Once we are done, the photographer is still snapping away as I move out of the room and up to get my dress on. Paige helps me to fasten the buttons and slip on my shoes because it's hard to see my feet with all the fabric.

"Oh I almost forget," she says, leaving the room. I take a look in the mirror. I can't believe I am getting married. Even to my own eyes I look beautiful and the smile on my face could light up a room.

"Here you go," Paige hands me a velvet box.

"What's this?"

"Open it and find out," she rolls her eyes at me.

Opening the box, I almost ruin my makeup. Nestled in the blue satin inside is a small charm. It is a bride and groom holding each other.

"Knox asked me to give it to you before you left."

"Thanks," I whisper. She helps me put it on my bracelet and we do one last mirror check.

"You look amazing, Bailey."

"Thanks, so do you." We hug for a few minutes and then leave the room. On the way down the stairs, I have to stop for a photograph. My mom is crying again and Dad looks pale.

"You okay Dad?"

Nodding he smiles at me, a little teary-eyed himself. After another round of photographs, I usher everyone out of the house. Dad locks up for me and puts my bag in the limo for tonight. I wave to Mom and Paige as their car pulls away and I climb into mine.

"All set?" Dad asks as we begin our journey. "You can always turn back, it's not too late," he teases, while pouring each of us a glass of champagne.

"No way, Dad. Wild horses couldn't keep me away."

Taking the glass, we toast to my happily ever after. Dad holds my hand for the whole journey while we drink and reminisce about the 'old days.' When we pull up to the hotel, my stomach summersaults with excitement. Paige is already waiting for me by the doors with the wedding coordinator. Getting out of the car takes a few minutes and some serious maneuvering.

"This is it," Dad whispers.

"Are trying to make me run old man?" I ask, gripping his arm. We both laugh nervously and walk over to Paige.

"Ready?" her eyes are gleaming as she looks at me.

"Yes," I nod. We follow the coordinator through the lobby and out to the side of the building to the bottom of the stone steps. The sun is almost setting and I can hardly stand still, every part of me wants to be in Knox's arms already. When the music begins, Paige smiles one last time and takes off. Dad holds out his arm for me and I take it, letting out a long breath.

We climb the five short steps and stop beside the coordinator. She smiles at us while talking into her headset. "Okay, get ready." Dad and I both nod, the music changes and she nods to us waving her hand for us to walk. As soon as my feet hit the cream runner, my body shivers. My eyes lift and I find the love of my life standing up at the flower covered arch waiting for me. My breath is stolen from my lungs and my heart falters when I see him.

His black tux and black hair stand out against his megawatt smile. Our eyes lock together and my feet hurry me towards him.

"Slow down, sweetheart," Dad whispers to me.

"I can't, Dad. Do you see what is waiting for me?"

My hearts speeds up with each step I take. As we reach the flower arch, Knox reaches out for my hand. Dad places my hand in Knox's and my whole body electrifies.

"Hi," he whispers to me.

"Hi."

"You look beautiful darlin'," his eyes glisten as he looks at me.

"So do you babe."

We are both smiling like it's our first meeting. The priest clears his throat and gets our attention. During the ceremony I half tune out, all I want to do is say I do.

249

"Knox would you like to say something?" the priest asks.

I'm a little confused because we never said we were doing this, but Knox winks at me and clears his throat.

"Bailey, from the moment I saw you, I knew you were mine. Although it wasn't plain sailing for us, there is no one I'd rather be with during hard times. No one I'd rather hold every night. No one I'd rather own my heart so completely as you do. I promise to love you always, to keep you close, and protect you with every part of me. I love you more than I ever thought possible to love another person. You're my whole world darlin' and I give you every part of me. I trust you to take care of my heart and I yours. I love you, so much. I do."

"I love you," I whisper. Tears blur my vision as Knox gently wipes my eyes.

"Do you Bailey Grace Mortenson, take Knox Andrew Porter to be your lawful wedded husband? To have and to hold till death do you part?"

"I do."

"Do you Knox Andrew Porter, take Bailey Grace Mortenson to be your lawful wedded wife? To have and to hold till death do you part?"

"I do."

"You may kiss the bride."

Our lips meet with a slow urgency, hungry to taste each other. My heart beats out of my chest as Knox wraps me in his arms. After a few minutes our friends and family clap and cheer. Breaking apart, Knox closes his eyes and resting his forehead against mine.

"We did it darlin'," he whispers.

"Yeah, we did."

Opening his eyes, he smiles at me and takes my hand. We walk down the aisle and out into the gardens of the hotel for our photographs. Max grabs me in a hug.

"Congrats sis," he smiles at me, then he hugs Knox.

We take our official photographs and soon it turns into a photo shoot of craziness. We do stupid poses and make each other laugh. Knox and Max take a few together while Paige and I do the same. I manage to get one of me standing between my husband and brother-in-law. Once the photos are over we head back up to the dining room for our reception. Sitting at the table, I look around the room, seeing for the first time all the people who came to celebrate with us. I don't know most of the Porter or Marshall side, which are his mom's side.

I find my cousins and my friends. Some of my mom's family and, of course, the Andersons. Roger looks happy sitting beside his wife as they talk to Corey. It's a mixture of my past, present, and future. Knox slips his hand into mine as Max stands to make his speech.

"Evening everyone. I'd like to start off by congratulating my brother and his new wife." He holds up his glass and winks at us.

"Also I want to say, ha ha, I won bro." Knox laughs and nods in agreement. Max gets a serious look on his face and clears his throat again.

"On behalf of my dad and I, I want to officially welcome Bailey to the Porter family, although she has been around for four years now, we are glad to have you. When my brother and Bailey first met, it went off like a bomb. They grew close fast and I could tell how happy they made each other. But they have been through some crazy stuff. The good, the bad and the ugly, but they made it through, and a love like that, is worth holding onto.

I'm happy my brother found his soul mate and Bailey you are the sister I never had. I love you for that. I love you for loving my brother and bringing him happiness. I can't say how much seeing him this happy, makes Dad and me happy. I love you, bro. Now please raise your glasses and toast to Knox and Bailey."

Everyone, raises their glasses, and toasts to us. Knox stands to hug Max and whispers in his ear. My heart is ready to explode from all the love pouring my way. Standing, I hug Max and kiss his cheek, taking the microphone I begin to speak.

"Four years ago, I honestly thought I'd never love anyone again. Never have a best friend again, but then I met three amazing people who quickly became my friends. One of them was a girl who, at first wouldn't leave me alone but she soon

251

became one of my closest friends," turning, I smile down to Paige, who wipes her eyes.

"The other two, drove me crazy but in a good way. Max, I love you and I'm happy to say that you have become one of my best friends. We can act crazy together and fight but at the end of it all, I know you'll always be the brother I never had. And Knox, I can't imagine my life without you. We have been through so much together and I just wanted to say thank you. Because without you I wouldn't even be here, I love you with all my heart and I promise to love you forever."

Knox stands, wrapping me in his arms. "I love you too darlin'."

After our meal, the DJ calls Knox and I to the floor. The music begins and I laugh at him. "Nickleback?"

"Of course darlin'. What else would we dance to?"

"I love you, Knox Porter."

"I love you, Bailey Porter," he smiles at me.

Our arms wrap around each other as we sway to the sound of Satellite by Nickelback.

Our first dance of many as husband and wife.

Epilogue

Christmas Eve.

"When is that wife of yours coming home?" Max asks.

"Soon," I reply, checking my watch for the hundredth time in ten minutes.

He laughs at me and shakes his head. I know what he's thinking and he's right. I am a pussy, but I don't care; I'll be a pussy any day if it means I get to come home every night to the most beautiful woman in the world.

"How long has it been?" He laughs.

"Fuck off Max," I grumble. He only laughs harder.

"C'mon bro, let's finish this so you can get home and wait by the door."

I punch him on the arm and follow him up on stage. We are playing at the bar tonight for something to do really. I haven't seen my wife for three weeks because she has been in DC with her dad. But they land soon and I'm dying for this night to be over so I can feel her in my arms again. The bar is not too full, but the night is good fun, it's been a long time since we played together. Max and I usually lock ourselves in my music room at home, but as a band it's been months.

We rock out together and sing more songs than we usually do. It's turned into a jamming session but it's fun. After we finish, we have a beer and lock up the bar.

"So what time will I be over tomorrow?" Max asks.

"You can just come with me now, Max."

"Nah, I'll let you two have your reunion," he smirks.

"Yeah fine, about noon if you want breakfast," I laugh.

"Bro, you're disgusting," he laughs while walking over to his bike. I climb on mine, still laughing and wave to him.

Riding up the hill, I feel the wind on my face and shiver. I'm tired, but I want to get home fast. Pulling up to the house I frown, noticing all the lights are off. Parking in the garage, I walk into the house, silencing the alarm. I don't see the suitcase by the door where Bailey usually drops it after a trip. Flipping on the lights I feel sad that she is not home yet. I check my phone, but there are no texts or missed calls. I hate all this traveling she does.

Kicking off my boots, I grab a beer and walk into the sitting room, to turn on the Christmas tree lights. After a few sips from the bottle, I notice a huge ass box by the tree. I know that wasn't there earlier. Jumping out of the seat, I put the bottle down on the table and run up to my room.

"Darlin'?" I call out as I burst into our room. She's not in here, neither is the suitcase. "What the fuck?" Running my hands through my hair, I start to walk back down to the sitting room to finish my beer.

"See something you like, darlin'?"

Looking up, I almost fall down the stairs. She is standing by the door to the music room in, let's face it, not very much. Turning, I run back and grab her into my arms.

"You frightened the crap out of me," I scold, as my lips trail down her neck.

"God I missed you, babe."

"I missed you too darlin'." My hands roam all over her body, all I want to do is make love to her right now, right here.

"Whoa, babe slow down. I want to give you your present."

"You are my present darlin'. The rest can wait."

"No Knox, its Christmas, come on." Slipping out of my grasp, she runs down the stairs laughing. I am wide awake now, and racing after her.

"Oh, you're going to get it darlin'."

I walk slowly into the sitting room, finding her smiling at me. She looks beautiful, standing by the tree with all the lights reflecting off her skin. I watch as she spreads her hands over the huge box.

"What's that?" I ask, my feet inching towards her again.

"Open it and find out."

254

Kneeling down, I begin to pull off the wrapping paper. Opening the box, I am a little curious. I know what I asked for, and it's not this size for sure. Looking inside I find another wrapped box. I frown at her, but she gives me her killer smile, and I open this one. After three boxes of boxes, I look up at her.

"Darlin', what is this?" I shake the last box.

"Don't shake it!" she grabs my hand.

"Okay," I answer. My brain is not functioning right now because sleep has finally caught up with me.

"I promise this is the last one." She smiles.

Believing her, I open the wrapping paper and the box. My eyes stare at the gift, uncomprehending. I look up at her, biting her lower lip and looking worried.

"Merry Christmas." She says.

I look back at the gift again, "Seriously?" I ask. She nods her head and I stand up grabbing her in my arms. I don't know why but tears fall from my eyes as I squeeze her.

"Really darlin'?" She nods again. "Thank you, thank you. I love you, I love you so damn much."

"I love you too babe." She wipes the tears from my eyes and smiles at me.

We both look into the box sitting on the coffee table, seeing a pair of little white booties.

Infinity and Always

The End

Made in the USA
Charleston, SC
25 June 2015